J.M.J.

I0630375

RANSOM

Shadow of an Empire

~

Book III

~

Shards of Crystal

By Thérèse Judeana

~

illustrated by Grace Bourget

En Route Books and Media, LLC

Saint Louis, MO

⊕ENROUTE
Make the time

En Route Books and Media, LLC

5705 Rhodes Avenue

St. Louis, MO 63109

Contact us at **contact@enroutebooksandmedia.com**

Cover Credit: Grace Bourget

Copyright 2023 Thérèse Judeana

ISBN-13: 979-8-88870-028-0

Library of Congress Control Number: 2023930334

All rights reserved. No part of this book may be reproduced, stored in a retrieval system, or transmitted in any form, or by any means, electronic, mechanical, photocopying, or otherwise, without the prior written permission of the author.

Acknowledgments

The author would like to thank her friends and acquaintances who made suggestions and gave advice; thanks to Chantal LaFortune for feedback and her enthusiasm in reading it.

Most of all, thanks to Christ the True Ransomer for rescuing us all, in time, eternity, and every day of our lives.

Dedication

O Lord I offer Thee This work through Thy only Son,
in the power of the Holy Spirit,
to the praise of Thy eternal Majesty.
- St. Gertrude the Great

To the Hearts of the Holy Family.
In honor of the Holy Face of Christ and Our Lady of La Salette,
that it might help to dry their tears.
For those searching for the key to freedom from sin and hope in
this vale of tears.
And to my Ransomer and my Daystar.

Book III

Shards of Crystal

RANSOM

Book III: Shards of Crystal

~~~

"Nothing can happen to me that God doesn't want.
And all that He wants, no matter how bad it may appear to us,
is really for the best."

- St. Thomas More

I

Interrogation

As soon as they were back in Mal'lon, business resumed as usual, but with the marked change of mildly chaotic energy. Medrhos seemed to always be in a dozen places at once, with his military duties, building projects, reconnaissance, petitions, the senate, the fleet, and half a dozen other items including the slave trade.

Coran took the time to inform Samantha that things would be twice as hectic once the interrogators arrived.

Samantha, for her part, watched serenely and waited. Medrhos had indeed become hard and cold again, not having time to even speak to her. He seemingly had forgotten most of what had happened in Almedran-town, though the one time she ran into him and managed to give him a hug, reminding him to keep his promise, he smiled slightly and nodded.

In the midst of her own duties – matters of the court, the royal table, her own senate duties in presiding over the women's side, and, of course, caring for the people and the slaves – Samantha searched for a way to save her 'husband.'

Clearly, since being at his own wedding Mass hadn't had the same effect as the valley did, he would need something more. She managed to catch a word with Ransomme, and told him everything that had occurred. The priest listened attentively but simply told her that he would keep praying.

"Continue with your work as you must," he said, "and try to let me know if anything else happens." He blessed her and then she had to run.

Her duties as Medrhos' queen were indeed important. She had pulled at the laws until the slaves were well-cared for, well-housed, clothed, treated, and fed. The law to keep slaves treated as less than human had been changed as much as Medrhos would humor her with. The law that they should not speak unless spoken to, especially the women, had also been removed and Samantha had been wonderfully surprised at Silvestra's courage in striking up her first conversation with her. But there was much more to be done.

Soon she was as lost in her duties as Medrhos was in his – for she, too, had to make sure everything was secure for the Interrogators' arrival. And then, the fifth day after their return to Mal-lon, a fanged ship landed in the elite spaceport.

Medrhos had his men out in full ceremonial battleguard as the ramp lowered and the Marauder King himself stood before it, every inch the warlord emperor. He knew how to let these Interrogators know that their terrorism would not intimidate him; he was in command, not they.

Samantha stood behind him in her queenly array with Silmä and Gelert on either side, realizing now that once again, Medrhos' fear was only for her. The madness of the past week had been spent by all for her protection. But these Interrogators *couldn't* be worse than Karthos.

Two men stepped out of the ship, dressed all in burgundy and ebony. One was short, the other tall; both looked unassuming until they spoke. Their accents were heavy, and Samantha guessed that they were accustomed to the ancient tongue and had only learned the modern form to carry out their work. They tried at first to frighten Medrhos, but seeing that he would have none of it, they approved and granted him their respect.

"The Cult greets its chosen son," the shorter one, Melkos, said approvingly, and bowed to him.

"From Karthos' reports, the Cult has never had such a worthy prince," the other, Pvettkar, noted. "We shall find out for ourselves whether that is the truth."

Medrhos looked vaguely amused, for he was scarcely a 'worthy son.' He didn't even listen to half the laws of the Cult. He could only imagine what they had thought of his predecessors.

"We will inspect your work and your Empire, and then, if we deem it right, we will mark you as the Lord of the Empire for life."

"I'm sure you'll find everything in good enough order," Medrhos murmured dryly. "My lords, this is your Queen. I warn you not to get under her feet; you'd rather not be on her bad side. Ancilla, Melkos and Pvettkar. They may decide to inspect your Queenship as well. Be gentle with these babysitters, I mean, *interrogators*, if you can," he winked.

Samantha bit back a smile and turned a look of mock condescension on the two Interrogators. There was a brief silence in which the men scorned to acknowledge her in due reverence, in part from the sting of Medrhos' words.

Samantha was unfazed and locked eyes with them until their gazes flickered and they turned back to the King. Silmä offered a growl and Gelert joined in. Medrhos waited, making it very clear that it would be wise to treat the woman with respect.

At last, Melkos and Pvettkar grudgingly bowed their heads to Samantha but insisted that she had no title until they had approved Medrhos' reign.

"And she wears unacceptable dress for her rank," Melkos added with displeasure. "You will change into something more fitting for your peasantry, until we are sure that you are truly a Marauder woman."

Medrhos' lip curled. "Who do you think she is? A slave, or my wife? Wear what *you* think is fitting, Ancilla."

"I'm thinking Almedran gowns would do just fine," Samantha said breezily, passing him as they all turned to walk up the grand stairs to the palace. "Unless you'd rather that I change into my engineering dress and start taking their ships apart and making toys with the pieces, just to keep them occupied. Oh, or I could *really* go for a Galatkan courtdress."

Her eyes twinkled. The Galatkan clan was a south quadrant group from 2700 A.D., which had gone to a strange blend of what was basically Victorian, Earth Mod, and Circuswear, which made for a bizarre appearance. Individuality and lack of formality were hated by the Cult. Both interrogators looked annoyed and then disgusted. Medrhos met Samantha's eyes, struggling not to laugh.

"I said wear what you think is fitting," he managed to say. "If that means wearing a crown of peacock feathers and a ridiculous ballgown, I think we can let you do that."

"Ugh, please tell me I'm hearing things," Melkos muttered to Pvettkar.

"I was hoping you'd tell me that instead," Pvettkar sighed.

"Oh, wonderful."

~~~

The Interrogators spent many hours reviewing Medrhos' acts as king, the state of the city and Imperial relations and affairs, finances, military, the slave trade, and the like. Three days of this while Samantha continued her own work and then she was summoned to Medrhos' side.

"You are doing well," Melkos said to the King. "You are a worthy Emperor. . . our only request is a little more respect for tradition, and you will do even better."

"I'm glad that the thoughts of the Cult are in fair accordance with mine," Medrhos replied, and turned a warning gaze on Samantha. "There you are, my Queen," he said. "I believe these men have a request to make of you." He turned with her and was pleased when the men courteously acknowledged the Queen.

"We hope it would not be too much trouble to take an account of your queenly affairs?"

Samantha looked at them and glanced at Medrhos. "You may, as long as you don't interfere with my work," she granted.

Medrhos was silently warning her to do none of the things that the Cult would surely disapprove of. Samantha would have to figure out what she could fill her time with.

She spent the next twenty-four hours wearying of being followed, every movement watched. Keeping up her queenly, Marauder façade was not easy. It was even harder to avoid those responsibilities for which the Interrogators would discredit her. She tried to focus on the elaborate royal meal that night - Medrhos had suggested to her that they turn out a full-fledged Royal Marauder dinner, complete with the intimidating flaming decor, so perfect for those royal 'baby-sitters.'

Thus, Samantha allowed Melkos and Pvettkar to trail her to the massive kitchens that fed Medrhos' thousands of men, and many of the cities' people, including the slaves. It was the latter point that was soon to cause Samantha trouble. It came as she was discussing the warlord's menu for that night with the royal chef.

The servants' chef, Luka, whom she had placed in charge of feeding slaves who did not have enough rations, jumped in the moment the menu was settled. Luka himself had been a slave, until Samantha had used a portion of her monthly allowance to free him and his young family.

"My Queen," he murmured, with an anxious glance at the Interrogators. He realized too late the possible danger he was putting them in, but Samantha signed for him to continue. "The King's orders this morning regarding banquets for the entire court, and fairs for all the citizens, will inevitably lead to many of the slaves going hungry tonight. There will be more than my kitchen is able to provide for. What would you have me do?"

Samantha was thinking quickly, feeling as though she was watching the faces of the men behind her. A pain flashed through her forehead but she resisted the urge to touch her scar. They would attack her for this, she knew; for servants must not speak to masters, and royalty not feed slaves more than their due, that is, just enough to keep them alive. It couldn't be helped; God's timing could seem the worst, but He certainly had His reasons.

"Hugo!" Samantha called the military chef away from the vat of stew he was preparing for the guards. "Hugo, the servants' kitchens are unable to provide for the number of slaves who need to be fed this evening. I would have you grant Luka a third of the rations he needs."

Hugo nodded curtly and grabbing the list from Luka, ducked away into his storeroom to order his twenty aides to carry out the Queen's orders. Samantha then called the royal chef, Derek, who was overseeing the computer that was shaping the rustic loaves he always served with chili. She commanded him to fulfill not one-third, but two-thirds of Luka's request. The royal kitchens were too well stocked for how few were fed; it was merely for herself and the king, Medrhos' brethren, Samantha's handmaids, and royal guests.

Samantha watched as the kitchen servants carried out the task; all the while she was refusing to turn and accept whatever scathing or triumphant looks the Interrogators might have for her. She turned back to Luka, whose eyes left the kitchen activity to study the two men.

"You may go, Luka," she said kindly. "Thank you for bringing this to my attention. See to it that the slaves are fed well, and that not one leaves without something to take home. If you run out or need any assistance, Hugo and Derek will be glad to aid you." She dismissed him and turned at last to the Interrogators.

Melkos looked amused; clearly he was looking forward to putting Samantha 'in her place.' Pvettkar, on the other hand, looked mildly disgusted as he made a note on his digipad.

"Shall we continue?" Melkos asked politely. "What is next on your agenda, *Ancilla*? I believe I heard the King speak of petitions being in your line of duty. Don't you normally hear petitions at about this time every morning?"

Samantha looked directly into his eyes, knowing perfectly well what he was thinking, and noticing his patronizing tone.

"Indeed," was her only reply, and she departed for her chambers to change into the traditional robe of state.

She had intended to postpone that morning's petitions until the Interrogators had ceased to watch her every move, for she knew it would only offer them more occasions to spite her. Her heart was sinking and she grimaced as she thought of Medrhos' warning.

Again, nothing could be done. She still hoped that Medrhos would deflect whatever the Interrogators might throw at her, and that he would be able to understand why she hadn't been able to do as he had asked.

Samantha took her throne in the hall of petitions, adjacent to the throne room. Marauder custom dictated that warlords remove themselves from their intimidating surroundings when hearing petitions of their people.

The stream of petitioners, always light on Thursdays, began to trickle in. Even her citizens were afraid of the Interrogators' power, and so Samantha found that she had only half a dozen people to serve. These were a mix of the boldest as well as the most innocent in the city; too desperate or too naïve to fear what their missteps could do to the Queen.

Samantha, for her part, did not silence them when their words only further proved the law she had amended of a servant's speech. She saw further notes of the gravity of the situation, and of the Queen's 'excess' charity to slaves and the gentle reins she used on non-Marauder citizens. This alone wouldn't be enough for them to remove her as Medrhos' 'wife', she knew. It wasn't a moment later that the worst happened.

It came in the form of the captain whom she had accompanied on her escapade, and whom she hadn't seen since. He was off-duty, and so wore the casual uniform of the Marauder men, with the addition of gold stripes on his shoulders. He smiled and bowed, but there was a strange look in his eyes. He was as kind and courteous as he had been in aiding her, but now he threw caution to the winds.

"Ah, I haven't seen you since your escapade," he said with a charming smile as he kissed her hand. "I'm glad to see the Sand Monsters didn't get you."

"Ah, you don't think a Queen can handle herself alone?" Samantha paled slightly, trying to save the subject.

"Mm, no, as I recall you intended to. The King tells me you did find your friends down South; it's a wonder you didn't stay with them."

The blood was draining quickly from Samantha's face as she discreetly motioned for him to cease. She didn't dare to look to the Interrogators who stood on either side of her throne.

"Didn't you come for a petition, Captain," she reminded him gently. Why was he being so bold, endangering both her and the Realtra? He had promised to help her – but then, as Medrhos had said, he didn't dare to cross the Emperor. Maybe the same was not true for the Empress.

"I just wanted a chance to speak with you about the Realtra," he said calmly. He was leaning forward, gazing into her anxious eyes. "I know you're doing your best, my Queen, but I was wondering if you could share your ideas with me. So far you haven't brought your men into this, but as the one who knows you, I thought maybe you could trust me, since I know you feel alone."

Emerald eyes stared into golden-gray. It wasn't the worst he could have said, but it was like a death-knell. What the Interrogators wouldn't do, to pull the information from her that Medrhos had not-! And yet the Captain's tender concern, mingled with that strange glance, was very real.

A dark shadow seemed to lurk at the back of Samantha's mind, threatening to grow with every thought – it had returned at last since the peace of Almedran-town. Any trifling moment of despair would give it power over her. Samantha tried to breathe, and found it hard, quickly realizing how long and suspicious the silence was growing.

"I have not yet discussed it in full with the Emperor," she replied, feeling that she were choking. Somehow her words were audible, just barely.

Father help me, don't let me bring any of Your people to harm. Let this pass, or let Thy will be done, no matter how terrifying it might be.

Aloud, as she placed a hand on the Captain's shoulder, she thanked him for being there for her. If she could trust him that much.

It was clear to her that the power of the crystals was being utilized to draw her out into danger. If only her words would soothe the Interrogators enough to save her, and the Realtra.

But no, they were likely to bring it up at dinner, and Medrhos would surely begin to change under the power of the crystals as well. There was no telling what he would do, despite his disdain of his 'babysitters'. Now that his reign was approved and only hers was left in the balance, perhaps he would change. . . .

She watched the Captain as he strode out of the hall, and the great doors were shut behind him, leaving Samantha alone with Melkos and Pvettkar. She left them no time to speak, making a swift exit out the back doors, leaving them to follow in her wake as she swept her way down the hall.

In scarcely an hour it would be time for the royal dinner; she had every excuse to hasten to her chambers and be free for that short time. That is, if she could shut the door quickly enough.

The Interrogators were right on her heels, with the obvious intention of, well, interrogating her. When she waved her hand to signal the door to slide shut behind her, Melkos caught it with a stern glance, and opened his mouth to say something as he and Pvettkar pushed their way into her parlor.

A crash and a sudden swirl of capes and robes left both men in a heap, jammed in the doorway, with Coran's face appearing through the opening above them. He peered in to see if Samantha was alright, then with a grin quickly apologized to the pair and precipitated them out into the hallway as the door closed with a soft hiss.

Samantha echoed the sound with a sigh of relief. Coran, at least, was still on her side for now. Silvestra's companionship seemed to be having a healing effect – it was as though the Marauder side of him was lessening, and from this incident maybe even the effect of the crystals – was it possible? If so, was there a chance that Medrhos would remain a safe haven even when the subject of the Realtra came up at the table?

Her thoughts twisted and turned in every possible direction as she exchanged the heavy robe for a dinner gown of crushed velvet in shades of carmine and blackberry. It hadn't escaped the golden ornamentation of Marauder royalty, for it was draped with metallic lace and adorned by a crystalline geometric applique on the bodice and at the waist where the overskirt was swept aside.

Samantha gathered up her hair and held it there with a jeweled comb; no crown was required, but Medrhos had requested that she wear the gilded band of thorns and winter berries he had recently ordered for her, so she slipped it into her hair. That was all she needed; she still had time.

The Queen drew the medal from around her neck and clasped it in her hand. She paused long enough to breathe her troubles out in a long, wordless sigh, and stood for a few moments as her petitions were heard. All would go as He planned, no matter how violent it might be. The Empress left her chambers.

The towering oaken doors of the banquet hall, with their bronze scrollwork of vines, swung open to reveal savage, dark firelight. It was traditional Marauder style; heatless torches flickered on the walls, a rainbow crackled in the massive fireplace, and stone-held channels of flame criss-crossed the room, causing deep shadows to tremble on the walls and ceiling. They were intimidating, but heatless and due to the meddling of their scientists, nearly painless as well.

Medrhos was already lounging in his throne at the table. Melkos and Pvettkar were consulting with him, it seemed, and none had seen her enter. Samantha stood still, trying to discern whether they were speaking of her, but the crackling of the flames made their words indistinguishable. There was nothing left but for her to steal up behind the two men and give them a fright. She succeeded, leaving Medrhos laughing as he tried to sip his wine.

"Good evening, boys," she greeted them, chuckling at their indignant expressions. She slipped between them and glided up the little stairway to her throne beside Medrhos. She seated herself and the Emperor dropped his hand lightly on hers as it rested on the arm of her throne.

"These two fine-feathered fellows were detailing your day to me," he remarked. "They don't seem happy with you, my dear, but it is a matter we will soon clear up." But his eyes flashed, asking why she hadn't taken more care.

"Duty doesn't pause for interrogations, it seems," Samantha said lightly. "I will welcome your understanding and counsel, my lord."

Satisfied, Medrhos sent a message to the kitchens that they were ready to dine. He turned to Melkos and Pvettkar, who were still standing, eyes locked on Samantha.

"Ah, you must be exhausted," he purred. "Please take your seats. And don't gawk at your Queen; that's her King's privilege only."

"I thought we held that close relationships are not things of kings, sire," Melkos said dryly.

"Indeed," Medrhos murmured, eyeing him, "but any man who doesn't guard his woman with jealousy is a fool. Worse than fools are those who try to hinder his protection. I advise you to keep your names from that category."

There was no more time for talk then, for the meal was brought in, and Coran and Silvestra took their places beside their master and mistress. Samantha tried to concentrate on watching the food being served, but her mind was laughing at sight of the Interrogators on the other side of the table; for their chairs were not on a dais as were the royal seats, and were so low they looked like children.

She stifled a giggle as she silently blessed her food and dipped a piece of the rustic dark loaf into her chili. Medrhos toasted to her with his glass of wine but she merrily raised her glass of cherry cider, which seemed to annoy the Interrogators further. Medrhos shrugged at her and stole a sip from her glass.

The meal was, to Samantha's relief, not as terrible as had been the wedding feast, at least in the way of food. The wine-sauced chili was paired with garlic bread, fried potatoes and stuffed peppers, and a chocolate lemon cake for dessert.

The Interrogators ate in silence, with a glance at Samantha now and then if Medrhos wasn't looking. The King carried on most of the conversation while the Queen was content to listen. Unlike the terrifying tales Karthos had told, the King confined his speech to the comfortingly dull topic of routine state affairs.

Whenever the Interrogators were not watching him, he would turn his gaze to Samantha. She couldn't tell whether it was out of concern, or if he were thinking of the talk they were going to have to have once the meal was over.

At last, the dishes were cleared away, leaving them with glasses of delicate rose and raspberry wines – a gift they had received in Almedran-town. Melkos and Pvettkar pretended not to enjoy it.

The group listened to the crackling flames for a few minutes as they drank deeply, looking out the massive windows. It had begun to storm, and the rain covered the city in a thick cloak of mist.

"We have something to discuss," Medrhos said at last, quaffing the last of his wine with a reassuring glance at Samantha. Melkos and Pvettkar exchanged a look before Melkos offered a slimy smile.

"We need not go over our notes again, I think; she needs some correction, but you may keep her, for now, and we will watch her and see that she improves."

The thought of having to carry out her necessary duties for her people, *all* of the citizens of the Empire, under the evil eyes of those men made Samantha shudder. There would be no escape – if only Medrhos would find a way out of it for her!

But then, he was a Marauder, and though he loved her, he gave only one suspicious glance to the men before nodding with satisfaction. After all, what did he care about the changes Samantha had made? All he cared was that she was his queen, and that she remain safe. All else he saw with Marauder eyes.

Samantha bit back an involuntary sob, completely missing whatever it was that Melkos and Pvettkar were saying to her. Medrhos must have seen her state of mind, for he stretched out his hand and gently touched her scarred brow with his gloved fingers.

"I think," he said, "that I gave you a bit of homework to do tonight. Would you please do that for me, Ancilla."

Samantha had no idea what he was talking about but bowed her head in reply, bidding the men goodnight and soon found herself in the safe haven of her own rooms. She sank down in an armchair. This was quite a state of things; would she somehow have to accomplish her designs in secret, or somehow request every citizen in the city to comply and pretend that all was as it had been before?

Well, those were possibilities, showing that the latest test was not impossible. She was glad that Medrhos had not been worse. It was strange, she thought, since he had warned her that she might have difficulty keeping her promise to him. As yet, though he was indeed a Marauder, he had not become cruel and unpredictable once more. Yet something gave her the feeling that this was a very false sense of security.

Samantha was so overwhelmed by all she had learned of the Cult, the darkness behind the Marauders, her anxiety over the Realtra and Medrhos – and now thoughts of gentle Aiyra came back to her mind – that she sank into a deep silence from which Silvestra could not rouse her. At last, the handmaiden left her lady, resolving to return shortly and put her to bed. It didn't happen.

Scarcely had Silvestra exited than a cackle shocked Samantha out of her stupor and she leapt to her feet, looking wildly for the laughing skull. She thought she caught a glimpse of it in the face of the moon as she turned and found herself confronted by the Interrogators. She caught her gasp before it escaped from her lips.

Samantha wished now that Gelert didn't remain in Medrhos' quarters every night, and that Silmä didn't have her own chamber in the royal menagerie. A guardian with sharp teeth would have been greatly comforting just now. She drew herself to her full height and tried to regain her composure.

"How did you enter, and why?" she demanded. "There *is* a doorbell, and a lock, and a rule." She gave them an insulting glance but the two only smiled grimly.

"You have much to learn, *Ancilla*."

Pvettkar moved around her and Samantha's instinct to fight kicked in, but something pricked her arm and when she blinked, she was bound in a chair, no longer in her own room but in Melkos' suite. How they had gotten her there without raising hell was the first question that came to her dizzy mind, but it didn't make it to her lips.

Melkos leaned in and stared into her eyes. "You vowed as Queen to uphold our laws yet what have you done?"

Samantha summoned all her strength to think clearly. "I have. I improved them."

"But treating slaves as equals, Ancilla, puts you among them. . . or betrays your foreign allegiances. You have been working against the slave trade the supports your entire empire."

"If you want an Empire to run without rebellion, you are attentive to those most likely to rebel," she answered. "I have spent my time cultivating the better trades that will soon support it twice as well."

"Then you are a Marauder woman. The Marauders are your people alone, and you would not try to escape, insulting your Emperor and your people to whom you have a duty. . . would you?" His eyes glowed like a cat's.

"Ah, then I am a Queen." Samantha smiled. "You know I do my duty as a Marauder sees fit."

Melkos looked mildly annoyed but could say nothing to the latter; he motioned Pvettkar to write down her answer. "Whether you are a Queen remains to be seen, Ancilla. There is something about you Rätha finds most distasteful. You have too often overstepped your boundaries as a woman, wife, and queen with too little silence and obedience, and too much freedom. Medrhos' mark against him is in being far too lenient with you."

"Why did you let him marry me?"

Melkos and Pvettkar both bit their tongues and did not reply. Quickly recovering, Melkos turned to her again.

"Tell us of the Realtra, and your charming little escapade."

"Reconciliation is important, don't you think," Samantha sighed. Her vision was blurry from fear and whatever drug had been used on her, but she tried not to blink as the men kept their eyes fastened upon her. "Wouldn't you rather root out rebellion without wasting Marauder lives?"

"Rebellious and cunning, the marks of a Marauder," Melkos smirked, "but mingled with your love for the poor, lack of favoritism, adherence to the Being you believe supreme over Rätha, and mingling with rebels?" He took the bracelet from her wrist and revealed the tracker beneath the ornate silver plating. "Karthos recommended tracking you, if not with an RFID chip, using what you already wear."

With a smile he took a small electronic tablet from his robe and scanned the tracker. Once the computer locked onto the signal, he put the device away, closing the bracelet's capsule and locking it tightly on Samantha's wrist – breaking the mechanism which allowed it to be removable. It was painfully tight now, and would never slide off her hand. Whatever Talitha had woven it of, it was almost uncuttable, and she'd have to slice her own wrist to get a blade beneath it.

"And now we come to the verdict."

Pvettkar handed a solid crystal bracelet to Melkos. The gem was white with a lurid red glow that frightened Samantha. It seemed to her that it would be far worse than the one she had been forced to wear already.

As Melkos reached for her left hand, the girl instinctively kicked him. If only she were free! How could she keep them from placing it on her hand – Melkos struck her face savagely as Pvettkar pushed her back.

"You'll be leaving with us, Ancilla, to be trained as a Marauder woman; and if you fail, you will die for having been on the throne," Melkos snarled, but he didn't manage to finish, for the door had slid open just as he had struck the Queen, and Medrhos had thrown him aside.

The smell of burnt velvet filled the air – Melkos' sleeve was sizzling where the Emperor's hand had grasped him.

Medrhos' eyes were like fire as he faced the Interrogators.

"*Don't touch my wife,*" he hissed. His right hand was raised and clenched, the gems on his gauntlet blazing furiously as he held the bracelet. With a crack the crystal band burst into flames and fell to the floor in ashes. Medrhos turned and touched the bonds that held Samantha to the chair, tearing her free as the bonds disintegrated. With his left hand he lifted her to her feet, but Samantha's muscles were too weak to support her.

"What have you done to her?" Medrhos growled, lowering the girl gently to the ground, for he only had one free hand and couldn't carry her yet.

"It's only a drug," Pvettkar said quickly, seeing that it would be wise to give an answer. "It will wear off in a few hours."

"It was to last long enough for you to take her away, wasn't it. You were going to force me to let her go and take another, and submit her to slavery."

Medrhos' voice was dripping with cold fury. His right hand clenched restlessly as the jewels on his wrist throbbed with a painful intensity.

"Coran!" he said sharply. His aide entered. "Take your Queen to her chambers. I have. . . business to discuss with these *gentlemen*."

Coran gave a silent nod and, in a moment, was bearing Samantha out of the room. Upon reaching the Queen's suite, he stood just inside the entrance, eyes dark but almost tender as Silvestra put her mistress to bed.

Little Estill was there, and tried to help, brushing Samantha's hair and singing the way her own mother used to. Then she crept away with Silvestra. They joined Coran and waited.

It was some twenty minutes before a soft beep announced Medrhos' arrival. A soft murmured discussion between the three, and then the Emperor came and stooped over Samantha. She had been nearly asleep, although a pricking of her nerves and the sensation of being watched by a silent skull kept her from entering dreamland.

"Ah, can't sleep," Medrhos muttered. "It doesn't matter then."

He slipped his arms beneath her and lifted her up to his shoulder as Silvestra tucked a dark, heavy mantle around Samantha. That done, and without a word of explanation, Medrhos took the girl from her bed as Coran and Silvestra followed. Gelert bounded down the corridor and joined them.

The cool night breeze quickly woke Samantha. Red and white lights glimmered through the city and down the wet roads, and the air was cold and heavy after the rainfall. She saw now that Silvestra, Estill, and the other handmaids that now joined them, were all dressed in traveling mantles. Each carried a satchel with Samantha's Marauder initials embroidered upon it. Estill, meanwhile, was carrying Lyona, and Silmä prowled gracefully alongside. This removed any surprise from Samantha's mind at their arrival in the spaceport. But where were they traveling to, and why?

Medrhos bore her up into the *Harbinger;* the ship's engines were already purring softly, the crew already waiting for them. The Ensign stood at the door, awaiting orders. Medrhos paused only a moment on his way to Samantha's garden chamber.

"Ensign. Put out Code 1-600. We'll be off the ground in ten minutes."

The Ensign saluted and vanished into the bridge. Coran opened the door to the Almedran room. The handmaidens slipped in and quickly began arranging the Empress' sofa among the flowers, and taking her garments from their satchels, hung them in the arched ivory wardrobe. Lyona was set free to explore the koi pond and Gelert took up a post at the door. Silmä settled at the foot of the bed.

Medrhos laid his Queen to rest beneath the velvet coverlet and kissed her brow.

"You will feel well in the morning, Ancilla," he said softly. "And then we will discuss what to do about you."

Medrhos walked out. His mind still raced with the adrenaline of having to save Samantha. The Cult was getting increasingly out of hand. To please Samantha, he would not destroy them. But he would prove her worth as his Queen.

II

Maeris

Upon awakening, after Medrhos had given orders that his Queen must eat before she arise, Samantha was ushered into the study. They had not yet left the planet's orbit, as though waiting for something, she knew not what.

The Emperor was standing there, his hands clasped behind his back as he looked out into the void. He had exchanged his kingly garments for that of a warlord. Samantha's heart sank when she saw this. Medrhos motioned her to a seat. They locked eyes, Medrhos calculating, Samantha worrying.

"What are you willing to do to save your life?"

"What?"

Medrhos moved around the desk.

"The Cult has a mind to kill you. I alone can plead for your life. You don't wish me to destroy them, so what will you do?"

Samantha only raised her perturbed eyes to his face.

"There is only one thing you can do, Ancilla. You must fulfill what Karthos saw in you. This very moment, we are setting out on a course for the Great Galaxy. My fleet is ready to obey our every command. Ancilla, you must become a war-queen and bring down Vestar with me. You must work with me as has been the tradition of our people. Before now I let you mold part of my world to your will, but now you must follow mine. From henceforth you will be Maeris, not Ancilla, not Samantha. You are my Queen and we will be of the same mind. Help me, Maeris. Let me save you."

"Medrhos, you know I can't and I won't, not to save my life."

"To save another life?"

"Medrhos, stop."

"You wish them to die."

"No, but to fight them, yes!"

"Maeris, you force my hand."

He motioned to the guards. They stepped outside and returned with her handmaids.

"Medrhos, no!"

"Maeris."

"Medrhos, I *can't*! You *know* I can't."

Medrhos flicked his hand and the guards struck the girls so that they fell.

"*No! Medrhos, don't do this!*" Samantha flung herself forward to receive the next two blows that fell, leaving her dizzy. The guards pulled back, horrified that they had struck their queen. Medrhos dragged her upright and held her firmly.

"Maeris, I would kill a thousand slaves to make you save your life, and the Realtra would perish. I will spare them all if you let me save you. Don't make me strike!"

The handmaids didn't make a sound.

What could she do? If she said no, Medrhos would carry out his threats and more until there was nothing left but her own life. But if she complied there was a chance she could stop him still.

"Okay," she whispered. "Just please don't strike!" She felt she had betrayed Samantha to a terrified Ancilla, but no matter how she felt she had to believe she could still do this. What choice did she have?

Medrhos lowered his hand and let the handmaidens leave. Then he pulled Samantha into his arms and held her close, pressing her cheek to his heart, covered by the warlord medallion that clasped his cloak. The claw of the tiger-like image scratched her cheek, but she was too upset to notice.

Medrhos, the cunning tiger that he was, knew that comforting Samantha now would bring her further under his power. And though Samantha knew it too, his strong arms and heartbeat still comforted her, and she could hardly help but lean on him. Somehow, she would have to turn this to his good!

III

Void

The cruiser glided through the night sky. Mal'lon shrank behind them, glowing with sunset hues. Samantha sank down beside the rippling pool in her garden chamber. Her skull was tingling from stress. Her cheek stung where she had taken the blow intended for her handmaids, and as she raised her eyes she saw in her reflection the mark left by Medrhos' medallion. Was Medrhos truly too far gone?

All her hopes seemed to have been dashed, but there was *always* hope! If he were lost, if his people were lost forever, why was she put in this position by God? Why had He chosen not to have it come down to a battle between Vestar and the Marauders? Well, there was no use questioning for answers she could not find.

Samantha sat for some time, trying to collect herself again. Lyona was curled up close by, and Estill knelt there in silence, stroking the cat's head. Their presence and the sound of the bubbling fountain soothed the Queen but did not aid her mind.

Gelert then pushed his cold nose into her hand and playfully pulled at her bracelet with his teeth. It was still painfully tight, thanks to the Interrogators. Of course, Medrhos had not realized. Despite his protests about literally keeping track of Samantha, he was a Marauder at heart and would not stir to remove the device from her wrist.

"Maybe you could call Uncle Orion?" Estill whispered timidly. Samantha raised her eyes, surprised, and then she remembered the other device she wore clipped to the inside collar of her gown. In the swirling fear of recent events she had forgotten it.

Her heart leapt. Yes, she could call Marc! The Marauders would not detect her signal, and she could ask him for advice.

"Oh Estill, you're a Godsend!" she breathed, reaching up and unpinning it. She fumbled with it, praying that no one would come to her door at an inopportune moment. She slid the switch. Three soft beeps came from the device and three green lights lit up in succession and faded away.

"-Samantha?" A familiar voice immediately bathed her in relief.

"Konstan!"

"Sis, what's wrong? Are you safe?" he asked urgently.

"Not exactly," Samantha groaned. "I need advice. Is Marc with you?"

"No, he's off on another raid. I rerouted most of his messages to myself. He should be returning now. One moment, dear, and I'll see if I can patch him into a three-way." His voice faded and she heard faint clicking and a hum on the other end.

"Samantha, Konstan?" Marc's voice came sharply, wasting no time, though he was currently zipping over the snowy flatland. "Sahma, are you alright? What do you need of me?"

"I'm – alright," Samantha hesitated, not wanting to waste time on describing all that had occurred. "Marc, Konstan, I need advice. The Cult has led Medrhos to instigate a raid on Earth. We're on our way now, and he says I need to help him, or the Cult will kill me. I don't know what to do. I can't stop him, I already tried, and he threatened to destroy all of you, Estill, my handmaidens, and all the slaves in Mal'lon."

There was dead silence for a space of five seconds. She knew what was running through the men's minds: images of Talitha, murdered through so similar a situation.

"I'm coming to get you," Marc broke the strained silence. "In our time, you're still in Mal'lon. If we take you away from the city and hide you, Medrhos won't be able to force you into anything and we'll do everything in our power to keep you safe."

"Five hours ago," Samantha replied, "I was drugged and being interrogated. It's too late to save me from this. It would bring too much danger to the Realtra." She glanced nervously towards the door, half imagining that she heard someone in the hall outside. "I'm so afraid that Medrhos is destroying himself, and that everything is in danger of becoming irreparable - please, what should I do?" she begged.

"Do you know what time period he's taking you into?"

"Our own," she replied. "He said he doesn't want to 'undermine' Vestar but to destroy it as it is in our time."

Even the Marauders had a sense of the delicacy of time, and were unsure as to what would become of themselves if they crushed the beginning of Vestar. Besides, clearing the Queen's name would be easiest if she faced those who were supposedly her friends.

"Lucky for us he isn't going back in time to destroy it," Konstan muttered. "Or we might not have the Captain to save you. Do you know *anything* specific about his plans?"

Samantha paused, remembering the nightmarish images imparted by the influence of the crystal while she had worn it.

"I think," she said slowly, "that he's intending for me to trick Vestar into thinking that we're no threat, perhaps not even Marauders but escaped slaves, and take over any Vestar ships that meet us."

"If that happens," Marc said briefly, "use the Vestar code for emergency plans and no questions asked. Do you remember it?"

Samantha gave the affirmative, her heart rate relaxing ever so slightly.

"I'm afraid you're going to have to play this by ear, Samantha, but be brave!" Marc urged her. "As soon as you find out anything, call us if you can. In the meantime. . . I have an idea, and luckily, we have five hours to work with. We're going to do everything we can to help you. I'm not going to lose you, Samantha. We'll save you, I promise."

"If all else fails, sis, trust your judgment and keep praying," Konstan told her. "I haven't known you to make the wrong decision often. Trust, and everything will work out."

"I know," Samantha whispered. She took a deep breath and promised to call if she was given the chance. She slipped the device into the collar of her gown, tearing a small hole in the lining to place it in, and pinned it closed. She had a vague terror that Medrhos would somehow already know of it. Marc and Konstan were right. She had to try and discover as much as she could; only then could she make any kind of a plan.

Arising, she paused briefly in front of her mirror and tried to rub away the red mark on her cheek. It was stubborn, but finally, for lack of ice, she pulled the cold medal from the chain around her neck. The dull pain and the redness faded at last.

Rubbing the medal thoughtfully, she slipped from her room, finally ready to confront her 'husband' again. He was in his throne on the bridge, watching the tunnel-light flicker through the cracks of the heat-shielded viewport.

"A few hours more, Maeris," he said without turning. "Then your chance will come."

"My chance of what," she replied, joining him and forcing herself to lay her hand on his arm.

"To prove yourself a true Marauder Queen," Medrhos smiled softly. "To fulfill all that we knew you to be, those long ago days on Almedra. I can't wait to see how you do it."

Samantha bit her lip and let her eyes focus on the dancing shadows. "If you want me to work with you, Rhos, I think you should share your plan with me so I know what to do." She steeled herself to hide the worry in her eyes and tilted her head back to glance at him. His eyes sparked in reply and he was once more the cruel and calculating king that had taken her from Marc's side.

"I hope you don't think you can find a way around me," he purred softly. "I've already sealed off any escape you could take, Maeris. I won't lose you. Not this time."

Samantha's heart crashed painfully as though it had dropped from a twenty-story palace window. It was as she feared.

"No," she whispered. "You're always two steps ahead." Medrhos softened for a moment and he kissed her brow again.

"It will be over soon enough, and we'll be home again and all will be well," he soothed her. He told her then that once they arrived at the edge of the Great Galaxy, in her own time, they would surely be greeted by Vestar. Then, Samantha would be left to her own devices. She must obtain their entry to the galaxy, and in making the Great Raid possible, her worth would be proven to all who distrusted her.

Now the warlord took her arm and placed her in the Queen's carpeted flat, raised a few feet above the bridge. It was spacious enough, at two-hundred square feet, open-walled and empty save for her couch that looked out over the bridge and her own bay viewports.

Medrhos intended to keep an eye on her. She would have no opportunity to call Marc again. Perhaps it was just as well; what could he do? She would just have to pray that she would be given the opportunity to use the emergency code.

Medrhos lightly touched Samantha's scar and it stung faintly, like salt on a wound.

"Remember your promise, Maeris. I will protect you. If you try to work against me, I will block you. I won't let you lose your life for so low a price; the Cult will never touch you."

But his eyes were gleaming with the same light that glowed in those kingly gems bound upon his hands. Slowly, slowly, they were drawing him back down the darker path he had tread before Samantha's arrival. She was losing the ability to influence him towards good!

Oh, that this would be the last journey, that somehow, somewhere, God would place Medrhos on His Calvary. She would have given her life for it. She would just have to wait and see.

IV

Straits

Samantha stood alone, looking out at the pitch-black sky, sprinkled with diamond dots that were galaxies. The long time-flight was over, and now they were crossing the narrow void between Andromeda and the Great Galaxy. She stared out into the blackness as if for an answer to her predicament.

It was such a difference from the whirling, colored confusion of the time-flight. Now there was silence except for the distant, internal hum of the engines mingling with the murmur of the air flowing through life-support. Every sound that did fall was quickly caught by her ears, even faintly.

The soldiers had left her entirely alone, and Medrhos didn't come near her, either. The flat was wide and open, with the lingering smell of newly laid carpet.

She had thought that once she was alone, an answer would come, that God would surely aid her, at least noticeably. It was not so; nothing came, not to her mind, nor to her heart. It was as though the rushing river of her thoughts had stopped, leaving her mind and heart silent and clear, but without the answers that usually come with clarity.

Was there an answer? If there was no answer, did that mean she had to follow through? Or should she return to Medrhos and let him strike her with the fury of the Cult that would surely consume him if she did not acquiesce? Her fingers found the medal around her neck for the hundredth time.

She heard the hum of the engines grow louder and realized the ship was moving ever faster towards the bright opal band that was the arm of the Great Galaxy. Medrhos swept into the flat and stood beside her.

"They're coming," he said. He gave her a sideways glance. "Don't back down, Maeris."

Samantha kept watching and waiting, wondering what Marc would have done in her place. Now the clouds were sweeping over them, and there! Two great battleships and three lighter-class carriers were coming upon them.

Medrhos did not order the *Harbinger* to stop until the Vestar ships held their position. Samantha stood waiting for her cue, without knowing what she would say or do when the call came through. The code was all she was armed with.

She mentally stood before the tabernacle in the chapel aboard the *Lumenara* and wished He'd say something. But sometimes, she supposed, she'd just have to trust herself. She had free will and sometimes God was just going to let her choose without saying a word.

The largest battleship hailed them.

"This is General Altarra of the Vestar Fleet. You Marauders are trespassing in our galaxy; you will not be allowed to enter in further. Turn back now and return whence you came! Entrance here means death."

Medrhos smiled languidly at the dramatic message and signaled Samantha. She took a moment to answer. She still didn't know what to say.

For an instant, she saw His Face as her fingers brushed the medal around her neck. Her heart beat faster as it hit her. She flipped the switch to open the channel.

"This is Samantha Mariel Anselle, #612-41A of the *Lumenara V*, Vestar fleet #31097, code 5501. We are not here to harm or take captives. I wish to be taken to Earth; the Marauders have given their word that no harm will come to anyone on the way. Will you stand down?"

Medrhos was looking at her in suspicion. If Altarra listened, he would bring Samantha on board his ship unaccompanied. Samantha gestured to the blaster that even she now wore. There was no reason to avoid using them to gain entrance to the ship. Medrhos shook his head, but he was smiling and she knew he understood.

From Altarra's brief silence, she could tell that he, too, understood; for she had replaced the *Lumenara's* fleet code, 6971, with the code 5501, the code which Marc had commanded her to give. Would Altarra trust her?

"To clear you, we must clear it with Vestar headquarters," he said warily. "If you care to wait."

Medrhos nodded. Samantha answered the question positively. Twenty minutes ticked by. At last Altarra said he had been ordered to take Samantha aboard.

"You're an engineer, Ms. Anselle, I trust you can pilot a shuttle," he said. "Bring yourself and no one else, and we'll take you to your destination." Samantha thanked him and turned to look at Medrhos.

"Keep your promise, Rhos, don't hurt them," she warned.

"M'lady, I wouldn't dream of it," he answered with a twisted smile, and helped her into the shuttle.

Samantha took the controls and prayed that Medrhos would keep himself in hand and find some sensible way of getting something done, that wouldn't wreak too much havoc yet might keep the Interrogators off him long enough for her to save him. It wasn't in her hands now. . . all she could do was pilot her way to the ship and warn Altarra.

She locked the hatch and kicked the swift little shuttle into gear. Five minutes' time found her docked, and she disembarked to be greeted by Altarra, his first lieutenant, and five men with pistols set to stun.

"Anselle, just what exactly are you doing that requires code 5501?" Altarra demanded, grabbing her arm and pulling her along to the bridge as the shuttle was inspected.

"I'm trying to save a million lives, General, and unfortunately I can't by a hop, skip, and a jump."

She briefly told him the situation – would he understand? Altarra frowned darkly when warned that Medrhos and several men were probably already onboard, though the Marauder ships were already retreating.

"By the stars, I *hope* you know what you're doing! If headquarters had any idea what I just let you do they might haul us all in. Just how do you think you're going to make him keep his word?"

They were entering the bridge now.

"I don't think," Samantha replied. "I pray. I'm going to try and have him take something, not some*one*, mind you, that will help turn him. I'm going to have him steal the Resurrection Veil."

Altarra exploded. "The Resurrection Veil, are you *insane*? Just how do you think you're going to do that?" he spluttered. "Look, I'm not even much of a practicer, but on our modern Earth, with the majority of the crazies and the power-hungry Red Stars having left to make a planet in their own image, *everyone* knows what the Resurrection Veil is, and *no one* is going to let you walk in and take it! Alright, maybe there are quite a few of them left, but historians and architects and snake-tongued politicians use it for themselves too. And I'm not about to help you steal it, either. I'll take you down, but that is all. I thought you'd be decent enough to–"

"I feel the same way, Captain," Samantha said gently. "But would you rather have all those on Earth enslaved, or worse?"

Altarra fell silent, looking at the wedding ring on his hand. He clenched his fist and sighed. "I can't believe that I'm going to steal a relic with you, but you're right. What am I doing?" he groaned.

Samantha put her hand on his shoulder. "If God wills it to go well, your family, and everyone else, will be safe. But if I fail and any harm comes to anyone, I won't stand in the way of your duty, Altarra. . . I'm sure you'd have me in a cell by then."

"Perhaps," Altarra muttered, looking out into space as the course was set for Earth. "But I guess I'll pray with you, Anselle. Pray that we're not going to destroy our own world."

V

Risk

Samantha shaded her eyes from the sunlight that darkened her vision after the long voyage. She was greeted by the mulberry-sapphire haze of the Atlantic. The sun was sinking in the east, leaving a trail that glittered on the water and the city that crowned the waves. This was Arce'Atelane, City of the Sea, the birthplace and home of the original Vestar Fleet.

The spirals of silver and crystal melted into the waves and looked to be born of them. The island had been constructed ages ago, and had grown from a small, secret outpost to a city filled with the hum of a thousand languages – those who guarded the galaxy.

Samantha stepped from the causeway of the *Czar* with Altarra, who had been summoned with her to Point Alise, the home base of Vestar's highest ranking officers and the so-called 'Galactic Embassy'. But before they could get there, they had to get through the crowd.

The port's gracefully lit piazza, which flowed in from where both sea and space vessels docked, was now swarming. Apparently, the news of the 'quiet' Marauder incident had been leaked, and everyone wanted to know who the Marauders had either planted in the Ocean City, or, preferably, had been intimidated by enough to release. Either way, Samantha's arrival was a long overdue sensation. Things had been quiet in the city before now, without the pirating troubles faced by the Vestar Fleet of Andromeda.

There was a murmur of anxiety and excitement as Altarra, greatly agitated, swept a path through the crowd for his newly acquired charge. A Vestar armored sedan was waiting at the edge of the piazza, an officer leaning against the door. He looked keenly at Samantha.

Altarra had asked the girl to exchange her royal Marauder gown for a less intimidating dress of white and seafoam green. It still bore obvious Marauder elements, as Samantha realized that it would be better to show some connection to their culture than to hide it completely. The first thought on everyone's mind would be that she was a spy, as well as they may; so, she would be honest even in her dress.

Altarra slid into the backseat with her and the officer shut them in, starting the engine. The sedan used the force of magnetism to glide smoothly a few inches above the road, passing other sedans and commercial and private vehicles that graced the city like an ever-moving silver ribbon.

The usually happy streets, with couples taking evening strolls, and families attending festivals on the beach, were quieter with the strangeness of the day. No one was quite sure what the news meant – an invasion perhaps, and so no one felt like celebrating. There were still many out for a walk, but they were in earnest conversation, and their eyes kept darting to the sky as if expecting to see fire fall.

"So," Altarra murmured, leaning over to Samantha. "Are you going to lie to Governor-General Vereon? Or will you tell him what's really going on?"

Samantha nervously beat her hand on the armrest of her seat. "I don't know," she said softly. "I won't lie. But how do you expect the Governor-General might react if I tell him the whole truth?"

Altarra sighed and shook his head. "He's a wise and cautious man, kind too, but if you tell him that you're dragging a bunch of Marauders here, he'll have the same conflict as I had. I can promise you, it will be harder to convince him. His responsibilities to protect our world are far greater than my own. He would feel that he must speak to every head of state, unless you have the perfect method of convincing him, Anselle."

Samantha drew a deep breath. "Then I don't know what I'm going to do. I guess we'll see what comes to mind when we face whatever interrogation we have waiting for us."

Altarra nodded and they lapsed into silence.

Samantha was thinking of Medrhos. After she had left her conference with Altarra, she had hunted down her 'husband' deep in the cargo bay of the *Czar*, with half a dozen of his men. The rest, he informed her, would come at a moment's call through any portal they chose.

For now, the group had safely hidden their life signs and the electronic signals of their gear, and had placed themselves in one of the hidden bulkheads where no one would look.

Looking into Medrhos' eyes had brought again that chill of fear. She could still feel that dark power trying to penetrate her – what if it knew all her plans? What if Medrhos would now play the same acting game and let her do her part, only to tear that world into pieces? She could only trust blindly.

She swiftly instructed him in the knowledge she possessed, of their first landfall on Earth, the plans Altarra had made for taking her to Vestar, and what she thought they could expect. But then she begged him not to steal anything sacred to her faith.

"It would be an awful thing," she had told him, "to have it on my heart, and far more because it would cause chaos on this Earth – for many who live there are of my faith, others having left to create their own worlds. But then. . . they are far too protected for you to be able to steal even one," she reassured herself.

Medrhos' eyes had narrowed as he looked at her in amusement. He laughed. "Show me how to take one, my Queen. If you do this, the Interrogators will be pleased, and then when I return for the true raid, you can help from home. No more torturing your soul by being present amidst the chaos."

Samantha tried to argue, but Medrhos insisted and she gave in. "Promise that you won't take any prisoners this time, then? That you won't hurt anyone? And can I please pick which one you take, because if you take it, it becomes mine; for what's yours is mine, isn't it? And perhaps. . . I can help you take it."

Medrhos had shaken his head, but seemed more pleased than before. "Cross my heart, Maeris, I shall do as you wish this once, and all of this shall save you quite well."

Samantha took him seriously, and gently crossed his heart, which made him soften for a moment.

"Maeris. . . well, this is your test. Pick the sacred item that will be the greatest feat, and get us there."

~~~

The evening sun still gilt the ocean surrounding the city and the stars had not yet started to show themselves when the sedan slipped through a spiraling gardenway, up the center hill of the island. Samantha stirred from her thoughts when she sensed the change in scenery.

The sedan came to a stop on the height, in a wide cobblestone courtyard before an old-fashioned villa. It was distantly flanked by two grand buildings: the offices and homes of some of Vestar's greatest men.

Five officers stood on the walk up to the house, waiting to greet those who rode within – or quite possibly, to congratulate Altarra and arrest Samantha.

The driver, Antoine was his name, opened the door for them both, having never said a word to either. His eyes still studied Samantha, looking for answers. Samantha looked to those who waited.

Three were officers, men and women of varying ranks, dressed in the accompanying shades of blue, red, and violet. The other two were a strongly-built, white-haired general, and a king. Or so Samantha supposed. She wasn't far off.

Altarra strode forward, leaving the girl to trail behind, kept moving by the fact that Antoine was on her heels.

"Governor-General Vereon, sir!" Altarra saluted.

Vereon gravely shook his hand.

"We are glad of your return. We have much to speak of." His eyes briefly met Samantha's, but he motioned Altarra's attention to the regal figure present. Altarra gave a curt bow, clearly unimpressed.

"An unexpected pleasure, your majesty."

"Unexpected times," was the reply from the man dressed in black and white. Something about his eyes reminded Samantha of Medrhos.

"Anselle!" Altarra said sharply. "The Emperor Serengoch of the United Nations, and Governor-General Vereon, commander of all of Vestar in the Great Galaxy. Sirs, this is Samantha Anselle, one of our engineers, who has been released by the Marauders."

Hard stares went all around, then Samantha gave a half-curtsy.

"Sirs," she murmured. "I know you don't wish to waste time on formalities. Shall we begin the interrogation you have in store for me?"

"Indeed," Vereon answered. "Come with us, Altarra, Anselle."

He led them into the massive villa, home of the Galactic Embassy and himself. The smooth mosaic marble floors cast echoes of their footsteps, and were softened by the tropical plants in every corner. Hues of cream, topaz, and jade melded with the view of the ocean through the crystal windows that stretched to the ceiling, flooding every room with the last light of the setting sun.

Vereon's office was starkly contrasted with the rest of the house by its white modernity, built of sea-stone and equipped with all the necessary resources for a man who commanded a fleet of millions of men and women, and thousands of ships. Here on Arce'Atelane, he was as his own king, free of the jurisdiction even of Emperor Serengoch.

Vereon bade them all to sit as he took the chair behind his desk. Samantha was seated directly across from him, Altarra nearby, while Serengoch lounged on a window seat.

"I know already how you came to be here with Altarra," Vereon informed her, wasting no time. "What we don't know, is the story of your capture and why the Marauders would release you. It is unprecedented that they, tyrants and slave traders that they are, should release anyone they captured. Moreover, with the information that Altarra gave us, we know that you are not from Earth. You know, of course, what we suspect."

"I understand your train of thought," Samantha said simply. She was eyeing Serengoch. She needed almost as many answers as they did. She sensed that she could not trust him. "It is also my understanding that here, you own your own jurisdiction."

Vereon frowned but nodded.

"Then, with all due respect, I ask that the Emperor not be present. As you can imagine, after being amongst the Marauders, the only men I trust are of Vestar. If, afterwards, you conclude that what I have to say is of import to him, then by all means. . . "

"We hardly think you need distrust us," Serengoch said with a strange mix of flattery and frustration. "We're sure the Governor-General and ourselves understand the trauma you've suffered."

He arose and came to her with a pitying look, which he quickly found didn't suit the engineer's knowing expression. The Emperor dropped it hastily, but offered the girl his hand, trying to be reassuring.

"Anselle, we're trying to help you. We'll do everything in our power to keep you from suffering at their hands again, but we need to know everything. Trust us."

"Forgive me, but I don't," Samantha drawled, pulling her hand away. "Somehow I get the feeling you're more likely to put me back with them than to help me any. Good day, your majesty, I'm sure you know where the door is." She turned away from him and caught Altarra's eyes twinkling.

"I'm afraid I side with the girl on this one, your majesty," Vereon agreed, arising. "Please leave us. I shall inform you if there is anything that you should know."

Serengoch's eyes sparked but he languidly acquiesced. Vereon, Samantha, and Altarra waited tensely until the door clicked shut, and the stormy footsteps receded down the hall.

"Anselle, what on earth is going on?"

"Overall, in the universe, more like," Altarra muttered, straightening in his chair and looking anxiously at his charge.

"Earth is in grave danger."

"So I surmised."

Samantha arose and slowly went to the window.

"I was not released." She was afraid she wasn't doing the right thing by telling him. What if Medrhos was somehow hearing everything? The only sound was the clicking of one of the computers.

"Anselle, what have you done?"

"As you know, I have been among the Marauders for some months now. I know the darkness that binds them, but I believe I have also found the key to breaking it. I need to go to Italy. I need the Resurrection Veil."

Version stared. "You mean. . . to take it."

"Yes. With or without permission I will take it. It is the only chance anyone has in these two galaxies of ours, and Vestar won't be able to stop them from taking all that they desire. General. . . the Emperor is here. If you value all that you love – you need not even help me – only set me free for Italy. I can't promise to keep the Marauders in check, but this is our only chance. Please, tell no one of this, and let me go."

Vereon stood with clenched hands, looking at her. But his gaze trembled. He turned his eyes out the window to see the moonlight glinting off the ocean below, the city lights twinkling, and Vestar patrols returning.

"General," Altarra whispered. "The danger is here. It's a risk that can no longer be avoided, and one that never could have been. All we can do is our duty, in trying to save what we can, and end this battle now."

Vereon turned back to them. "This could be the end of time," he murmured. "The end of all things as we know it. The end of our lives, the world, the universe. Altarra is right. There is no longer a choice, or a path of perfect safety for any of us." He exhaled. "The Emperor-"

"Which one."

"Good question. The Marauder King. Where is he now?"

"I can't be sure. Most likely onboard the *Czar*, unless he decided to enjoy the nightlife incognito."

Altarra noted the anxiety in the general's eyes. "Sir, I think you can trust that all is well for now. Anselle is-" He looked at her.

"He considers me his wife," she supplied. "I am not, but I am able to sway him slightly. He promised that no harm would come to anyone, this time, and that the only thing he would take is the relic I have chosen."

Vereon breathed a sigh. "Very well. Anselle, I don't advise informing Serengoch. I'm sure he would try his own questionable methods. As for you, tonight you may take a suite in the International Apartments next door. You'll find every means of making yourself at home. For now, I would ask that you locate the Marauder King and ensure that all goes well before you retire. Of course, we will find a suitable reason for your departure in the morning, that he might not suspect our conversation. We will message your room tonight with such words." He took her to the door.

"There being a need for me to keep Altarra here," he said quietly, "we will need to trust someone else with this situation. We'll have to move our troops into position, of course, just in case, but perhaps in the dark. There are few we can trust not to talk even to their families, and that would put you in grave peril."

"I understand. I'll be fine on my own, and it perhaps would be better. If he sees me by myself, he'll understand that you trust me, and it won't raise his suspicions."

"Very well. There is a network of trains running beneath the city, and you'll find digital maps all around the streets. Here is my number, if you need to reach me for any reason. *Any* reason."

He sent a text to the com-watch Altarra had given her onboard the *Czar*. Samantha thanked him and slipped out of the office.

Now that it was dark, all the lights glowed throughout the corridors of the house. She exited and paused on the edge of the terrace to get her bearings.

There was the distant murmur and clink of glasses and plates, coming from the massive dining room of the Galactic Embassy. It mingled with the faint sighing of the waves, and the sound of cars and music down below. The people in the city only had a vague fear of what might be happening; a fear vague enough that it seemed one to be laughed off, one that would vanish in the morning light. And so, nightlife was returning to normal.

Samantha hoped that this vague fear would be all they would ever know, but something warned her that Medrhos was going to have to be more than silent on this Earth. She took a deep breath and gently silenced her worried thoughts. All she could do was what she felt she must do.

At the moment, that was checking in on Medrhos and making sure he was sticking to the script. Which was hardly likely.

It took several minutes for Samantha to hurry down the spiraling gardenway and finally come out into the busy streets of Arce'Atelane. She checked the nearest digi-map for the route back to the harbor, deciding to forego the train. It would be a long, enjoyable walk, minus her mind trying to imagine what Medrhos might be getting into.

As she proceeded down the busy sidewalk, she didn't notice the dark limo that slid from the shadows of an alley beside the gardenway's entrance. A white square was on the door, cut in half by a red sickle moon.

Samantha tried to study her surroundings as she walked. She also tried to act as though she belonged there. Those who had seen her that morning when she had disembarked the *Czar*, she worried, would not easily forget her. To her relief, no one seemed to remember her, and those whom she passed gave her a smile as they went on their way.

Jazz music serenaded the giant palm fronds that swayed over the sidewalk as children ran by, plucking sea grapes from the vines on the way to the nearest diner or the magic show in the square. There were theaters, hotels, stores, and restaurants unlike any that Samantha had seen on any of the planets she had recently visited.

So this was the birthplace of the human race, she marveled. It was strange, but still she could discern pieces of life that had been woven throughout every subsequent culture in the galaxy. These were webs that made these places home. The surroundings might be different, she thought, laughing as children ran by chasing a parrot, and nearly pushed the engineer into a tangle of papayas and hibiscus. Yet it seemed lovingly familiar. She was nearing the heart of the city now, not more than a mile from the harbor.

A commotion by a nearby fountain pulled her to a halt. It was the magic show. Children were gathered around the magician, who declared that he could make a carrot disappear in three seconds. He held up the carrot and all the children began to count – but at the count of three, instead of a puff of smoke, the carrot went flying into the water, where it was promptly devoured by a family of ducks. The children screamed with laughter and begged for another.

Suddenly a prickly feeling crept up Samantha's spine as though someone was behind her.

"Fun, isn't it?" a soft whisper came from just beside her. The limo was at the curb. Serengoch smiled from inside. The door was open, and something cold was pressed against her shoulderblade.

VI

Aurora

From the expression on the guard's face, and the prick of the stun-gun she felt in her shoulder, Samantha had no choice. She slid into the back seat with the Emperor. The door was slammed shut and the limo pulled back into traffic.

White, gold and ruby lights flowed to and fro in a steady stream on either side of them as they left the harbor behind. Samantha glanced at Serengoch. He was watching her, with eyes not unlike Medrhos when he was in his Warlord frame of mind.

"I would call this kidnapping," Samantha stated.

Serengoch smiled with a shadow over his face. "It would be wise to trust us. But wait until we have stopped."

The limo pulled into a shadowy street. Ahead there was a glimpse of the water, behind the distant glow of the streetlights, and high stone walls pressing in on either side. The engine was turned off, and the lights of the limo as well. They sat in darkness. Serengoch turned to his companion, weaving his fingers as he looked at her. The only light was a shaft of moonlight that fell through the glass roof of the car and cut across their faces.

"Now that we are away from Vereon and his self-jurisdiction, you may tell us everything."

Samantha looked at him, wondering what part of his memory had forgotten that *she* had been the one who didn't want to tell him anything.

"There is nothing to tell you," she said calmly. "What I had to say was for Vestar alone, and there is no need for you to know anything. I chose not to have you present, and it was agreed that it did not pertain to you."

"A Marauder threat to my empire is certainly my business. According to your record. . . ." Serengoch languidly flipped through a file. "Putting an entire world's population potentially at risk is unlike you."

Samantha pulled the file away from him and peered at it. "Pilfering private Vestar files is very much like you, apparently. You're right, I do not desire nor intend to put a population at risk." She shrugged. "I think you have wasted your time."

Serengoch leaned forward. "Anselle. . . we recommend that you tell us what you know."

"May I ask why?"

"Because," he whispered, "the Marauders aren't the only ones who know how to gain information. If you don't tell me everything I want to know, you'll find yourself conveniently kidnapped in the same manner they kidnapped you. Only, this time it will be my empire. "

Samantha slammed the file into his face and her elbow into the glass of the locked window, shattering it. She vaulted out but Serengoch caught her arm and she fell into the side of the car.

"I'll take that as my offer accepted. Arlan, handcuff her and put her in the back. We'll take her with us in the morn-"

He never finished his sentence. His words weren't able to catch up with him as he was thrown over the roof of the car and collapsed in an undignified heap on the street.

Arlan jerked out his pistol and found himself precipitated onto the nearest lamppost, where he hung like a broken marionette. The chauffeur took one look at the Vestar captain and ran.

The newcomer gently lifted Samantha to her feet and steadied her. She glanced up. Beneath the brim of his cap sparkled a familiar set of angry hazel eyes. The girl breathed a sigh that was only half in relief.

"Never thought I'd see the day where you'd don Vestar blue," she laughed faintly.

Medrhos smirked. "It came sooner than I thought," he admitted. "But you know, I just *had* to have clearance to go wherever I wish."

He slipped around the car and picked up Serengoch by the collar.

"Hm, smaller than I thought," he commented. "I'm sure someone will be quite interested in what you were trying to do. I recommend not trying it again."

He dropped a very weak and furious Serengoch back on the cobblestone street and returned to Samantha. He offered her his arm.

"May I buy you dinner, Anselle?"

"Of course," Samantha smiled, as they started down the alleyway.

Returning to the warmly lit downtown streets was a welcome relief. Medrhos steered her down the sidewalk and soon they were back in the comforting busyness of the city evening.

The Marauder looked down at Samantha's arm, feeling that she was still shaking. Her elbow was bleeding profusely from shattering the window. He pulled her to a stop under a blossoming wave of jasmine and passionflowers that stooped over the low wall.

With an almost curious look, he cupped his hand over the bloody area. It was then that Samantha realized he was not wearing his gloves; they were tucked into the pocket of his coat.

A soft warmth seemed to glaze the scrapes as though with beeswax and herbs, as was done on Almedra. Samantha had a sudden vivid memory of her mother rubbing such a salve on a scrape she had received the day Medrhos had saved her from the waterfall, and he had looked solicitously on to see if she would be alright.

Medrhos lifted his hand and smiled with pleasure, for the cuts were gone, blood cleansed from her sleeve, and the rents no longer visible.

Samantha studied it in surprise. This was not Medrhos' power of destruction, nor the dark power that he could bend to his will. It was warm and soft – the power he had used to create a vine to save her from her fall, unlike that used to destroy the spider. Samantha raised her eyes and found something had lifted from that hazel gaze. No, this power was not dark. It was something far better. He was not completely gone!

Just as Coran and Silvestra's love was healing, Medrhos' love for her was still keeping him alive, deep inside. Samantha trembled with a rush of relief. She took his ungloved hand.

"Thank you, Rhos."

He smiled back, relieved that she was not distressed.

"You're still shaking. How about that dinner I promised you?"

Samantha nodded and they continued down the street toward the harbor, where Medrhos had seen several eateries that had interested him.

As they came out of the downtown streets, the buildings fell away into wide open spaces: parks, plazas, the harbor – a distant clatter and the laughing shriek of several dozen voices pulled their gaze to the left where, tucked around the tropical trees, strange constructions, flashing signs, and many colored lights danced.

A track ran high above into the sky, twisting and turning with sudden drops and hills. A tram sped along it, full of laughing passengers. A dozen other strange amusements were in motion, and the large sign called it 'Atlantis Borealis, Land of Stars and Sea: an Amusement Park.'

"What in the universe is that thing?" Medrhos asked, tilting his head back to see the starship-shaped carts flying overhead, seemingly reaching for the stars.

"I have no idea, but apparently it's for fun?" Samantha suggested, examining the sign.

"I'm curious," Medrhos said. "But never mind, you need something to eat."

Just then they caught a tantalizing scent coming from the park.

"Smells like they have food," Samantha commented. "I'm up for it if you are."

They hesitated no further and ran through the archway entrance. Samantha looked at the cost and almost turned around, but Medrhos mischievously took the Vestar access card from his pocket, showed it to the ticket master, and pulled her through the gate before she could argue. Samantha, of course, had lost her card way back when she had been taken to Mal'lon. Only, now it belonged to Medrhos.

They stopped and looked around. Dancing lights mimicked the aurora borealis overhead, glowing soft greens, blues, and purples, while the waves crashed in the distance. Men and women, workers apparently, passed by in astro costumes and aquatic regalia. There were simulators, carousels, and gift shops in the front. Medrhos led the way deeper into the park, where they found a museum, aquarium, and a monorail, and all around were booths with carnival games and prizes.

Food stands were everywhere, and Medrhos took duty before fun. He looked with skeptical interest at the strange items on the menu. They came away with a corn dog, fries, pickles, and a 'rocket engine' double waffle cone with orange and honeybell ice cream. Samantha stared even more skeptically at the amount of food she was expected to eat while Medrhos would surely go hunt up a steak.

"Um, Rhos? I can't eat all of that," she reminded him dubiously.

"Certainly not," he said loftily. "I intend to try it and see what this culture's tastes are like. That's what tourists do, isn't it?"

So saying, he munched on half the corndog in between acquiring the majority of the fries and pickles. Samantha stared. This was not Marauder food in the slightest. She found herself wanting to laugh at the sight, so she hastily stuffed a few fries into her mouth, nearly choking. Once the salty foods had been polished off they snapped the double cone apart and set off again, enjoying the tart sweetness.

Down by the waterfront they found a map revealing that the Atlantis rides lay beneath the water. A few, including a plexiglass water slide, began above water and disappeared below for a tour of underwater ruins. Others had to be reached via a long deck that stretched out to a plexiglass elevator.

Along the beach a great deal of vegetation had washed up and was being collected by workers from the seafood grill. Medrhos picked up a piece.

"Is this. . . lettuce?" he asked in confusion. Clearly he had never seen seaweed, hence his confusion; but Samantha could hardly keep herself from giggling.

"No, it's sea-lettuce," she said. "The lettuce sea."

"Let us see what?"

Samantha laughed and shook her head, pointing to the sign she had been reading from. On the ocean bed there was a field of seaweed, so vast it had jokingly been christened the lettuce sea.

"Ah," said Medrhos, and threw the piece of seaweed away. He still wasn't interested in eating it. Samantha picked up another piece and rinsed it in a nearby cleansing fountain, dedicated to the purpose.

"You said you want to act like a tourist! Eat it."

After much protesting Medrhos finally did, albeit with an expression that revealed his distaste. Probably because it was green.

After being forced to finish it, he dragged her through the park to their original reason for entering: the roller coaster. The line was long, and it seemed to creep along like a starfish on the ocean floor. They leaned on the rails that hemmed in the straggling would-be riders and busied themselves watching the false aurora overhead.

Children in the line ogled at Medrhos' captain's costume, complete with the badges of honor he had vainly chosen to add, representing, of course, the victories he had won as a Marauder.

Finally, after much elbowing, the children got up the courage to inquire whether he had been in many space battles. Medrhos was flattered.

"A few," he admitted.

"How many?" they still begged.

"Oh, just a handful. . . Alright, alright! Maybe a few dozen," he exclaimed, as the children jumped and tugged on his sleeve, shouting that they needed to know. Then they cried that he must recount tales of his deeds, but their parents apologetically herded them back to their places in the line. Samantha looked at the Emperor and smiled.

"Don't you wish children looked up to you like that?"

Medrhos straightened his coat, trying not to smile. "I do have children looking up to me," he said calmly.

"Not in the best way. Oh, come on Rhos, you know that, don't you ever wish you were a normal person and could ride roller coasters as often as you like?" she asked laughingly.

"Pfft, I can ride roller coasters whenever I like anyway. I can build one if I want to. Except I haven't been on one yet, so I can't say that I actually want to ride one whenever I like," he retorted.

The teasing continued to pass the time it took to finally reach the side of the track and climb into one of the silver carts. Medrhos casually tucked one arm around Samantha's shoulder, ignoring the children who were ignoring the beginning of the ride to turn around and stare at him. The magnetic tram began to glide along the track, creeping up the first incline.

"You know, you're *really* going to attract attention if anyone remembers that I got here this morning," Samantha began, but whatever she or Medrhos were about to say was cut off as the carts ignited a fiery tail and plunged down the steep incline.

Medrhos nearly lost his cap but Samantha barely managed to catch it by the brim; she nearly lost her stomach as the cart took a sharp turn and twisted onto the bottom of the track several times before righting itself. It slowed and they glided along among the aurora borealis and the stars overhead, before plummeting up and down again, dodging holographic asteroids, and coming to a dizzying stop on the ground.

Medrhos and Samantha stumbled out, laughing when they found they had lost their sense of balance and direction. It took them, and all the passengers, a few minutes to regain their balance in the mock de-con chamber before they could make it out of the park without tripping over a pebble.

"I'll stick to falling from a waterfall, thank you very much," Samantha panted, her hand on her still concerned stomach.

"I'll stick to rescuing you from falling from said waterfall, thank you very much," Medrhos joked, putting on his cap and trying to fix his slightly crossed vision.

He declared that it was time for a real dinner, if only to get the taste of sea lettuce out of his mouth. They found a restaurant called Pizzeria Under the Sea. While Samantha was familiar with pizza, Medrhos wasn't; he only that he thought Samantha would enjoy the place from its looks. It was painted soft shades with an ocean theme, and when they entered, they found themselves viewing the kitchens.

Their signature dough, made with refined oceanwater, was deftly being thrown in the air to form the pizza crusts, and they could smell sausages and veggies frying in butter. A stairway led down to the underground dining room. It was surrounded by four glass walls, behind which swam brightly-colored fish that played hide and seek amongst jewel-like corals.

Fascinated, Samantha only half paid attention to the waitress who seated them near the southern wall and handed Medrhos the menu. He looked blankly at it and had to ask Samantha what half of it said. Samantha couldn't resist. She ordered for him.

When the pizza arrived, Medrhos' eyes widened and he wondered who in the galaxy put such things on a dinner entrée. Half of the saltwater crust was topped with glorious mounds of cheese and tomato sauce, piled high with raspberries, pepperoni, and chocolate chips, while the other half was coated with olive oil, fried potatoes, feta, and drizzled with maple syrup.

"You said you wanted to eat like a tourist," Samantha teased. "You might want to eat some humble pie."

She put a forkful in her mouth and tried not to choke as she watched Medrhos gingerly attempting to eat his slice. A little girl, only a few years old, was watching from a nearby table. She scooted off her chair and tugged on his sleeve.

"You eat like dis," she demonstrated, with messy hands. Medrhos looked at her fingers and reluctantly gave it a try. The child took a chocolate chip from his slice and munched on it, with a piece of potato in her other hand.

"Learns fast," she admired, while tugging curiously at the gloves in his pocket. Medrhos hurriedly dropped his pizza upside-down on his plate and caught her hand.

"Don't touch, little one," he said, tucking them back away before she could pull at the gems.

"They pwetty, are they hers?" She cocked her head at Samantha.

"No, they're mine for. . .work," Medrhos sighed.

The girl studied him. "Only pwinces wear pwetty things, are you a pwince?" she asked with sudden excitement. Medrhos coughed as he nearly choked on a raspberry.

"Momeeeeee!" the girl squealed running back to her mother. "Momeeeee he's a real *pwince* and he's *choking*!"

She grabbed her chocolate milk and raced back to the unfortunate Medrhos, who had completely neglected to order anything but lemon water, thanks to Samantha. Medrhos wouldn't take the glass but the girl was persistent.

"Dwink!" she insisted. "Den you won't choke."

Samantha accepted the glass and put it in Medrhos' hand as she thumped him on the back. He gave in and drank it, and managed to dislodge the miscreant raspberry from his throat. He grinned sheepishly when he saw that Samantha was laughing – laughing at the fact that Medrhos the warlord sat there drinking not beer nor wine, but chocolate milk from a toddler's cup.

"Sometimes, I think I care about you," Samantha said to him, leaning her head on her hand as she watched him. "The rest of the time, you're the person I most want the *least* to do with."

Medrhos gave her a roguish grin. "That's the definition of most marriages, or so I've heard. But you might try it the other way around."

He froze when the waitress returned with two platefuls of a red and white mound. Samantha hid a smile and dug into hers. She wondered whether Medrhos was about to overdo his sugar intake; oh well, she thought.

The angel food cake, filled with creamy vanilla pudding, was dripping with fresh strawberries in syrup, strawberry ice cream, and a glorious height of whipped cream. She figured she'd give half of her oversized portion to the child who had lost her chocolate milk to Medrhos. The little girl was overjoyed at the free dessert. Medrhos made a sound of indignant disbelief.

"Why didn't you let me give her mine?" he complained. "I can't eat this. . . whatever it is."

"It's called a tourist dessert and you're eating it because I paid for it," Samantha smiled impishly. Surely using his powers burned so many calories that he could use the boost. Poor Medrhos was tortured through layer after layer of the dessert, in between wounded glares at Samantha, who was busy choking on her ice water.

But now that the subject of his gloves had been brought to mind, she watched as Medrhos' eyes darkened little by little, and as the last bite was eaten, and the tables nearby cleared, she knew the lighthearted evening had come to an end.

"Now," said Medrhos, turning to her with glittering eyes. "Tell me of your progress, Mae." He called her that in public, just as she only called him Rhos, to hide their full Marauder names.

Indeed, the fun was gone, and war had returned to his mind. Samantha straightened as she met his gaze. The respite had given her the strength to continue for his sake, and the sake of many.

"They were wary but they seem to trust me. I believe they will let me depart for Italy on the morrow, but I am waiting to hear from them. They gave me a room at the International Apartments next to the Galactic Embassy."

It was certain that he already knew that. He had made good use of his time, studying the city and its people, as well as their destination.

"But I don't advise that you visit me there, even with your Vestar trappings. I'm sure they will be keeping close surveillance on my apartment."

Medrhos eyed her for a moment but nodded. "Contact me when you have news. I will be blocking the transmission of any microphones that may have been placed in your room. If they do not allow your departure, we will do this my way."

With that final chill, he stood. "I'll walk you to your apartment."

"There is a system of subways that will take me there quickly enough. Serengoch won't cause any more trouble tonight."

Samantha tossed her napkin on the table, gently tugged the brim of Medrhos' cap, and departed the restaurant with a slowly beating heart.

The dark cloud had again shrouded her heart as it had shrouded Medrhos' soul. What she wanted most was for Marc to be at her side, to take the reins from her weary hands. But she knew it was far important that he be where God had placed him, wherever that was. She was sure the device he had given her would never be able to reach him across so vast a distance, and even if it could, it would take many hours.

The train was just pulling in as Samantha descended the stairs to the underground station and she found a seat in the emptiest compartment. It had been long since she had meditated and she knew she needed a reminder of God's presence. She closed her eyes.

The silky clack-clack of the magnetic track stirred Samantha from her meditation. Passengers disembarked on the underground level of the Apartments. She showed her room ticket to the concierge, and he sent her up to her apartment on the eleventh floor.

Gauzy curtains, soft sofas, and a flowing fountain greeted her. There were a few complimentary items of food and toiletries, a satin nightrobe which she donned, and a change of clothing for the morrow since she had brought nothing with her. She surveyed the room with tired eyes.

It would have been a comfortable haven on an exciting vacation. But silken pillows and satin coverlets would bring no warmth that night. Tomorrow she had to engineer the theft of one of the most precious relics of all time. It would be a herculean task on which the fate of the entire universe might rest.

VII

Web

The sea cruiser *Marinette* hummed over the waves, barely grazing the water, sending up rainbow sprays in its wake. Dolphins leapt in the foam, playing carefree; for they did not have to worry about how to live and how to die, only how to dance as they had been made to do.

The sun was rising, and most of the fifteen hundred passengers were still asleep, for the vessel had departed at four in the morning and was making good time to the Mediterranean Sea. Some early risers sat quietly, sipping on fragrant cups of coffee as they watched the sunrise.

Samantha was awake. Her corner of the vast cabin, with its luxuriously wide aisles and a beautiful distance between each little personal nook, was only faintly tinged by the morning rays. Her eyes stung from lack of sleep.

Her moon scars had failed to glow that night, and so she didn't even have that way of knowing whether God truly approved what she was doing. She had procrastinated her study of the relic house they would have to infiltrate, hoping for some confirmation. But He, while present, was as silent as He had been onboard the *Harbinger*.

It felt like waiting. But can one ever simply wait? Or was she searching, reaching, and pursuing? Why did He seem so distant? Was she getting no closer to Him? Was He as silent as the night on which He had been born. . . was she searching as the Wise Kings and the shepherds? There were some things she might never know, and many questions that she might never have answered. All she could do was her best, and pray that it was good.

She sighed as she brought up the datapad in her lap. She was alone. Medrhos and his men had declined sneaking onto the ship. He had messaged her in the middle of the night to say that he was not feeling well and that he would be waiting for her at their destination, via vortex, and thus would arrive at the same instant as she.

She had not heard the details, but apparently the walls of Medrhos' stolen room were not padded to match the level of sugar insanity he had reached after their culinary adventure. Sugar, it would seem, would drive a Marauder king crazy if he had too much after a life spent feasting on meat. Thankfully most of the crew of the *Czar* had been enjoying themselves in Arce'Atelane and had not heard the noise.

The cruiser was nearing the Pillars of Hercules now, and Samantha knew she had only a few hours to plan her mission. The relic she sought was going to be more difficult to take than she had expected.

Modern-day Europe was a fascinating but dangerous place; only the major cities and a few villages were inhabited now, and had grown to twice their ancient size or more. Many had abandoned Earth in search of better worlds to make their mark on, and to escape the supposed onset of 'over-population' and 'global warming'. All this left beautifully overgrown ruins throughout the European landscape.

Over the past two hundred years, the map of Europe had gradually shifted, and governments secretly led by the Red Stars had come into power in many of the reshaped countries. Altarra's remark that even politicians protected the relic for their own uses was an understatement.

All the most important relics of Rome and the surrounding area, including the Resurrection Veil, had been locked inside Castel Sant'Angelo, which had also been seized by the state. Red Star politicians of the Italian Republic had no desire to see these relics 'perform' miracles that would drive their voters away by acts of faith and virtue. No, the only miracles that happened would be kept under lock and key, and made to serve their own purposes. Samantha was not surprised to see that the republic's president, Antoni Altomi, was a close friend of Serengoch.

The Castel itself was protected by an electronic fence and was patrolled 24/7 by four guards on each side of the building. Each interior chapel – for even politicians had to appease their followers by housing the relics properly – was, when empty, guarded by a laser gate and high frequency sound emitters. If the lasers failed to catch the intruder painfully, the emitters would be tripped and create high pitched tones that would render any man unconscious. Floors were electrified. Cameras were everywhere.

Furthermore, the only place where there was easy access to hack the system was in the external control room, a recent addition which was set upon the roof: surrounded by an electrified wall four feet thick, and inside, the floor was electrified as well. Every instrument was calibrated to specific fingerprints. The slightest touch in the wrong spot and the consequences could be fatal. That was not the worst of it.

Even though Samantha could think of ways to get past all these security measures and get to the wires she needed to remove, there would be a hidden wire somewhere, through which 30,000 volts pulsed at intervals of five seconds. This wire would carry the shock through every surface surrounding the wires being tampered with.

Samantha shut her datapad with a sigh. The schematics she had been studying had been uploaded by the republic's government to prove that the precious relics were 'safe'. There was, however, one useful loophole.

Because the people of Italy loved these relics and still possessed deep devotion to them, when the republic had taken them away they did not dare keep them from the people. The people, in turn, could hardly complain about where the relics were kept, since it had been Church property.

Visiting hours were allowed every day. One hour in the morning, one in the afternoon, and one in the evening, except on Sundays and feast days, when most of the day was allowed with hidden supervision. The Italian people did not enjoy this set-up, nor being spied upon during their devotions, hence there were fewer physical guards and most of the chapel cameras were generally turned off. Certainly, all the electrical dangers were turned off as well.

The *Marinette* would arrive in the port of Civitavecchia, which was just an hour's train ride to Rome, in time for her to make it to the 10 am visiting period. Getting the group inside would be easy, then. It was Samantha's role that would be difficult. There was no more time for studying, however; most of the passengers were awake now, and the chattering and clattering of breakfast dishes were enough to ruin any train of thought.

One piece of her studies lingered in her thoughts, not unpleasantly, as she took to gazing out over the Mediterranean. If the relics had, in truth, been stolen from the people and the Church to be locked up to spite devotion and the possibility of miracles, then there was a chance that her theft could free the relics and place them back in the hands of those who loved them.

Perhaps this was why God had not answered her. Perhaps He needed to use her here. . . she could only hope and pray that she could help Him. She closed her eyes and let the sound of the waves sweep her away, for the little bit of peace that was left. Darkness and Light were closing in and the clash was not far away. Her mind kept singing, *Calvary*!

~~~

The scent of vine-ripened tomatoes, fresh focaccia, and sweet wine filled the ancient cobblestone streets of Rome. Samantha was loitering near a modern shopping mall on the corner of Via dello Spirito Santo, and in the distance she could see the Castel and Italy's supreme court. She didn't seem surprised when Medrhos and three of his men, Cehros, Landon, and Varcel, appeared around her.

Samantha gave her would-be husband a look of amusement. He had again borrowed the costume of the people. He sported a casual linen jacket over a gauze tunic and linen trousers, with sharp cuffs and seams to fit his character. Leather bands on the shoulder seams, cap, and cuffs were the only ornamentations. He and his men looked more Italian than the modernized men around them.

"I see you're playing tourist again," she observed.

"Well, *il mio Tesoro,* you stand out so that I could find you in the middle of a street festival," Medrhos greeted her. "I can't have my *ragazza ladra* being as obvious as a magpie among doves."

"Precisely so that you could find me. You don't need to blend in so well as to speak Italian, especially to me since I already know you aren't," Samantha retorted. "Most people know the common tongue here, you know, and we have pocket translators."

"Precisely, I've been using mine to translate my thoughts," Medrhos answered, and nudged her into the lobby of the mall. "Now, we'll begin once you've played chameleon, my dear."

Samantha glanced at her watch, heart beginning to race. Even if it took her only five minutes to find something suitable to wear, which was impossible in the maze of the mall, the one hour visiting period at the Castel had already begun. She took a deep breath and plunged into the nearest fashion store, which was up the escalator on the opposite side of the mall.

With the aid of a friendly fashion stylist who recognized tourists who wanted to play Italian, she had soon discovered the brand *Futuristi* and splurged Medrhos' Earth-converted cash on it. With thirty minutes to spare, she returned to the Emperor's side, clad in an asymmetrically draped white linen dress and similarly styled chestnut brown vest. Cut-out leather vambraces, purse, and a headband were her chosen accessories, made to match with the sturdy heels she had purchased.

Medrhos approved her choices merely by offering his arm. No one would have guessed that this couple had come from one ancient alien city to raid another. The Via dello Spirito Santo seemed endless. The beautiful Pont Sant'Angelo crossed the river to the Castel. No vehicles were allowed, and so devoted pedestrians streamed to and fro between the towering angel statues that guarded the bridge's sides.

A chill went up Samantha's spine, the sort that came with beauty, when she saw what the angels bore. Each held within their hands an instrument of Christ's Death. And she came face to face with the one that held the very relic she sought to take. She glanced into the carven eyes and felt her heart pleading with any angel whose image it could be.

No, it wasn't assigned to any angel in particular, but heaven's ears would hear, and an angel would answer. If only he would grant a sign, and not a scourge upon her for what she was doing. If only these ten angels would assuage the crucifixion her soul was undergoing and lead Medrhos to his own Calvary, through the grace shed by the wielding of those dreaded, and now beloved, instruments.

Samantha watched as their slow steps finally brought them to the entrance of the Castel, and the hundredth glance at her watch told her that the limits of her abilities were about to be tested. She had twenty-five minutes to infiltrate the fortress that was the security system, and she still didn't know how she was going to do it.

"Plan?" Medrhos whispered, as they showed their passes to the guard at the entrance.

"Don't have one," Samantha hissed, as they grabbed their stamped passes and entered the Castel.

"That's the best kind," Medrhos laughed quietly.

Within the outer walls of the fortress was a grand and ancient maze of elevated walkways, ancient stairways, and mysterious entrances. Its majesty was clouded by the modern presence of security cameras on every corner, and the invisible electric fence that barred every wall from being climbed.

Samantha took a deep breath and pulled Medrhos along, his men following. She had memorized the layout of the Castel and knew where the relic she desired was kept.

"Hey, no stragglers allowed!" a voice boomed over the speaker. The group stopped short and found themselves being hustled into the nearest gaggle of tourists. "You may split up once we reach the café, but then and *only* then," the tour guide reprimanded the confused couple and their bewildered brethren.

"Oh great," Samantha muttered.

"They have a café?" Medrhos looked mildly interested.

Samantha shook her head and the tour crept leisurely along through a massive spiral staircase, the tomb of an ancient emperor, and St. Michael's courtyard, while the guide droned on. The history he told of would have been fascinating if Samantha's brain hadn't been struggling to work out some kind of plan. Medrhos was halfway listening, enthralled by the Emperor's mausoleum, as was natural for him.

What could she do? Samantha panicked. Ideas were few and far between, and all she could hear was the guide speaking of princes, popes, and plagues. She was going to have to make it up as she went. She slipped her hand into her purse and found the few gadgets she had taken possession of while in Arce'Atelane.

One was a recorder remote, that would lock onto the signal of the security cameras and copy the footage before layering it on top of what the camera was actually viewing. The other two were a pair of rubber shoe covers, not unlike old-fashioned drizzle boots, and fitted rubber gloves covered over with quartz fibers. Hopefully these would protect her from the 5,000 volt charge of the wall and floor of the security tower.

Medrhos was bumping her arm.

"Move!" he muttered. "We're at the café already. I think your brain needs some espresso before you become my *piccolo ladra,* Ancilla."

"There's no time," Samantha protested, but found herself shouldered into the little café in the two-millennia-old stone wall. With fifteen minutes left, an espresso with whipped cream and chocolate was shoved into her hand along with a slice of anything-goes pizza.

"Rhos!" she groaned.

"Plan?" he asked, under the cover of the noisy atmosphere.

"Um. . ." She hastily took a sip of her espresso. "I'm going to take care of the security. Right now there aren't that many guards, and most of the security cameras aren't recording. Once the Castel is closed, all of that will change. I'll take care of the cameras, but I need. . . a distraction, just as the changing of the guards in the control room occurs. In precisely 14 minutes and 30 seconds. And in order to take the relic, we're going to have to wait until there's no one in the museum. Which means that somehow you're going to have to hide until then."

"Piece of focaccia."

"What?"

Medrhos shrugged. "Makes more sense than cake to me." His hand was fingering the blaster hidden in his coat.

"You're making *zero* sense to me," Samantha grumbled, gulping down her espresso to get the cup out of her hands. "Alright, now listen, we only have a few minutes to do this."

"Are you going to eat that or not," Medrhos interrupted.

Samantha glared at him.

"Do you want to get the Veil, or not? Now listen! The floors will be electrified as soon as the museum is emptied. There are high frequency sound emitters and laser gates on every doorway, so you'll need to appear directly inside, but only *after* I've been able to disable the floor. I'm going to need at least five minutes after it's closed. The floor will be easy, but the sensors around the relic won't be. You're going to have to hang in there as long as you can without being spotted. Understand?"

"It doesn't sound like much of a plan, but I understand the little bit that there is," Medrhos said wryly.

"You're the one getting on my nerves," Samantha muttered. "I need to head out. Remember, don't get into the chapel until-"

"What chapel?"

Samantha smacked her forehead. "Oh for Andromeda's sake, Rhos! It's in the Library Hall, which we didn't pass through. Check a map on your way out."

"Got it. And I'll take that pizza off your hands if you're not going to use the energy. My powers take quite a bit out of me," he said, flexing his arm.

Samantha eyed him. He didn't know it, but it was quite possible he wouldn't be using his powers again. She hoped that was the case. She pushed the slice of pizza into his hand and darted off through the crowd.

A corridor on the floor above was empty, save for a few wandering couples, as well as guards posted at some of the doorways. Samantha halted, heart beating in her throat, and pretended to study the digi-map on the wall. Her recorder remote was in her hand.

With a few clicks of the dial, it found the electronic frequency of the livestream security cameras and was recording each innocent moment. Ten minutes of footage would be enough, she prayed. She put the device back into her purse and allowed it to continue to work as she meandered down the hall.

"The museum is closing in five minutes," a voice came over the speakers. "Please proceed to the nearest exit. The museum is closing in five minutes. . . ."

VIII

Voltage

Samantha would have to get out of the way of the guards, who would make sure the corridors and halls were empty. She waited for the nearest guard to turn his head and slipped up the narrow stairwell to the rooftop.

A strong breeze was blowing and the sun warmed her dark hair as she came out into the square tower that looked down upon the Tiber. All of Rome spread out as far as she could see, gleaming white, silver, and ivory, reminding her of the silken patchwork quilt her mother had made for her cabin on the *Lumenara*.

The control house was not here – it was in the exact center of the roof, which rose in a tower some fifteen feet above where she stood. She looked furtively at the tourists who were reluctantly leaving the rooftops, and checked for any guards. There were none.

She dropped a glance on her watch. She had three minutes. She was going to have to find a place to hide while the guards made their way down from the tower. Samantha turned and froze.

Above her towered the bronze angel St. Michael, guardian of that tower for millennia. His eyes blazed like fire in the glare of the sun and his hair seemed to move in the gust of the wind. The blood in Samantha's veins chilled like icy rain despite the warmth of the sun on her skin. Michael loomed over her, larger than life and more terrifying than she had ever known an angel could be.

Angelic wrath! Beautiful but terrible and her ideas came crashing down in her terror of what she would do now. Everything had been in vain, and if those eyes told her anything, then her plan – she stopped and the chill was strangely fading, and the terror with it. She met his gaze again and looked hard, asking if she could really be seeing him as he had appeared, to end the ancient plague. His eyes said yes, and his sword was held at the ready.

But then the look gentled, and as the wind stirred his hair, the bronze arm moved and the sword was sheathed. His anger was not for her, but for those who had brought her to her Calvary. And then bronze was shining in the sun again, and all was still.

Samantha drew a shaky breath and laughed, as one could not help doing after finding such a terrible thing was only love. This was her sign, then, that she was on the right path and that God's ways were strange!

She bowed her head and touched her brow in respect to the image of her new guardian. The statue might have been only a statue again, but the warmth he had given her was not leaving her yet.

The blood rushed back to Samantha's heart and her mind clicked back into gear. She had less than a minute now. The stairway! It was made of stone, but there was a cavity underneath where the statue of a seated woman had been placed, to match the odd modern images seen scattered throughout the Castel. She hastily climbed behind it, finding the recess full of spider's nests, but they didn't care and neither did she. It was none too soon, for now she heard the great door of the control room sliding open, and the voices of the guards as they came out into the fresh air.

"It's a beautiful day, Alessio!" one was saying.

"And a quiet one, Marcello," a calm voice replied. He seemed to be enjoying the breeze and Samantha heard their steps pause at the top of the stairs.

"Too quiet. Sometimes I wonder why we need to guard this place so thoroughly. The only ones who want these relics are the ones they belong to, and I think they ought to have more than three hours a day," Alessio sighed.

"Well, until such a time as Altomi and Serengoch change their ways, at least we get extra free time in the chapels ourselves," Marcello pointed out. "But you're right, let's hope they change their tune. Or that someone else does it for them."

They descended the stairs and vanished inside the Castel. Samantha found herself smiling and she glanced at the angel as she raced up the steps. It was another piece of proof that somehow this could work out for the best, if he had a hand in it. She was sure he would.

Samantha went to the steel door of the control center. A soft beep and the light on her watch told her Medrhos' men had gone into action. Shouts and the buzzing of electric wires below confirmed it. If her guess that the replacement guards would check it out was correct, since they were some of the few guards present during the end of the visiting hour, she would have five minutes to get Medrhos access to the relic.

It took thirty seconds to snap on her gloves and boots. She grabbed a thin file from her bag. The heavy door had one loophole, a simple internal locking mechanism which she could pick, if she could slide the file into the crack and find the gears. This crack was so minuscule that the engineer had great difficulty pushing the file through. She probed around for the gears.

There was only one problem. The schematics she had seen had not told her that there was a live wire inside, designed to counteract just such a measure. And Samantha found it before she found the gears.

A sharp tingling pain jumped up her arm, her body recoiling so sharply that she was flung away from the door as it faded from her vision in swirling colors. There was a thud as she hit something soft instead of the sharp stones of the wall behind her.

The pain cleared and the colors steadied; Samantha sat up in bafflement. There was nothing beneath her that would have softened her fall. She raised her eyes, the question of how to bypass the live wire not yet coming to her mind. It proved not to be needed.

The door stood open, wrenched on the hinges as though by a great and forceful hand. A caerulean glow shimmered where the metal had been bent, flaming into gold like the Egyptian lotus.

Samantha dragged herself to her feet. She had three minutes now before she would be discovered. But the rent door had saved her time. She gingerly placed one foot on the copper flooring. Nothing happened. Her boots would keep her safe, as long as that was the only contact she had with the floor's surface.

The engineer crossed the room and scanned the various instruments and control panels. There was a click and she saw the video footage switch to her recording. All was going well.

Now she needed to pull the plug on the defenses of the library hall. Avoiding tampering with the main wiring would be her first desire, but if she couldn't make progress within the first minute, she would have to risk it. She peeled back the panel on the computer that controlled the electric flooring. To her dismay, even this was guarded by a series of electrified coils. She began to bypass them.

"Samantha, aren't you done yet?" Medrhos' strained voice came over her watch.

Frustrated, Samantha dropped her screwdriver.

"Hardly, I told you how much time it would take and I need a few more minutes. What's wrong?"

"Uh, long story," the King muttered. "It's best to be focused on where you're traveling to when you open a vortex."

Currently, the Emperor was precariously perched on the ivory cornice lining the upper walls of the library hall. After mingling with the crowd observing his men's diversion, he had carelessly dropped into the nearest vortex, and accidentally transported himself to the middle of a chapel full of quietly praying mothers and their children. In his ensuing panic he had leapt into the hall early, and was now forced to cling to the wall lest he fall to the electrified flooring below.

"They probably think I'm an angel," he growled, staring in annoyance at the room below.

Samantha nearly snapped her hand trying to remove the coils from the computer.

"That would be ironic," she commented. She silenced her watch and slammed the panel back on the computer. There was no time for it; she would have to try cutting the main wires. With her trusty alligator clips in hand, she followed the tell-tale removable panels along the walls until she came to one that bore the faint danger mark. She pried it off.

A mass of multicolored wires twisted and turned through the wall. The red controlled the lasers and sensors, and the blue, the flooring. She could cut them easily enough. But where was the hidden wire? Was it inside of the cables? Or did it run through the walls? Exactly how would she find it and how would she avoid it? If she touched that live wire, she would surely die. . . and Medrhos' plans would change. He would destroy Earth and take all of its people, and the relic would never be in his hands.

"Samantha!" Medrhos' voice rang out impatiently.

"Oh, be patient! I'm about to get electrocuted," Samantha snapped.

"You what?"

"I *said*, I'm about to get electrocuted, especially if you keep talking." She reached into the wall and her fingers grazed a hidden channel within it, and a clear cable that she had not seen –

"Samantha, stop." The Marauder King's voice was calm and chilled now.

The girl pulled back just in time.

"Leave the tower. I have a simpler way."

IX

Collision

"Rhos-"

The signal cut off and Samantha threw everything down and ran from the control room. The sunlight seemed to have dimmed since she had entered and an unspoken fear was stabbing at her heart. She scanned the skies and felt her heart drop. Something was descending in the distance, sparkling black and silver in the sun.

Medrhos' forces! Five warships, two star cruisers, and within them dozens of sun snipers. War had come to Earth. It was an invasion!

The stones around her surged and she found herself dragged into an inescapable vortex. A feeling of walking on smooth glass surrounded by an ocean of pink, and she tumbled out into the library hall.

A black-gloved hand caught her wrist as an eruption of sparks ripped up the floor. The sound of crunching metal mingled with the ever-increasing drone of the ships that now were overshadowing the city. Medrhos, clothed in his warlord garb once more, dropped down to the floor and pulled Samantha down with him.

"The relic," he said, and turning towards its veiled resting place, he stretched out his hand and clenched it. The protective sensors and glass case imploded.

"Sire!" Cehros' voice came over Medrhos' com-watch. "We have a problem – one of our ships isn't manned by our men-"

Medrhos stopped, halfway to the veil.

"What do you mean?" he demanded.

"It's the Realtra, sir, and Orion and Kadmos are with them."

"I'm on my way!"

Medrhos whirled and grabbing Samantha, dragged her out of the hall and out of the Castel.

"Rhos, the relic!" she begged.

"It can wait," he snapped, standing on the ramparts and surveying the city.

As yet, little was happening. The early warning systems had mistaken Medrhos' forces for friendly ships due to the codes they had sent upon entering the atmosphere, a fact which he had counted on.

But a fray was beginning where one streamlined ship had pulled away from the others, its camouflaging paint transforming from black and silver to ice blue. Southwards, silver gleamed in the morning sunlight as a Vestar squadron flew into the city, summoned by Orion's call.

"Hell's fire!" Medrhos snarled.

He spun on his heel and scanned the city skyline in vain for a place of safety. He found the lack of Rapunzelesque towers most disturbing and it only fueled his fury. He seized Samantha around her waist and the crystals flashed as he threw out his arm. A cable snaked its way into being and hurtled across the breadth of the street, pulling them from the ramparts and swinging them to the top of the Chiesa di Santa Maria Annunziata. But Medrhos wasn't satisfied.

He flung them onwards, and the crystals burned again as flaming steppingstones appeared mid-air, leading him by leaps and bounds from rooftop to rooftop. The cable whipped out again and with a whistling rush of wind, he precipitated Samantha onto the colossal dome of St. Peter's.

"Queran, Anjus, Percel, bring your squadrons to the Great Dome and shield the Queen!" Medrhos barked, watch raised as he viewed the beginning skirmishes. "Don't let anything harm the building or she'll get hurt!"

"You have shields?" Samantha asked incredulously. Even now, the engineer in her couldn't resist the question.

"I told you, I've seen better tech on my side of the fields," Medrhos said impatiently. Snatching Samantha's arm, he shoved her into the doorway that led inside the dome. "Go inside and stay!" he commanded. "I'll be back for you when this is over. Don't move!"

"Medrhos, I –" But in an instant he was gone. "I can't help you if I'm stuck on a roof," Samantha groaned.

She raised her eyes as three dozen Shielded Strikers wheeled overhead and hovered in locked positions marking the perimeter of the church, a loud hum echoing off the buildings as a chartreuse bubble masked the façade and rooftop. But the back and gardens were not protected. Samantha slipped her hand into her bag and found her silken rope.

"To each their own," she muttered, and slipped out of sight.

~~~

Plasma blasts began to ring out over the city and engines were starting on fire. Pedestrians were running, looking up into the sky, for there was little danger of flying shards of glass and metal and it seemed to them a spectacle.

Medrhos leapt from the glimmering spire of the modern Chiesa della Galassia di Dio, which dared to mock the ancient skyline with its spear-like towers and glass façade that blinded passerby. But the Emperor took no notice as he plummeted towards the river six hundred feet below.

A yellow light was flashing rapidly on his watch as it discovered a vehicle hurtling towards him at terrific speed – Medrhos caught the wing of his speeder and vaulted into the seat. Only one thing was in his mind now: Orion! The Realtra could hardly help but be defeated, and he wanted that cunning, pantheresque prince to fall by his own hand.

The wind whistled through his hair as he shot down the Tiber, ducking and weaving through the skyways that spanned its breadth. Just ahead, a swarm of sun snipers and the Realtra's Cascadian jets were dogfighting, mixing their firing with missiles of fractaled ice. The Star Cruisers and warships were encircling the city, trading furious firepower with the Vestar ships and preventing them from entering, lest the plans fail, the Queen be injured, and Rätha forbid that anything should happen to the Emperor! Not that anything would, Medrhos smiled darkly. He had all of Rätha's destruction at his bidding.

"Orion's been spotted in Piazza Navona," a voice crackled over his speeder's radio. "He seems to be heading for the Queen!"

"Not on my watch," Medrhos muttered with a dark laugh, and spun the speeder around sharply to the left, buildings and personal transports whizzing by on either side as he wove through the maze of streets until they crumbled away into what had been an ancient stadium.

There in the monumental piazza before him was a melee of Vestar combatants, Marauder warriors, and foot soldiers. Everywhere he looked, Roman police were trying to convince spectators to get inside the nearest building before they were shot. The blaster fire, the zing of plasma blades, and the noisy whir of the Supernova news helicopters overhead left Medrhos unfazed. It was a fitting place to crush this tenacious rebellion.

The warlord caught sight of a masked helmet, gleaming icy hues in the sunlight, and the tall figure of Orion broke through the fracas as a sea-creature through a wave. He stopped on the outskirts of the crowd, ghostly blue cloak swirling in the violent breeze, metal armor gleaming like pearl and ocean skies, as he gave a silent challenge.

Medrhos' eyes narrowed as a smile played over his lips. He dismounted his speeder. A hiss of smoke, and black and burgundy leather and molten steel crept over his garments, curling and flaming into plating, and webbed into a horrible helmet that concealed his face. It was a haunting visage that looked upon Orion now, that would have sent a death chill to any other heart that saw it.

If Samantha had glimpsed the warlord then, she would have discerned it as Rätha's imprint upon his heart and known that he was close to falling fast. But if it had any affect on the heart of Orion, he did not show it. A blade of molten crystal braced by plasma and steel bloomed in Medrhos' hand. Orion ignited his plasma blade in reply.

"Look out!" someone screamed.

~~~

The silver silken rope slid soundlessly from the heights of the basilica and swung in the breeze. Samantha had run its length around the nearest balustrade, and safely secured by both ends in her hands, she rappelled down the wall, with just a grimace of guilt for having to do it on a basilica instead of a cliff. With her skills it was but a short time until she stood at the foot of the great church.

What had once been meandering parking lots and private byways were now lush concrete ruins, bejeweled with snapdragons, roses, and cherry trees, for the clergy's modest sedans no longer took up much parking space.

Samantha pulled the datapad from her purse and brought up the digital map of Rome she had been using. She didn't know where the nearest exit from this gardened maze was, or how she was going to reach the Castel and retrieve the relic, now that it was surely under guard.

Indeed, at that very moment, chaos was growing in the city, and the Republic Guard was heading out in full battle array. So desperate did the situation seem, that the outdated iron cannons and trebuchets of the Castel were being used haphazardly to the danger of anyone on the other side of the Tiber.

Samantha found that the Porta del Perugino was only the distance of two Vestar service jets from where she stood. She rounded the building and dashed past a bubbling fountain, ducking cherry tree branches as she went. The greenery was so dense that she didn't realize that she was on a collision path until it happened.

"Hey!" a startled voice cried out, and the man she had run into grabbed her shoulders to keep her from falling. She looked up to see a youth clad in a black cap with a scarlet plume, and a uniform striped in yellow, royal blue, and red. Behind him were six others, and half a dozen clergy, stirring in apparent frustration.

"What are you doing here?" the guard asked sharply. His comrades circled them. "This is restricted property! Anyone caught here in such a time as this falls under suspicion."

"I don't mean to trespass," Samantha panted.

"Why then, do you have this?" He pulled the coiled rope from her hand. "You were seizing the moment to take home a prize, weren't you. Marcos, Luka, take her to the bastion! I'll take the rest to the Castel. Whatever she says, don't believe her until I return, is that understood?"

"Ancillo!" a man's voice said firmly, but it was kind. "Leave my daughter be."

The murmuring ceased, and for a moment there was only the sound of distant gunpower. Samantha's breath caught in her throat as the guard released her and everyone stepped aside. It was the man in white!

X

Rupture

The snap of breaking stone was the cause of the cry. Medrhos had made a crushing gesture with his free hand and a violent crack drew everyone's eyes to the colossal obelisk standing in the center of the piazza just behind Orion. Marauders and Vestar men alike ran anywhere that wasn't in the growing shadow. In the split-second that he had, Orion lunged out of the way, rolled, and sprang up again.

A nod of approval from the ghastly helmet meant that this was only a test of the enemy's reflexes. . . a test of how and where he would choose to fight. He raised his hand again but the rebellion's leader had other ideas. With a whistling hum, his speeder whizzed into the piazza, drawn to his signal, and took him out of the square with it.

A faint snarl escaped the helmet of Rätha's Emperor. He jumped onto his speeder and with a spark of the engine, sped off in pursuit. Skyscrapers and markets flashed by as they zipped around the Pantheon. Orion led the warrior king on a merry high-speed chase past the legendary cake-like tomb dedicated to the war-dead, through and under crumbling ruins, over skyways, and towards a colossal, crumbling amphitheater of copper stone, filled with archways like eyelet lace.

How they managed to navigate through a thousand pillars at such speed, they never quite knew, as they shot back out into the sunlight and found the stadium falling away beneath them. Their crafts plunged with the sudden change in their energy fields and both men leapt from them to avoid the inevitable collision with the marble seats before them. The crunch of metal, and sizzling sparks showered through the colonnades.

Massive arches and triple walls punctured by a hundred corridors slanted down towards the arena floor. It was covered in glass, and half scattered with sand; and down below they could see the ruins of many-halled storage areas where animals and fighters had been kept, and slaves had worked.

The men slipped on the sand-strewn glass as they vaulted through crumbling colonnades. Their blades sparked and clashed against the other and upon stone, cleaving ancient blocks in two.

Both warriors paused to take a breath in the center of the arena, chests heaving. They eyed each other invisibly, their helmets so fully enclosing their faces that they seemed more machine than man; at least, until the first blood would be spilled.

The Emperor's heart was beating with the joy of war just as the hearts of ancient crowds had thrilled there long ago. But the emperors then had not crushed their enemies in such a way as he intended to.

Medrhos drew his head back; it was time to test his prey further. Crystals flashed, and with a thundering roar, the sands shifted and swelled, and lions of blazing gold, red, and ebony leapt from the glass and descended upon Orion. The fighter kicked one away with a strike to the jaw, turning it back only momentarily, and vaulted backwards. He drew his blade and slammed it into the glass beneath his feet, piercing it through.

For a moment it hummed there and an aqua cast crept through the glass, coupled with meandering cracks. The lions leapt forward – he leapt back and let their weight crash down upon the fissure he had formed. The floor shattered and hurled them into the labyrinth of broken corridors below. Medrhos met Orion head on and they sparred once more, skirting the jagged arena edge.

Between blows, they glimpsed ship after ship rising into the sky. Random selections were being made and filled with soldiers. The metal monster that was Medrhos paused mid-swing of his blade. A space-going winery had just vanished into the clouds, fully commandeered by the Republic in the hopes of boarding one of the enemy vessels. Had there been enough time left in the battle, it might have worked; the Marauders couldn't have resisted the anomaly of a winery in space.

"I want that ship!" he said, and for one moment it was his true voice that Orion heard. Then it was shrouded in guttural shadows once more, and as he clenched his hand and sent rubble hurtling towards Orion, the subject matter changed with it.

"A rebel captain following his Emperor to the Great Galaxy, and for what?" he snarled, chest heaving as Orion leapt on top of the flying blocks of stone and landed in front of him. They drew back into the center of the arena. "Did you fall in love with Rätha's daughter when she escaped from me?"

"Not when she escaped, no," Orion's voice came with an even chill. "She is *God's* daughter, and I loved her long before you could ever have laid claim to."

"Your head is shrouded in a Magellenic fog," the Emperor growled. "Rätha chose her before you did."

"It was God who chose her. Rätha didn't even know she existed."

The embered eyes of the grotesque visage eyed Orion in calculating silence.

"I see how that is now . . . *Hesslin*."

His blade whistled through the space between them. Before the rebel captain could move, it cracked the faceplate of his helmet. Orion's blade whipped upwards not a moment too soon, locking against Medrhos' and barely saving his own eyes. Icily-tinged plasma was leaking from his visor as he flung the villain's sword away from his face.

"I've come back to torment you, Medrhos, with the lives of all those you've murdered. You won't break free of me!"

"Nor will you take my Queen from me!" and Medrhos laughed a horrible laugh. His voice morphed once more, flickering between reality and shade. "I have all of time at my bidding, but I have no more time for you! I must save your precious Samantha from being canceled by the Cult. Your hands. . . could never save her!"

The black hand was raised. The stone archways overhead swayed in an unfelt wind and ruptured. Fifty tons of limestone plummeted down over Orion's head. Amidst the rolling thunder and billowing dust, the face of Rätha gave one last leering glance.

"Queran, Anjus, Percel, cease your shields and collect the Queen from the Great Dome. It's time."

Medrhos stretched his hands out before him and his speeder recreated itself before his eyes. It was time for him to accomplish the theft that would protect his Queen from the Cult. As he cleared the edge of the Colosseum's heights, he didn't see a haze of cyan growing beneath the wreckage.

Chunks of columns and archways trembled and then were launched in every direction. An orb of glassy, marbled azure hummed and faded. Orion stepped from his proposed tomb and watched the Emperor's speeder shrink into the skyline.

"Perhaps you've forgotten why your people have feared me...."

He snapped his blade in half. It bloomed into a plasma bike and he set off in pursuit of the man who had taken his Queen.

~~~

The new addition to the labyrinth beneath the city smelled of cold steel and the acrid lighting. Samantha's footsteps rang off the plated walls and ceiling. She had passed several terminals already, and she wasn't the only one using the tunnels. A number of bureaucrats had mingled with clergy, some escaping, others guiding families to the Vatican, temporarily made safe by Medrhos' shields.

The engineer glanced at the guidance plaques on the wall and ducked into the next transept. She could have taken the ancient corridor to the Castel, but it had grown dangerous and was in need of repairs. Besides, the man in white had reminded her that the men on the other side of the door wouldn't be in a welcoming mood. But they didn't know of the more recent entrance from Michael's pedestal.

Samantha thought of the man's eyes when she had confessed her mission. The white brows had furrowed. His eyes had reminded her of a placid sea at dawn, yet with the ocean's depth. They were the kind of eyes in which you couldn't discern the color for the soul that was in them.

"Those of the Red Star never doubt that they who hold the key are those who are the rightful kings of what is locked inside," he said at last. "The Face of God cannot be taken from Him, as the clouds cannot be taken from the sky nor the stars from the heavens. The key is mine alone to give. . . His countenance is our shield, my daughter. Take it, if you trust that by it many will be saved."

He had laid his hand on her hair and taken her to the labyrinth door. "When you reach the other side, you will find whether God has unlocked the door for you. Go now, my daughter, and may His blessing save His children."

A door of bronze and oak confronted Samantha now. She pressed the keypad. She had lost all sense of time, but as she stepped out into the day once again, she saw the state of affairs. The city was shrouded in haze as ships took shots at each other like a swarm of wasps. Samantha's stomach churned for a moment.

If she acquired the relic, she could hold Medrhos to his promise and they would return. Or would he fight until Orion had succumbed? And surely Marc meant to save her from the snare she was in. Could she heal Medrhos and join her captain?

Chills ran through her nerves and she pushed her thoughts away as she descended the stairs. She knew what she had to do first, and whatever was next would have its turn; but it was not to be. The shadow eyes that penetrated her as she stumbled were familiar.

"I hope you like to travel, Anselle."

Samantha's blaster raised to meet Serengoch's gaze. She wasn't quick enough. He ripped a cry of agony from her lips as a jolt of electricity scalded her right arm. Her blaster clattered to the ground and two guards cloaked in white and obsidian seized the girl as she crumpled.

"Tsk, tsk. You don't look well, Anselle. Allow me to take you home. . . my dear ex-Queen."

XI

Crucible

Chunks of rock and masonry charged the air. Electrified fences were ripped apart with a sound to shock a timid heart, as the wall of the Castel shattered inwards. Alarms railed against the intruder, but he silenced them as he swatted Castel defenders away with a stroke of his hand.

The chapel was a silent oasis when he reached it. The distant sounds of panicking guards and the noise of the battle faded away. Glass still strewed the ground like winter crystals, crunching underfoot as he moved down the walk. Long ago, an earthquake had rent the ceiling and the room had been reinforced by jasper columns, from the crowns of which silent faces stared down.

Save for the echoing footsteps, the chapel was a strangely cool and quiet haven from the outer chaos. There was the faint hum of the air conditioning system, enough to make one feel drowsy.

A shimmer of iridescence riveted Medrhos' attention. His mind was too locked to feel the onset of such peace. A breath of near smoke escaped the lips of his helmet, and it curled away, peeling from his skin with a sound that was almost a seething hiss, leaving the Emperor to face the unprotected veil.

The air seemed dense here, muffling even the hum of the generators. The Face on the veil seemed to float, neither touching the fabric nor the surrounding atmosphere. The eyes seemed to change with every glance, so soft but strong, so ethereal, yet he felt the distant tug of foreboding and the soft whisper of love. The Face melted in and out of view at every angle. It was the Face he had glimpsed deep within the vortex with every glance.

Medrhos' eyes seemed mesmerized but his ears didn't miss the sound of an ice cloak being shed behind him. Medrhos didn't blink. He fired a casual blast over his shoulder. The sound was followed by a vibrant hum.

"How did you think that you could get rid of me so easily?" Orion's voice broke the hum. "I will haunt you with all the souls of those whom you've sentenced."

"Are you dead, then?" Medrhos inquired, barely turning his head.

Orion's dark laugh rippled through the chamber. "The number of times I've wondered that is breathtaking! You know why I'm here, Medrhos. I can't save Talitha from the black hole of your Empire, but I won't let Samantha be erased as she was. Let your stars rain their fury! Tell me where she is and let her go, Medrhos, if you love her, or face me."

Medrhos briefly envisioned the edge of Marc's voice simultaneously slicing a glacier and hurling a hundred ships on tour in the depths of a black hole.

"How did you think that I would tell you?"

"I didn't. All your darkness can't hide her; I'll find her no matter your words. I think that you've forgotten to understand why your people bear me hatred."

"I'm hardly capable of fearing you, Hesslin."

"It's my heart you should fear, not my blade. My love could destroy a galaxy as you do, if I so chose. If you choose to keep her, you will soon learn, if you haven't already."

"Do me a favor," the other returned. "Don't kill me with your drama. That's not the heroic death I imagined. For your information, Samantha is safe and she'll remain that way... from *you*. Don't forget whose fault Talitha's death was, not to mention whatever happened to your little one."

"You tried that on me once before. The fault was neither mine nor yours." Orion's voice was even, yet strained. "Neither of us could save her if we chose."

"Hardly worth considering now, is it." Medrhos turned at last.

The leader of the Realtra was still clad in the dust of the makeshift tomb in which he had been buried, blood running down his unmasked face. A plasma burn streaked white across his brow and marked his blond hair with frost.

"You're right, I'm not sure you're not dead."

Medrhos made as though to re-arm himself but the sound of a screeching siren ripped from his watch. A frantic voice came through. It was Queran.

"Sire! We've lost the Queen." The man's voice faded for a moment in trepidation. "We can't find her anywhere in the vicinity of the Great Dome or its grounds."

"Then trace her!" the Emperor snapped. "Honestly, that webweaver can't listen to me for two seconds sometimes-"

Static cut through his sentence.

"Sire, she's nowhere, we can't trace her signal – she must have shut it down."

Medrhos spun to face Marc.

"You took her," he snarled. "You have her! Where is she? You'll pay for taking her, Hesslin, and every man and woman of my people will see to it!"

"I don't have her!" Marc replied. His blue eyes divulged his concern. They both stopped and stared at each other, the energy in the room quivering like gelatin, unsure whether to shatter in anger or fear or to cease its shivering.

"Call your people," Medrhos said, voice stretched thin. Of one mind, for once, each man hastily patched a call through to their entire force to find out who had Samantha. A tinge of gray stole into their faces when the answer came back that no one did.

Creeping fingers of chill stole over Medrhos' skin and ran up his spine. All his royal blood seemed lost in the vacuum of space. There was only one way that Samantha could vanish–

Medrhos grimaced as a shock wave seemed to echo through his brain. He saw a fiery vortex yawning open, a gleam of platinum, and then it slammed shut. He realized what happened and his body shuddered, forcing his eyes shut. His clenched hands fell against the altar as the air left his lungs with a rattling sound. The metal plating with its spikes fell from his shoulders and chest in ashes, leaving him as unprotected as the relic.

The foundations of everything he knew came crashing down, leaving him holding nothing but the relic before him. The darkness had swallowed the only star in his empire. He had been betrayed by all he knew. Every decision meant death.

He raised his eyes to meet the gaze of the veil and its intensity forced him to make the gravest decision of his life, one that could cost him his own life, the lives of his people, and of Samantha – but which if he didn't make it, he and all that he loved would be locked in the darkness in which he had been bound, and the Cult would destroy everything he valued in his Empire. He raised his hand before the Face on the veil and suddenly the crystals burned white.

XII

Shock

Satellites and orbiting apartments flashed by as the *Icebreaker* and the *Harbinger* shot from Earth's atmosphere with Medrhos' fleet in tow, as though spit out by some massive maelstrom. The invasion had vanished from Rome's radar as quickly as it had arrived, and not even a dime had been taken from the city.

No matter the authorities' sentiments, they were glad at the swift exit. General Vereon had closed his eyes in relief at Samantha's apparent victory. The damage done in the city was mainly superficial and was being repaired as swiftly as the tension between Marc and Medrhos.

It had not come easily with the Emperor's pride and Marc's anger, but between Medrhos' newfound change of allegiance and Konstan's timely arrival, dropping between them at just the right moment to knock some sense into them, it was done.

"You both love Samantha and you both intend to save her, so please, try to work together for once! We'll never save her if you don't!" There were tears in his eyes, for he sensed the atrocious things that might happen to his sister.

The two men had glared at each other for a minute more.

Marc exhaled. "I can't save her without you. And if Samantha is right. . . you never meant to hurt my family and there is aught else I can do but forgive you."

Medrhos' condescending gaze flickered. "She's rarely wrong." He glanced away, struggling with himself before turning back and extending his hand. "I fear she needs your help as much as she does mine."

Marc had fought every fiber in his being that rebelled against trusting one of the men responsible – even unwillingly – for his family's pain, but had taken the Emperor's hand at last and gripped it firmly.

Now both men stood together on the bridge of the *Harbinger*, leaving the *Icebreaker* to Konstan. Near silence reigned among the Marauders. They were fearing the thoughts of what might happen to their queen, and their minds and hearts were filled with much more besides; for in his purging, Medrhos had broken the spell over his people.

The crystals he bore had been burned to white and golden starlight; but anyone who would have looked closely could have seen that a tinge of dragon-smoke lingered within the tiger's-eye. Medrhos took no notice of it. He should have destroyed those gems when he used them to free his people. His fear of insecurity would find danger within the halls of the Cult, but that was far from his mind.

For now, he and Marc both gazed into the cold void of the universe, waiting, waiting to clear inhabited space so they could dive through the vortex, lost in terrorized thoughts and unwhispered prayers.

"What will they do to her?" Marc asked softly, scarcely aware that his voice broke the emptiness.

Medrhos' eyes didn't leave the viewport before them. Moonlight was casting an ashen hue over his face as the ships raced around the dark side, looking in vain for truly empty space.

"You don't want to know."

His voice cracked and Marc could feel his pain, a pain that reminded him of Cajetan. A pain that was flooding his own soul with the agony of losing Talitha and the promise he had given Samantha, to protect her. He had come so close. . . it had spun out of his hands.

All any of them could do now was their best, and at the greatest possible speed. He closed his eyes and tried to pray, but all he could see was the Broken Heart and Bleeding Face that knew their pain all too well, and the deep woodland eyes filled with tears.

"Sire. . . ?" the officer on watch's voice came tentatively. Medrhos turned his eyes with a sullen glance that told the man to proceed. "There's a ship approaching. I'm afraid we can't make the jump from here."

Medrhos struck his hands on the railing before him and it shuddered with a ring. "Curse timing!" he muttered with gritted teeth. "If only the Cult weren't immune to time, we'd have her back and no need to worry about the dratted jump!" He descended the stairs and, striding over to the console, leaned over it.

"What is it, another Vestar ship?"

Marc joined him, wary of the Emperor's frustration.

"It seems to be. It's coming into our sights now," the officer replied, eyes on the viewport as the *Harbinger* swung out of the moon's orbit and came back into sunlight.

A distant star cruiser was coming towards them on a trajectory for Earth, moving slowly but at the speed of one who is wearying after a race. Marc stared hard, wondering whether the vessel was conscious of the *Harbinger's* origins. Then he gasped as though he had been burned by a live wire and punched the magnifying controls for the viewscreen. That sleek silver hull was unmistakable.

"That's my ship!"he cried wildly, and snatched up the communicator. "*Lumenara V*, this is your captain speaking! Do you copy?"

There was a crackle and two undignified shrieks came over the intercom. One was clearly Vidara. Then came Pell's voice.

"*Hesslin?* Captain is that -"

"A'da?! A'da!" a cry cut through whatever Pell was trying to say.

"Aiyra!" Marc nearly choked on his words in haste and relief. "Wait for me, Princess, I'll be right there!" He slammed down the receiver and whirled to find Medrhos seizing his shoulder.

"Hesslin!" His eyes snapped and there was no need for him to remind Marc about Samantha. But Aiyra was here now, at last, and his duty for her would scarcely interfere in God's timing.

"Need I remind you that your people are the reason my daughter has a destructive implant in her head?" Marc didn't need to raise his voice.

Medrhos released him and turned away. "Varclav, unlock shuttle A. Stay on your ship, Hesslin. We'll wait for you."

Marc gave a curt nod of thanks and abandoned ship. The *Lumenara's* shuttle bay drew him in and he nearly forgot to unbuckle his seatbelt until it stabbed his shoulder in his attempt to leap from his seat.

When he jumped out of the ship he found Aiyra already waiting. She flew into his arms with a cry that was as unintelligible as the one she had given six years ago on Aliros.

Pell, Vidara, Briggs, and Topping were all crowding the heavy glass doorway into the bay, with Truitt and Elise, as well as a number of others, trying to get through. Pell kept his hand on the switch for sealing the door, preventing their noise from disturbing the much-needed reunion of father and daughter.

Marc was once again at a loss for words. How to tell Aiyra everything, and to ask if she remembered; to tell her about Samantha, but not only to tell her of these things but also to find out what damage she had endured in his absence.

"How's my baby girl?" was all he could say. Tears were threatening to flow from his eyes and they certainly were cascading down Aiyra's cheeks.

"I am alright now that you are here!" she whispered, and buried her head in his shoulder. She knew, without his saying so, that he had experienced Aliros. He soon found that she did, indeed, now remember saying goodbye to her mother, yet likewise still retained her original memories. The look in her eyes was all the thanks he needed.

Marc learned, too, that the situation with the implant had been sliding downhill rapidly, and she was only able to somewhat control it with the help of Truitt and Elise. It was easy to see at a glance just how much her overall health had deteriorated. Timely was his luck that he had returned to her now, and not later. Perhaps now, with Konstan's knowledge and Talitha's remedies, they could save her.

"I think we're going to be able to help you now, Princess," he said softly. "And I will tell you all that I've been through, when we're in flight again. But first -" he raised his watch to his lips. "*Lumenara V* to *Icebreaker*. Your highness, would you care to join us? As in, *now*."

There was a strangled reply that Marc guessed was a yes, for the *Icebreaker* was only now coming up behind the *Harbinger* and had been given zero warning of the *Lumenara's* presence.

"So he's a prince, A'da?" Aiyra asked, trying to wipe the tear stains from her cheeks. Marc dried them with his sleeve.

"Mm, by accident," he grinned. He stopped, looking down at the familiarly colored captain's uniform she was wearing. She had traded the original Vestar violet for one of cranberry, not unlike Marc's favored uniform.

"Taking after me a little much, aren't you?" he laughed, and steered her to the doorway which Pell now opened. There were warm and somewhat damp greetings all around. Aiyra had to step aside for a moment, because Vidara needed a hug from her space father before all could settle on making their way to the bridge.

"Truitt!" Marc called over his shoulder. "A second shuttle will be arriving. Could you please wait for it and bring the occupant up when I call?"

Truitt nodded and dropped back to await the approaching shuttle.

As the door slid open to the bridge, Aiyra watched. The moment her father stepped inside, something in his bearing changed. His shoulders settled and something in his eyes was regained which he had lost and not found even as Orion. And yet, half the light was still missing, and Aiyra could only think of one cause.

"But how is it that you're here?" Marc quizzed her abruptly, as he took in the familiar consoles and his own seat, which Aiyra was happy to permanently vacate.

"I had my implant tied into the signals of yours and Samantha's tracking devices," she admitted. "We were going to create a disruptive energy field to be able to reach you and Samantha once you were in the same time and place, but then we found your signals coming from Earth before we lost track of Samantha's. Then we could no longer pinpoint your location." Her eyes deepened with concern and she cocked her head as she always did.

"Where is she, A'da?"

Her father looked into her eyes, bracing himself. "She was taken again, Aiyra."

He saw his pain begin to echo in her eyes. They had been so close! And now even she could not locate Samantha, and her throat began to close again so she could hardly speak.

"By Marauders?"

Marc shook his head. "Someone far worse than the Marauders. . ."

Aiyra's disbelief and sudden terror were apparent. He gripped her shoulders reassuringly.

"We'll get her back! I promise! We'll never abandon her, Aiyra. I swore I wouldn't lose either one of you again, the way I lost you and your mother so long ago. Everything will be alright once we have her back with us." His watch beeped softly; Truitt was signaling him.

"You're happy that I've returned, aren't you?" Marc asked. It seemed like an unnecessary question. His daughter nodded. "Then I will show you something that will prove that everything will be alright. Someone else whom you love is safe."

Marc told Truitt to send up their visitor. He knew Aiyra didn't dare to guess who it was, when it certainly wasn't her mother, nor Samantha. She couldn't take her eyes from the entrance.

At his swift step, the door had hardly the time to slide out of Konstan's way. His eyes met Aiyra's across the room and both were strangled, then half blinded, by tears. There were far too many to go around now.

"Daystar?" Aiyra trembled, hardly daring to believe that she wasn't seeing things.

The prince stretched out his arms and called her name, thinking of the seven long years since he had last dried the girl's tears, and the fourteen years since he had last been with the one he loved. The girl ran, stumbling, and found his arms holding her tight as though she had never lost him, let alone twice, and never, ever, would again.

"I told you I'd come back to you if it took me a thousand years, my Aurora!" Konstan whispered, unconcerned that his tears were falling like raindrops and pearling on Aiyra's hair. "And it did, Princess." He gently held her at arm's length.

"My heart ached so much," Aiyra whispered, meeting Konstan's eyes from behind the curtain of her dark tresses. She heard him let out his breath softly and his fingers gently brushed her curls away from her face and dried her tears.

"I know. So did mine. . . ."

Marc's arms encircled them both. "Come," he murmured. "Now that three of us are ransomed again, it's time to save the fourth part of our world."

Marc took his old seat once more, and Konstan and Aiyra took the guest sofa behind him.

"Aiyra, I'm going to need to send all the families and nonessential crewmembers to safety." The captain stopped. He wanted Aiyra where it was safe, but if he abandoned her again, how could he trust that he'd not lose her to the implant? Only he and Konstan knew how to help her now. Aiyra must have read his mind.

"A'da, I am not leaving you! I have spent too much of my life alone, please do not make me leave," she begged. "I will not lose you and Konstan again! Besides, the *Lumenara* is half my ship now." She smiled, waiting for her father's inevitable incredulous exclamation.

He only laughed a little, shaking his head. "I suppose she is, isn't she. I can't abandon you again, Aiyra. Whatever danger we're heading into, Konstan and I will always protect you." The captain squeezed her hand and put through the link to the *Harbinger*.

"Medrhos, where we're headed, I need to discharge all nonessential personnel. It will take an hour. Are you willing to wait?"

Medrhos' reply came in a reluctant affirmative. As Konstan held Aiyra's hand, he found her fingers beginning to dig into his palm. Aiyra had heard that name too often in the last decade of her life to be ignorant of who it belonged to. The wideness of her eyes and the rapidity of her breathing outwardly belied her thoughts as she turned her eyes to her father.

"There are Marauders on that ship," she surmised. Marc swiveled his seat and dropped down in front of her.

"Yes," he said quietly, gripping her hands.

Aiyra could feel the pain creeping through the nerves in her head and streaking down her shoulders.

"A'da," she began, as the panic set in.

"Aiyra, I know! We know your pain and your fear, and we feel the same way," he whispered, forcing her to hold his gaze. If she continued in terror there was no telling what her implant would do to either ship.

"Aiyra, they love Samantha as much as we do. We can't get her back without their help. And . . ." he hesitated, praying that the change in Medrhos was true. "I think they've begun hearing God's call. I promise you, Aiyra, that we won't let you be harmed again. As insane as it is to say this. . . we need to trust them this once, and I need you to pray for them."

Aiyra looked from her father to the hulking shadow of a ship that loomed over them even now.

"I never stopped," she said softly, and settled back against the seat, her fingers touching the woven ring on Konstan's hand. Her mother's prayer lived in her heart. Aiyra wasn't about to let it die.

XIII

Vital

"*Icebreaker, Lumenara*, are you ready?"

Medrhos stood at the *Harbinger's* helm. The hour had been spent listening to the not yet silenced ticking of the grand clock, with its face of gold and ebony like a swarm of battleships preying on a harvest moon. It was one of the few moments in his life that time was not on his side.

He had strayed into the flat on the bridge that he had designed for Samantha, and found himself in her chambers, looking at the wilted blossoms which fell and floated in the pool as in mourning. It was not quite abandoned yet.

Samantha's handmaids sat in silence among the greenery, and little Estill was curled up on the bed, weeping as she comforted lonely Lyona, and was in turn comforted by Gelert and the tiger. When given the choice to join Marc's people, who were being transferred to Lune, a hospice city on the surface of the moon, they had all refused. Medrhos had not pushed them.

He saw the way Estill looked at him, all the disappointment and resentment mingling with her tears, and wondered why he laid his hand on her head. He saw the eyes soften. Samantha had adopted her in some form.

Medrhos sighed and lifted the covers over the girl and cat. The child was halfway to losing her family twice. The King's face was a study as he turned away, eyes closed as something drew back memories of the parents who had abandoned him in the way of wild things.

The days of his mother's love and care and his father's protection had been so sweet, yet they had abandoned him with hardly a care. *And whose fault was that*, Medrhos wondered darkly, rubbing the gem on the back of his hand. Estill's touch drew him out of his memories.

"We'll find her, won't we?" she whispered, looking up at him. Medrhos briefly questioned why she hadn't taken the chance to join her Uncle Orion onboard the *Lumenara*. "And then we won't be alone anymore."

Medrhos didn't answer her, for now, he could only hope. He thought of the Face he had seen in Rome, the eyes so full of love: the same love he had seen in Samantha's eyes many times before. And he wasn't about to resist. It was all he had left of her and surely He was the only one who could protect Samantha now.

The joint replies from the other two ships broke through and Medrhos shook his head, finding himself still on the bridge.

"Hesslin to *Harbinger*. All evacuations have been completed."

"We're ready when you are," Cobalt, commander of the *Icebreaker* replied.

"Then follow us in," Medrhos commanded. "Varclav, open a vortex to sector Alpha-Z, 239. You know the timeline. Gerion, send word to Coran that I want the fleet mobilized, locked and on standby for our signal. The crew of the *Delta IV* are to be returned to their ship and brought along."

Medrhos took his winged seat and the growing disk of rose flashed its light across his stony countenance. He had never imagined that he'd be on a witchhunt after twenty-seven years of life in Rätha's shadow. He knew he was risking everything. Destruction and deliverance were mighty weights to put on the scale. He gave the order to proceed.

The *Harbinger* glided forth, its wingtips seeming to graze the very walls of the portal. The Marauder's armada followed, and the *Lumenara* and *Icebreaker* closed the gap. As the gateway shut behind them, no one noticed that they were not alone.

Pulsing streams of rainbow colors cast blinding lights into the ships' viewports, and the order was given to close the metal shields over every window to spare numerous cases of migraines and seizures.

The *Lumenara* jostled and groaned with the tunnel's heartbeat. Marc raised his eyes to the screen that displayed the vessel's vital signs, praying she'd withstand the strain of traveling at nearly a decade a minute.

"Briggs, will she hold?"

The man's eyes were riveted on the lighted diagrams showing the status of every inch of the craft.

"At the current trend with seven and a half years passing every sixty seconds, with five-point-forty-seven hours to go, I don't know what to tell you. Maybe, but just barely. She's warping under the pressure waves. The peaks are pulling at her shell, but every trough is having the opposite effect of lowering the internal pressure. We stand equal chances of being turned into spaghetti or pulverized."

"I should have thought of this," Marc muttered with troubled gaze. "My ship was so small, all those years ago, that just as a single human body, it hardly caused a disturbance."

And then the *Lumenara* began to bump and sway, as an aircraft interacting with jet streams.

"Hesslin, can you hear me?" It was Medrhos. His voice came slurred, normally clear in inter-time communications, but the *Lumenara* was not built to catch his drift somewhere between the first manned flight to Mars and the Earthbound sighting of the most ancient, far-flung galaxy known to man.

"Barely, but enough."

"Kythonios is located in a dimensional warp, which we're heading into. It's creating turbulence within the tunnel that your ship cannot withstand. Get the *Lumenara* directly behind the *Harbinger*. We'll project a force field in front of you to shield you from the worst of it."

There was the danger of being caught in the wake turbulence of the *Harbinger* itself. It was like walking a tightrope that had a cut thread, trying to trust the Marauder King. Marc gripped the armrests of his seat and gave the order for the *Lumenara* to be eased behind the great jet-black warship. Now to find out if the shields were up and wide enough to save them from crashing and burning on the tunnel walls. But it was done, and only Konstan seemed to not be so surprised that they were intact.

According to Briggs' new reading, they probably would hold out, instead of maybe. The rest of the flight passed quietly, save for a pressure dent the *Lumenara* acquired on her hull, and an anomalous reading of the tunnel which Medrhos was sure was only a glitch.

At last, the tunnel began to fade and decelerate, until the bands of color blurred into the shocking stillness of space. This was sector Alpha Z, the outer rim of the galaxy, sparsely sprinkled with star systems. Waving bands of nearly invisible gray caused their vision to wobble ever so slightly; the skin of the rift was evident like the iridescent surface of a bubble. There were no obvious planets in sight.

"Well this has to be the emptiest corner of the galaxy! Where from here?" From his tone of voice, Cobalt clearly suffered severe symptoms of suspicion.

"Kythonios is only about a parsec from here," Medrhos said, with the sound of tilted patience. "Far enough to drop off your ship, Hesslin, before the Cult catches wind of it."

"Sire – I think they already have."

"Looks like someone ordered a hot welcome for us," Cobalt sneered. "Would that it were breakfast!"

He started pulling the *Icebreaker* out of formation as a squadron of Z-17 Starkindlers appeared at an ominous pace, their slightly smaller, wasp-like bodies reminiscent of their larger cousins which had attacked at the orbiting of Lythos.

"Cobalt, get back!" Konstan snapped. "You're a Marauder, remember?"

"I hate it when you say that."

"I know!"

It was a wonder that the collective holding of breath didn't slow the group's cruising speed, and the speed of the oncoming Starkindlers wasn't doing them any favors, either.

"Medrhos, can you call them off?" Marc asked tersely.

"Do you think they're mine?" Medrhos replied. "Mercenaries are like the wild right wing of the Cult, somewhere between murderous and malevolent. They don't have any rules; they only serve the Cult for the pay, rather like pet bats. They listen if they choose, and I hire them if I choose, but they'll scarcely choose to listen to me outside of my territory. If they attack you, I can't help you, and if they report you as my prisoners, you're sunk," he warned.

"Well, that would be disconcerting, considering sinking isn't a thing out here." Marc's voice was light despite the frown in his eyes as he fingered the onboard siren switch.

Medrhos snorted. "This is a sea like any other, Hesslin. Get shot down here and you'll enjoy finding the universe's floor."

A shiver of starlight passed over Aiyra's face with as much pain as a shadow, and Konstan gripped her hand as though reading her thoughts.

"If they fire on us, I won't abandon you again," he breathed with a smile that promised the world. He turned back to view the Starkindlers, now circling the group in vulture-like dizziness, searching for the worth in attacking the oddball ship. He bit his lip, knowing full well he was at risk of being forced to break his promise.

"Captain, they're locking onto us," Pell said, voice stretched to the breaking point.

"Lock ours, and we'll betray Medrhos to them," Marc muttered.

"He already betrayed us!" Cobalt snapped over the intercom. "Forget about what happens to him, we've got your back, Orion."

"If he's betrayed us, we're still not going to get out of this! If two took us down, what will a dozen do to us?" the captain muttered.

Sure, they were smaller, but they were no less deadly. They were verily the opposite. Marc was waiting for the inevitable crash and rocking repercussions from the ionic blasts that were sure to come at any moment. Once they did, defense would be forced. . . and Samantha may well be sentenced forever.

"I can give you shields, Hesslin." Medrhos' words came very low, and they knew he had been listening. "I'm trying to get through to the force captain now."

Medrhos flipped the communications switch again with one hand, the other clenching restlessly on the arm of his throne, remaining so. "Varclav, try catching their signal again." Varclav obeyed, and this time the force captain deigned to pick up.

"Raa, surely you wouldn't object, good sire, to let us have a bone such as this you carry with you?" the captain, Flotjvik, purred.

Medrhos knew him well, and answered warily, for he was the one known as Space Hawk, and the two were on equal terms with cunning, cruelty, and cutlasses.

"Verily, I object on the grounds that that ship is one of us, Hawk. If you are in such desperate straits, I'll have a bone to pick with you once I've met on the grounds of the Cult."

"I'm afraid such straits are much too narrow, my fine fyre, for your fleet to sail through," Flotjvik replied, and the Starkindlers darted over and under the *Harbinger's* surface, not daring to skin her, but with no pretense of believing that the *Lumenara* was anything but an intruder: an intruder which the Cult would order destroyed, or worse. One that would pay them and support their colonies, their families and the upkeep of the most wanted vessels in the galaxy, and all the better paid if they took it themselves and not for the Cult.

"May the fire fall on you, Hawk!" Medrhos spat, something in him instantly regretting it.

"Raa, by the powers, Medrhos, you know it will fall on you." There was an ominous curl in his voice. Both knew the other understood the reckless risk they were taking.

Then the Hawk called in the real danger. It was the mother of all mercenary ships, and the reason the Hawk was so feared in any territory. The *Callista* was like no other, no matter that she didn't match the *Harbinger* in size.

Green and black, drifting like the carcass of some ancient ghost craft, every side of her was speared with jagged plasma blades and turrets pierced by catalyzed cannons. It bore the skull-like visage of the Hawk's sobriquet.

"Curse you, Hawk!" Medrhos growled again. He ordered the *Harbinger* to break away from the *Lumenara*. No matter the repercussions, it was war now any way he looked at it. The *Callista* was giving birth to a dozen strikers and soon blasts were breaking on the shields cast over the *Lumenara*.

The Hawk drew his breath in softly with narrowing gaze. He knew all too well that the *Lumenara* had no shields of her own.

"Your method of piracy intrigues me, fyre," he murmured. "I know who else would pay dearly to know."

His craft spiraled and grazed the shields' surface, anti-gravity grenades locking to it and detonating as he spun away. The blasts rocked the ship and pain ran through Medrhos' still clenched hand.

"I-want-that-ship!" he snarled, teeth grit.

But Flotjvik was already leaving the other Starkindlers. His craft was swept into the *Callista*, and in a moment he was back at the helm of his pride. The *Harbinger* swung around and made for the *Callista* with all defenses and offenses set on her dripping wings. Flotjvik was happy to take more than blows on the solid iron shielding.

The *Callista* dove for the *Harbinger*, shields magnetized and the undersides of the ships crashed together as the *Harbinger* flipped back to meet it. All the outward plasma blades sheared into the force fields of the *Harbinger*, driving into her thick plating. Soon both were locked in a deadly gravitational spin in no direction other than down, to meet the universal seabed.

Marc slammed his hand on the siren. "Fire on the Starkindlers, now!" he barked. "Cobalt, we need to drive them away from each other – if our fields hold, the polarization -"

"I get you!"

The *Lumenara* and *Icebreaker* dove simultaneously, inching as close as they could beneath and between the two warships' wings. Four force fields collided with a crack and a burst of sparks that hurled each craft in separate directions. Glass splintered and instruments crashed into walls, heads spun and shots ricocheted every which way. Finally each captain jerked his ship out of the barrel roll they had put themselves in.

The Marauder fleet was doing well with the remaining Starkindlers and strikers. Flotjvik eyed their progress and drew the card that would, regrettably, take the *Lumenara* out of his grasp yet secure a lesser victory.

"Either give them to me, or I'll give them to the Cult, Medrhos. The choice is yours. You'll only profit one way out of two."

"I only throw bones to deserving dogs, Hawk."

"Pity, I think those dogs will come to chew on more than a bone now."

The *Callista* fired up the sulfur shields only given by the Cult. . . which could only be *broken* by the Cult. As the green haze began to bubble over the ship, Hawk reached for the communicator.

Without warning, a silent bolt of shimmering lightning streaked across their field of view, casting blinding white light as it collided with the Starkindlers, another blast took the strikers, and a third struck the *Callista* squarely where the shield had not yet grown, and it enveloped the mercenary ships with its sizzling glow.

"What the -" Marc leapt from his seat and everyone, Marauder, Vestar, and rebel alike searched for the origin of the blast.

The answer came when something massive materialized, uncloaking itself and overshadowing the entire battlespace. Swanlike wings wider than three *Harbingers* placed wingtip to wingtip glided overhead, coated in pearlescent sheets of some unearthly metal.

"No – in the heavens, it can't be!" Marc breathed, gazing upwards at a sight he had never dared think he'd see.

Medrhos was open-mouthed, for no one was meant to have a ship greater than he. The prized *Harbinger* was dwarfed by the ship that now embraced the group between her wings as a mother swan her cygnets, eyeing the still sparkling cloud drifting over the frozen mercenary craft.

Recovering from his spluttering, Marc heard Aiyra laughing behind him and found that she was easing her grip on Konstan's hand.

"How did you-?" he began, but Medrhos spoke at the same time.

"How did that ship get through with us?!" he shouted. "What-?! What *was* that?"

"It's the *Galateia*," Marc replied. "The only warship the Cythians ever built. . ." his voice trailed off for a moment, pausing the inquiry he had been about to put to his daughter. "Had she been functional the day of the burning, I doubt Cytha would ever have fallen." There was a tinge of bitterness to his voice still, and Medrhos took the words in silence.

"What kind of blasts *were* those?" Cobalt cried, with an excited exclamation, for the ships were still dead in space.

"Parasthesis. The Cythians call it the purgation beam – its general use knocks out all systems save life support, and paralyzes the ship for as long as necessary," Marc answered distractedly. "Primarily it functions to burn out dark matter." He turned back to Aiyra. "Aiyra, what in the galaxy are they doing here?"

She smiled. "We were on our way back from Alnilam when we ran into you, A'da. I asked them to follow us secretly, just in case."

Marc's expression softened by a smile and he touched his daughter's cheek.

"You saw them then. . . our people."

She nodded.

"I need to go home," Marc said, eyes closing briefly.

Aiyra laid her hand on his sleeve.

"A'da. . . A'ra Tryphena is here."

Marc's eyes flew open. "Tryphena?" he repeated.

Talitha's sister – he had been sure everyone had been taken, the royal family having refused to abandon those captured. But no. . . Tryphena and Talitha had been those set for coordinating and evacuating with the people if anything ever happened. The *Galateia* must have been taken to save the eight thousand souls she could carry, though her weapons had not yet been functional.

"Hesslin, we need to move. If you want to keep the *Lumenara* in one piece she needs to be hidden before this – cloud – wears off or another seeker finds them."

Marc stirred from his thoughts. "We'll follow you."

Aiyra slipped forward and rang the *Galateia,* leaving the communicator in her father's hands. A woman's voice answered with a vague lilt like Talitha's.

"Tryphena?"

"Marc!" Her voice was relieved like winter with the first breath of spring breezes. There was much to say, but no time.

"We need to take the *Lumenara* to safety, and you as well. Once that is done, I will come and see you, but briefly. . . will you follow us?"

It was agreed, and soon Medrhos was shepherding both ships into the atmosphere of an oceanic moon; the clouds of ice crystals would help to shield them from the Cult's gaze, refracting any scans should they even wander that far.

Marc had only a few minutes in which to make arrangements. He knew Aiyra was realizing that she was being set adrift again without him. What's worse, he was going to be taking Konstan, and she didn't need him to tell her that, either. He tried to avoid having her question him but felt her eyes following him as he gave instructions to his crew. He then took Aiyra with him to board the *Galateia* for the last of his preparations.

They found themselves in a lift within the great ship, Marc's heart pounding as they watched the white and gold lights ripple past with every floor of the vessel. The lift opened out into the ethereal softness of the Cythian warship, where all was reminiscent of pearls, starlight, water and clouds, and everything was soft, cool, and warm to the touch by turns.

A woman of stature equal to Marc's stood before them in the semi-circular hub that fell upon the bridge. A silver band circled her brow and the coat that fell to her feet was of the silken silver-taupe of swan's down, with a regal wing-like crest framing her slender neck and winging her arms in the Cythian equivalent of epaulettes.

"Tryphena!" Marc took her outstretched hands and bent his forehead to hers in the Cythian family greeting. Both were wordless a moment, having been sure all this time that the other perished or languished out of reach.

"Aiyra told me," Tryphena said at last. She studied Marc's face. "We have all seen too much. It has been so long since I have been with anyone so close to my heart. . . I feel your pain for Talitha-" She dropped her gaze. "-How you could not save her, just as I could not save my Elisav."

She had married sometime after starting again in Alnilam, but in their efforts to track down any and all Marauders in the hopes of finding the key to saving their people, Elisav had been shot down by mercenaries. Tryphena put her hands on Marc's shoulders.

"I will not let such a thing happen again if it be in our power. We will save your love, Marc, and bring her home. We *will* bring her home."

Marc grasped her hands and prayed that the promise would hold true. "I need to work with Medrhos, but I can't bring the *Lumenara* into danger again," he whispered. "Will you stay?"

Tryphena glanced at Aiyra, who had remained at a distance. The girl instinctively knew every word that was being spoken, and her eyes showed as much.

"I will protect her," Tryphena replied. "Do not fear for her, Marc."

Marc squeezed her hands and stepped back, bringing Aiyra to his side. They were interrupted by the lift door opening once more.

"Uncle Orion!" Estill threw her arms around him as three of the Queen's handmaids remained in the doorway.

"Estill! What are you doing here?"

Aiyra and Tryphena joined in mutual confusion as Marc pried the child from his knee and repeated his question.

"I wanted to stay with my daddy but he didn't want me to," the child replied, and now Marc's brow creased in confusion, knowing full well that the child was an orphan.

The handmaidens stepped forward, and the eldest, Dyra, spoke. "Medrhos has asked us to keep your daughter company. The rest of our sisters remain with him to care for the Queen, should she be returned." She and her companions, Zoryana and Lajariá, turned to Aiyra. "If you will accept us, little one."

Aiyra smiled and looked down at Estill, who was now examining the sparkling hem of the Vestar dress she wore.

"Thank you."

She looked at Marc for the dreaded words that had been interrupted. She already knew what he would say, but had no words of her own she could use. She may have realized that her implant would only increase the danger of the Cult's territory for them by tenfold. Marc exhaled, exchanging a look with Tryphena before drawing Aiyra close.

"Stay here with your A'ra, please dear? Pell can handle the *Lumenara*. I promise nothing will prevent me from returning to you, Princess."

"You know that you cannot promise me anything," Aiyra answered, voice hushed. "But please bring her home, A'da!"

At his command, the lonely maid remained on the *Galateia* with her aunt and new companions, and Marc found Konstan already waiting on the *Harbinger's* deck.

"I couldn't say goodbye to her again." The boy watched as the *Lumenara* and *Galateia* sank together below the clouds. Marc's eyes followed them too as the last glimmer on their hulls faded into the ice.

"I think she knew, Konstan. She always knows. . . ."

XIV

Twisted

Kythonios revolved in the outer rim like some abandoned marble set to spin. The planet's atmosphere had been drained away, leaving its bones bare to the heat of the sun.

"Looks like hell," Cobalt muttered.

"The mere mid-level of the Underworld is more like it. Save hell for elsewhere," Medrhos advised darkly.

The barren rocks were burning visibly, crackling and melting before solidifying again. Dark pinnacles dotted the landscape, long eroded.

"The Cult built their city of Morphos on the far side," the Emperor said, as the ships entered the planet's orbit. He glanced askance at Marc, who was now garbed as one of the royal guards. "Don't expect this to go well."

Only Marc's eyes were visible above the half mask as he answered. "I hope you have some idea of what you're doing since the rest of us don't?"

"Ha, I'm going to try and ask politely to begin with," Medrhos replied. "If that fails, I intend to remind them who banished them *here* to begin with."

Something came into view below them, suspended above the inhospitable terrain by what looked like an anti-gravity bridge. The shape glinted like glass and proved to be a sprawling city of iron and jasper. Sharp spires and creeping walkways made the city seem like a maze of extraterrestrial thorns. It was encapsulated by an immense dome that protected it from the non-existence of the atmosphere.

"I dare say they've always had a bone to pick with us over the location," Medrhos murmured dryly, as the *Harbinger* was cleared for landing by the portal that opened in the dome's side, just wide enough for her wingspan, and closed seamlessly behind them.

"That's some force field," Konstan commented as he joined them, identical in dress to Marc.

"It should be, because it isn't. Nothing functions in a sane way around here."

As if to prove his point, the *Harbinger* twisted upside-down and came to rest on a crescent-shaped port lined with red lights, jutting out from one great block-like building.

"Someone appears to have a lack of taste in architecture," was Konstan's next keen observation.

Medrhos must have agreed, by the look on his face, but he only ordered ten of his closest guards to follow them in formation, and Marc and Konstan fell in at their head. Silvestra and one of the other handmaids, Adora, were brought as well and placed between each line of men.

Meanwhile, the *Icebreaker* and her men remained fully camouflaged among the other Marauder ships, resting just within the barrier.

The group halted down the ramp as the sound of marching feet in the fabricated, falling rain met them. Two mages dressed in colors of smoke and ash appeared on the walkway, accompanied by four guards dressed in white and raven from head to foot. Medrhos turned his head ever so slightly and spoke, almost below his breath, to Marc and Konstan.

"We Marauders have not had cause to be here since the banishment of the Cult, so do not think that this is a routine sight. I have no cause to doubt they know why we're here. . . you can be sure they've planned something for us, quite possibly unpleasant."

One of the mages banged his bronze staff on the the tiles. Without a word, he motioned for Medrhos and his men to follow. Medrhos' eyes darkened and he swept down the walk, rain splattering on his shoulders.

"But if you've never been here before, how is it familiar to you?" Konstan questioned, whispering for fear the men ahead would hear.

Medrhos snorted. "The memory of the eyes is passed down between us emperors, so while it was my grand-predecessor, it is as though I have been here myself. Have no fear, I know exactly where we're going."

The path snaked its way at searing heights, the lower terraces of the city falling away below, and they could see the lights of strange vehicles passing through the cubed streets like the blip, blip, blip of data through a machine. It was not an uncommon question on everyone's mind that these walkways were far too dangerously placed a mile high, with no railings and frequent rain, acid at that, to set the mood.

What was worse, the walkway suddenly melded into a set of stairs that was insurmountable for the simple reason that it spiraled a hundred and eighty degrees. Marc and Konstan drew up short but Medrhos kept going.

"We can't walk on that!" Konstan said, flabbergasted. Everything about him suggested a puppy with ears flattened back in the confusion of arriving at the vet and not the nearest park. Medrhos' boots rang loudly as he defied Konstan's common sense and presently stood upside-down from them.

"Clearly we can," he retorted. "Everything is bi-gravitational here. Move!"

Marc and Konstan struggled to lift their feet onto each step, each muscle rebelling at the imminent danger of falling flat into the traffic below. At last they were level with Medrhos once more, the twisting stairs ending with a final spin that forced them to jump and abruptly switch the fall of their gravity.

Konstan landed on his feet, looking even more unnerved than before. Marc stumbled slightly, now looking upwards at the traffic and having lost all sense of up and down, for even the *Harbinger* had flipped upon entry. Was the sense of direction always so arbitrary?

"Please, do try to look like you know what you're doing," Medrhos hissed, and waved the rest of the guards to come quickly, holding the arms of Silvestra and Adora.

They tramped onward, now passing into the shadow of the temple mansion, a skyscraper of perfectly squared-off monoliths of black granite, the soaring edges of which ripped at the sky with their uncut jaggedness. This was Tapinak-Raebzalom, the house of the god of fear, the only one the Cult believed in.

A yawning symmetrical doorway swallowed them in midnight stone, penetrated at intervals by fiery lights suspended in the air. The walls seemed otherwise static, but as they proceeded, grotesque visages leapt out at them, only to melt away at another step with clever carving. Adora cried out the first instance and at a glare from Medrhos the guard beside her took her arm and kept her reassuringly shielded from any further images they might chance upon.

Other mages, guardsmen, and strangely clad men and women passed to and fro from crisscrossing corridors broken by lead-paned windows. They hardly deigned to give a frozen glance or bow to the Emperor as they may well should have.

Luckily for them, Medrhos was preoccupied with increasingly torturous images of Samantha, so close and yet so far from the painfully slow tramping of the guards ahead of them. One strike would send them out of his way and free him to continue at a run, or it might incur a heavier debt for Samantha.

A forest of temple columns, densely packed and wider than two men each, rose before them, carved and painted in ancient style not unlike some examples Marc had glimpsed on Aliros. Images of war and servitude to Rätha were the main glory here, among the flickering multicolored flames. The walls slanted inwards at narrowing heights, broken by spearish windows. Beneath their feet lay unevenly matched jet and jade tiles.

A low strumming sound emanated from somewhere ahead, mingling with metallic rain at a lulling pitch that softened the senses and dampened their thoughts. Through the shadows they caught glimpses of ugly metal pipes and structures covering much of the walls, and the faint acrid smell of various gases lingered in the air. Gases which the three men knew from experience was used in prisoner discomfort.

The perfume of the Cult drove the images of Samantha back into Medrhos' head and he lost his patience with the mindless pace set by the mages. He stormed through their ranks, sweeping them aside as the ocean tide with as many shattered shells, and his own men kept the ranks from reforming as they pushed through. Steps faltered again when the scarlet and fuschia mood lighting fell over them in the soaring wings of a throne room like a sorcerer's dream.

A blinding pale cast of white light fell into cerise and lavender as a wall of sheer crystal rose before them. It was fractaled and bound by metallic vines and spears resembling insect antennae. From within came the deep droning, and before the wall stood a throne reminiscent of frozen fireballs and flame in the drama of pagan drums. It was guarded by two drooping reptilian wings bearing cauldrons of rainbow fire.

A thick theatrical mist curled and lingered across the floor. Security television sets glowed and hovered in the air above, and Marc saw, with some unease, that two cameras were focused upon the *Harbinger* and her daughter ships.

Two beats of the mages' staves upon the tile sent peals of thunder rolling through the room, and the men could have sworn they felt the solid stone floor ripple beneath their feet like gelatin.

"Medrhos, my darling, how nice to see you!"

Medrhos' eyes jerked from one side of the room to the other as the voice seemed to bounce about. A figure vaporized from the cloud before the throne. The woman's robe of oily voile fell in pleats and presumably trailed off behind her, a detail that was missed in the mist. Her shoulders were bared by draping thorns dripping with strands of starstrung beads. The jeweled claws pinching the gathered straps of her gown, gunsmoke and gold diadem and the choker hung with a dangling half moon denoted her as royal, but the crescent sabre embroidered on the midriff, fringed scarf crisscrossing her hips, and the bubbled cape painted with celestial objects marked her as the high priestess.

Her lips, of which it could not be discerned as to whether they were dyed with a gradient of blood and wine, curled in a smile of the carnivorous sundew's sweetness. Medrhos grimaced and a thought flitted through his mind, wondering whether that smile was because of who stood next to her.

The chief of the Cult, sometimes known as the Doge of Deception, a man normally shrouded in mystery, was none other than Serengoch. Did he realize that he had been bested by the Emperor on Earth? The wicked, almost angry smile lurking over his own painted lips seemed to say as much, and Medrhos' misgivings turned to revengeful amusement.

"Aniceda," Medrhos replied, acknowledging the woman warily, spurning her companion. The last time he had seen the high priestess was long ago at his marking as royalty.

"It's been such a long time, my precious," the princess purred, floating down from the dais. "You've grown so well and you have become such a fine King."

"Naturally, and unnaturally you don't look a day older," Medrhos muttered, looking down at her, for while the princess was tall, even she had to look up at the Emperor. "You know why I'm here, Aniceda. Return my wife to me. *Now.*"

"Oh, don't make such a fuss; she's right down there." Aniceda waved a careless hand towards the crystal vault behind her throne, allowing him to mount the dais. He stepped up to the transparent wall and gazed down into Aniceda's special guest chamber.

Marc tensed and Konstan shifted uneasily. They saw Medrhos' shoulders pull back with a sharp breath and he turned on Aniceda.

"What did you do to her?" he cried, lunging down the stairs and seizing the priestess by the shoulders.

"Do calm down, darling, it *is* an issue of conformity, after all," she replied, extracting herself from his grasp.

"I swear, Aniceda, if you or any of your people come within five feet of her again -"

"An issue which must be addressed!" Aniceda's voice rose over his. "*Now.*"

"Bring my wife to me *now*, then I'll deign to listen to your pathetic defense. Or, I'll remind you why you're here," Medrhos threatened.

"You can't really think that we'd return her to you after what she's done?" Aniceda asked, almost amused. "Let's face it, my love. She single-handedly damaged much of Rätha's work in your Empire and has turned you further against our laws. You've always been rebellious, but it's always only better served the cause. . . up until she refused to submit to you and to us. She has refused to submit, would not serve, broke our laws and changed them, damaged our trade, conspired with our enemies and with rebels – in short, while she had the makings of the greatest Queen we have ever seen, she is what you would call a 'dud.' Thanks to your intervention, twice I might add, she is no longer programmable."

"If you've ever wanted to see hellfire, you'll soon see your city in flames," Medrhos snarled with the fire of the tiger he was. "Bring my Queen to me, now!"

The woman and her doge only smiled a little and watched as Medrhos, to drive his point home, made as though to strike a blow upon the crystal wall and shatter the barrier.

"I think your woman would rather you didn't touch the crystal, Medrhos," Aniceda said softly, examining one of the golden bands on her fingers.

Medrhos' hand halted mid-swing. He turned on his heel and looked her. His voice dripped with the passion of contempt.

"*Now*, Aniceda. You had no right to harm what is mine."

The Princess' eyes flickered and she, too, dropped her hand, perhaps in the knowledge that his threats were more than idle.

"Darling, you're just as dramatic as ever. Serept. . . have her brought in."

Serengoch, whose name seemed to be only an alias, signaled to the guards. They disappeared into a passageway to the left of the wall.

They returned, almost noiselessly from the opposite side, bearing between them a limp figure in stained ivory.

XV

Shattered

A sound escaped Marc's mask as though he were about to cry out. Konstan bit his own tongue viciously and jabbed the end of his stave into Marc's shin to silence him.

Bruises and burns littered Samantha's skin, and a charcoal and amaranth-colored stain spread over the right side of her face like the pockmark of an asteroid that had crashed and burned. Her hair, usually as perfect as the nature of Almedra, was disheveled and had been torn back from her brow to expose the deeply etched scar. She struggled to lift her listless eyes as the men flanking her halted at a supposedly safe distance from the King. They weren't far enough.

Medrhos had pulled the shackled girl from their grasp before they could blink, and stood back, loosely pressing her close with one arm. His shaking fingers unconsciously stroked the tattered ends of her hair, betraying his anxiety as he trained a frigid gaze on Aniceda and Serengoch.

"What. . . is this," he asked in that low voice that always denoted the threshold of danger at his hands.

The priestess shrugged carelessly, and with a wave of her hand, a vast table appeared between them, marked with inchingly spinning stars, moons, and galaxies. She motioned him to take a seat, and she sat down. Serengoch rested his hands on the back of her chair. Silvestra and Adora were drawing close, torn between fear and the need to be with their mistress. They flanked Medrhos' throne.

145

"This was her last chance, Medrhos," Aniceda said softly. "Since you wouldn't give it to her, we had to. Our hydrolizer liquefies crystal. . . so we did what even she is incapable of undoing. Once injected it carves a unique path and hardens. . . solidifying within nerves, veins, and the very cells of her brain."

The king's lip was curling; his breath whistled faintly between his teeth. "You and your implants!"

Aniceda raised an eyebrow at the implication that she had anything to do with another implant, but didn't deny it. No one could say whether Konstan and Marc were digging their nails into their own palms to try and curb their thoughts.

Medrhos' right hand covered the damaged half of Samantha's face but he didn't take his eyes from Aniceda. If she challenged him, she'd bring his wrath down upon her own head that much more swiftly.

"Don't think you can make me believe that you only meant to tame her, not to break her. You meant to destroy her," he murmured.

The stain was easing out of Samantha's face and her eyes opened in confusion. Medrhos took his hand away, pinching between his thumb and index finger a sticky ball of liquid crystal. He tossed it lazily at the priestess, whose quick reflexes swatted it away with a gust of wind that stirred her hair and the mist curling around their feet.

"Rhos?"

Medrhos looked down into Samantha's upturned face. Her eyes dizzily tried to lock onto his. After all the pain she had been through, his instinct was to comfort her and bring down the temple on

Aniceda's head, but here, raven's eyes watched to see that his bond to Samantha was distant at best.

"Be silent, Ancilla. It's fine."

"I'd hardly say so. . ." Serept murmured.

"You do realize, don't you darling, that you just destroyed her last chance?" Aniceda asked, taking a sip of some burgundy drink that had abruptly appeared before her. It bubbled and smoked like dragon's breath.

Samantha was now fully conscious and she turned her head, somewhat painfully, to look at the priestess, her fingers fumbling with the tiger pendant around Medrhos' neck as he opened his mouth to reply. Aniceda raised her hand and silenced him.

"Not to mention that you broke our most sacred rule, Medrhos, not to interfere with Rätha's adoption. That is a grave debt to pay on your own account. Also, I do wish you hadn't treated Melkos and Pvettkar so roughly. I hate to lose their fine skills."

Medrhos scorned her with a smile. "Allow me to remind you by whose power you are trapped here, save for your precious interrogators – and doge – who increasingly risk their lives with the privilege. As far as my people are concerned, your interrogators are dead if they enter my space."

Aniceda played with the holographic planets littering the table, sending several into unnatural orbits.

"Darling, darling," she murmured, her smoky eyelids lowered as she watched the twinkling stars play. "You do realize, do you not, that your power comes from us. . . all of it. . . and we may take it away? And you need not strain to pretend that this woman is your wife. . . she told me as much. She could not resist it."

Serengoch was noting, with pleasure, Samantha's horror-stricken pain at the revelation of her confession, and the sudden chill that crept into Medrhos' eyes.

"Which means, love. . . that you really aren't the Emperor. And your breakages have sentenced your people and ours to death. Even now, the men in your ships are slowly falling. . . one. . . by. . . one."

She fixed her eyes on the screens above her and Medrhos, pale, followed suit. The image flickered as Varclav slumped over the console, the men in the background beginning to stumble.

The chills were creeping ceaselessly through Samantha's skull as she feared for Medrhos' control and the hopelessness of their position. The tiger was being put in a cage, and would he sacrifice his freedom to merely escape the cage into a pen with high walls?

"Yet, Rätha is merciful. He loves you yet, Medrhos, for you and your rebellion are after his own heart. Karthos did his job well. You have two options that can yet save your position and your people. Less drastic would be to take a new Queen."

Medrhos was eyeing her as the blood crept back into his face. Samantha could feel him tensing as the flame, momentarily chilled, began to come back into him.

"Let me guess. You would have me crown you, and leave Samantha as a pet kitten."

Aniceda smiled then, still playing absentmindedly with the holograms.

"It would solve both our problems, my love. As Rätha's bride it would bring back harmony between us and I can hardly fail him."

"That would be like a fish wedding a worm."

"You dare call Rätha's princess -" Serengoch exclaimed, moving as though to throttle Medrhos.

The king flicked him away as easily as in Arce'Atelane. "Hold your peace, Serpent, or whatever your name is. I'm sure the thought is mutual between us. As for your offer, Princess, I wouldn't take it in the hundred-and-twenty years you've been around." He stood and glared down at the priestess.

"You and your forebears betrayed me, and my entire people. You've enslaved us and done everything you could to try and destroy all that is most precious to me." He laughed darkly. "But I've shattered the bond, thanks to my Queen." Samantha stared. "You no longer have power over us and we will destroy you."

For the first time, Aniceda's eyes flamed and she gripped the arms of her chair so tightly her pale skin turned to a glassy hue. Her gaze turned on Samantha so viciously that the girl wanted to cry, remembering the pain a lesser expression had led to.

"You *are* a little Disruptor, aren't you," Aniceda seethed under her breath, but her features were quickly softening as though the ripple had not been cast. Her lips twisted in a sweet smile that somehow made Samantha feel even worse.

The priestess turned back to the Marauder King, mindlessly fingering her pendant. The firelight flickered across its shivering surface and Samantha blinked, wondering if she had seen a skull peering from the metal.

"That's quite a turn, darling. . . is there anything *else* you'd like to tell me?"

A cold rush of air swirled the mist around their ankles. Medrhos dropped his hand from Samantha's shoulder as he straightened. The old arrogant smile began playing over his lips again. The smoke in the crystals had done its job. The white was fading, the smoke curling, and the red glare was flooding the room.

"Boys. . . bring them here."

Marc lashed out as he was seized from behind. For just a moment Konstan remained still, hoping somehow that he would be left free to intervene, but he soon found himself struck by dark energy and thrown to the ground beside Marc, their masks removed. Samantha gasped.

Medrhos smirked. "How does it feel to have the princes of our enemy here at last?"

"Lovely, darling. . . just lovely." Aniceda was looking them over and she smiled in approval at the return of the ruthless Marauder king.

"Serept, you may take them and do whatever you like."

Serengoch gloated like a child with a new toy, but only signaled the guards to remove the men from the room.

"Medrhos, please, if you love me, don't let them!"

The King gave the broken Queen a withering look.

"Be silent, Ancilla. My love for you doesn't interfere with my duty towards my enemy and the protection of my people!" His voice was rising. "Is that clear?"

Samantha didn't answer, only turned her head away and squeezed her eyes shut. Her heart shrank in fear as her world and her life began to shatter again.

"Serept, wait!" Aniceda called out. "Keep the men here." She arose and went to her throne. Reaching underneath, she drew out an iron case. "Medrhos, come here, my love."

The King complied, albeit lazily. Aniceda cast out her arm and the fire in the cauldrons blazed up, baring the dais and the steps of the mist. Marc and Konstan had been halted just inside the door and stood rooted, unable to move for some enchantment that had been laid upon them. Aniceda unlocked the box.

"There is one thing you must do to regain Rätha's complete faith in you. I will give you the greatest jewel of our tribe, the Eye of Eternity, given to our forebears by Rätha himself that he might never depart from them visibly."

She cracked open the case and the light glimmered off a diadem of woven iridium, darkened as if by smoke, and a heavy, inky-black jewel. So deep was its color that it scarcely reflected even a drop of the firelight

"By its power, it will gird you to perform the most difficult task of your life, and in doing so it will reinstate you as Emperor and heal those of your people who have fallen."

Medrhos bent his head with glowing eyes and Aniceda shaped the band to his brow.

A shadow crossed the room, briefly burning away the mist. When it passed, Medrhos had straightened. His garments, already black, were now so deep they seemed to be the shadow of nonexistence. His face in contrast seemed eerily white with his hazel eyes taking on an ember hue. He stood like a ghost, silent and motionless as Aniceda descended the stairs and placed her hand on his shoulder.

"Now, my dear Marauder, you must prove your loyalty to Rätha by sacrificing the one thing you love most."

Of one mind, both turned slowly to look at Samantha, frozen as she met the eyes of the man who was supposed to be her husband.

"No!" but the enchantment kept Konstan's voice at a whisper.

"There's only one way to break free of this curse," Marc said grimly, not taking his eyes away from the scene unfolding before them. "Try!"

"I am," Konstan moaned, and closed his eyes in prayer, digging deep into concentration and striving to ignore the fear and the torture that suddenly flamed through his already aching limbs.

At Aniceda's gaze, the table and chairs disappeared, hurling Samantha to the floor, and sending both handmaids tumbling backwards.

Feeling that both her knees were badly bruised by the landing, Samantha shook her head to clear it. She only felt further disoriented as the floor collapsed beneath her with a grinding sound.

The mist became a cloud rimming the sloping pit, not unlike the one in which she had been held. In front of her rose a fifteen-ton diamond-like table, marked with a triangular rise of sloping crystals. These met a square formation of long blocks framing a chunk of ruby like a lidless eye.

Medrhos and Aniceda were looking down at her, as a ring of the Cult joined them like dark ghosts.

"You know what you must do."

Medrhos swept his way down the floating stairway and stood before the girl, a dark smile lighting his otherwise shadowed face.

"Rhos-"

"Did you really think that I would risk everything to save you, Samantha? Did you really forget that I'm a Marauder? Did you really think, after all the times I've told you that close relationships are not things of kings, that I would travel nearly three thousand years into a time rift, to lose my crown, my throne, and my people to you?"

A second voice was layered deep and rattling beneath his own. His right hand was raised above his heart and an orb of furious light was blazing around the gems.

"Medrhos, please, this isn't you!" Samantha whispered. To see someone so close to her, so close to falling so far in a way that could never be fully repaired, was more than she could bear. Her heart wanted to break as she looked up into those eyes, so unfamiliar now in a face she had once known well.

"You promised that you would never hurt me! The Cult has betrayed you and used you, and stolen everything that you've loved! I swore I would be of your people, Rhos. . . if you kill me, it will not be you but whatever God wills, and by it we will free you. Remember!"

"Silence, Ancilla!" Aniceda cried from above. "And we'll never have to hear your voice again. Don't be afraid, Medrhos. This has become your destiny among all the paths that have been tragically broken for you."

Medrhos' face was twisted in pain and contention. His gaze strayed upwards and he saw that Marc and Konstan now stood at the edge, free and unnoticed by the wall of the Cult blocking them, but no less helpless to intervene. He hesitated for only a breath, but then his eyes were veiled and his face set, and his hand drew back -

The strumming grew louder, drowning out everything, Samantha's words falling silent, thoughts and breaths and one's own heartbeat -

Terror rippled through the ranks of the Cult as Marc and Konstan broke down and broke through.

Medrhos' hand crashed down in fury and Samantha's cry split the air; the room was washed out with a flare of light that blazed like a thousand suns contained in a dozen square feet.

XVI

Rift

One leather-gloved hand reached up and wrenched the smoking jewel from his brow and the other hand came down and pulled Samantha up out of the melted mass of her bonds.

Medrhos turned and faced the priestess who had traded the color in her cheeks for the whiteness that had previously stolen his.

"You. . . asked me to destroy the ONE thing I love most," he said, voice low and trembling. "How did you even *think* that was going to work?"

The priestess flung out her arms, a sibilant hiss coming through her teeth. "May Rätha take your power away as it was given to you!"

Medrhos looked at her and laughed. He tore the burnt gems from his gloves and flung them at her. "Plot twist. . . my powers are from you no longer!"

"Seize them, all of them!" Aniceda yowled, her once lovely face contorted. Her thick raven waves were strangling her like a woven snake.

Medrhos smashed his hand down on the altar and broke it, leaving the gathered sorcerers to shriek in physical pain.

"As for you-!" Aniceda began, raising one hand towards Samantha. She ducked to avoid a flying jinx that Medrhos had deflected up at the ceiling. "Don't think that this is the end!" She raised her arms again and pointed one perfectly sharpened nail at the girl. "This is only just beginning!"

And before Medrhos could read the spell on her lips, there was the sound of an old sci-fi disappearing act, and Aniceda vanished. Medrhos closed his eyes for a moment as he felt the onset of a headache, or was it a heartache?

"She took her, didn't she."

Silvestra's answer was a soft sob. Medrhos turned slowly, and looked from the silent melted metal that had once held the Empire's Queen, to the leering chaos above him.

Marc and Konstan, who had remained momentarily free while eyes recovered, found themselves dodging spells left and right, and curses soon ricocheted around the room, threatening everyone, including their originators.

"Keep concentrating!" Marc yelled, and Konstan found when next struck that the hex rolled off him like oil on water. Marc sent the nearest Cultsman tumbling down the pit as Medrhos' men barreled in.

For the second time, Medrhos doubted himself. It lasted only for a moment. Adora touched his arm with shaking fingers.

"You've saved her before," she trembled. "Please bring her back!"

Five minutes found the entire ring of the working Cult safely sealed within the crystal walls of what had been Samantha's prison. Exactly how he did it, Medrhos was not quite sure; he had half-tried to use his powers while remembering that he had broken their source, and something had happened. Whether it was of overwhelmingly good consequence, Medrhos was uncertain, and it left him abnormally ill at ease.

But whatever the circumstance, bands of unbreakable white energy were surrounding the crystal holding pen, preventing even the most powerful enchantment from breaking it. The source of the city's forcefield had been sensibly damaged in such a way as to lock it in place and prevent its mending for some time.

Now the group was racing back down the gravity-twisting path. Much to their relief, the *Icebreaker* had somehow remained unmolested and Varclav was improving after a literal dizzy spell. Apparently Rätha's curse had not yet come into effect.

Medrhos peeled back the protective dome just long enough to let the *Harbinger* and her colony of batships through. The atmosphere became what it had been before, a well-seasoned mixture of anger, fear, and desperation as silence cloaked their winged way once more.

"Where we're going, I hate to bring your daughter into danger, Hesslin, but we're going to need every ship just to make a valiant show of things. I have no doubt you'd rather see her the longer rather than the shorter."

Medrhos ordered the course set for the oceanic moon. Marc offered no objection. Somewhere inside, they all had an idea of what they were going to try and face, and what Samantha may well be facing right now.

Medrhos voiced their thoughts aloud, almost unconsciously as he thought of the blackness of the universe they sailed in, and the unruly whiteness of the moon that appeared before them. It danced slowly, ethereally as though equally unconscious of Aniceda's attempts to spin it out of control, maddeningly slow and sweet compared to the endless moments of sweat and terror they were drowning in.

"And Samantha thought one couldn't teleport to hell," he muttered. "I'm pretty sure she's finding out otherwise now."

"What do you mean?" Marc asked, dreading the confirmation of his fears.

Medrhos snorted and took up a forced announcer's voice. "That is to say, the bride of Rätha has dragged her captive before him to blame all her woes on the helpless and thereby force Rätha to solve her problems." He dropped the tone as instantly as he had taken it. "Take her in, Varclav."

"Meaning. . . Rätha is-"

"Precisely what you've been thinking he is all along," Medrhos finished.

There was silence for a few moments.

"I'm halfway in between thinking, this is horrible and we're all going to die, and, how bad can that be, considering that we deal with him every day," Konstan said finally.

Medrhos turned icy eyes on him. "Did you see *anything* that happened back there?" he asked, jerking his head in the direction of the distant wreck of a planet.

"Yeah. . . ."

"Imagine that level of ruination multiplied by a thousand. Yeah, we're all going to die, if we're lucky," Medrhos said darkly.

"And if we're blessed," Marc said quietly, "we just might save even a single soul from ever facing this physical darkness again."

~~~

It seemed that Aiyra did not need to be told the result of the mission. The *Lumenara* and the *Galateia* were surfacing among the clouds when the *Harbinger* swooped in. A shuttle was soon dispatched, returning Marc and Konstan to the *Lumenara's* bridge.

Shortly thereafter, Aiyra joined them. She didn't say anything; she only looked into their eyes and read the echoes of the shadows, weariness, and pain etched too deeply for any man to tell. She slipped under her father's arm the way Sage always did her, and took Konstan's hand to her heart.

The newly enlarged fleet was quickly on their way again. Aiyra let her father and Konstan spend approximately fifteen minutes silently steering the ship after Medrhos, before she sent them to bed.

"Heaven knows they would tell you," she said. "Mother and Samantha would. And so would I," she added, with a whisper of a smile.

They were too tired to argue that they were too wound up to rest. Yet sleep is medicine for many things in a man's soul, and there would be little they could do upon arrival at their bodies' current crash rate.

Medrhos had not yet disclosed just where, or how they were going to get to their destination. Medrhos himself wasn't quite sure how he knew where they were going, and that worried him.

The arrival of the great Marauder fleet, along with the *Delta* and the surprise addition of the three Realtra ships, was a good enough distraction when he couldn't rest. The journey was far shorter than anyone expected, perhaps because of the speed they were pushing their ships to, and perhaps in part from the emotional waves that seemed to be drowning out all sense of time.

When both princes returned to the helm, it was to the sight of something unsurpassable and suitably black lying ahead. Their ears were greeted by a five-way conference call with Pell, Cobalt, Tryphena, and Berron of the *Delta* arguing over Medrhos' plotted course. Aiyra seemed unsurprised by the Marauder's train of thought as she vacated her father's seat.

"Hold up!" Marc called, waving for Pell and the others on deck to shush. "What's the issue now?"

"I truly appreciate how you Rip-Van-Winkle your way into things, Hesslin." Medrhos' voice was vaguely sardonic.

"I see Samantha's been telling you Earth stories," Marc replied, with a pang. She liked to weave tales of all sorts, which he had occasionally had the privilege to overhear when hunting down a missing Aiyra after hours. Samantha certainly was weaving the mother of all of them now. But he was looking at the deathly silent maw in front of them and realizing what it was.

"You mean to enter this black hole."

No points of light shone anywhere within that sphere of shadow, but all around was a flickering red maelstrom. Konstan was squinting at it.

"Space lightning?" he muttered. "I didn't think it was ever visible."

"We'll be spaghettified before we can say an *Ave* if we go through it, and you know it," Cobalt objected.

"Since when did spaghetti come with a rosary attached?" Berron asked dryly. After his experience in the slave confines, he was debating whether or not he was in a hurry to agree with Medrhos amid the confusion of joining the fleet.

"I don't only intend to, Hesslin, we have to. But this is no black hole by our standards. This is Rätha's Gate, the only way to reach the beginning and the end of this." Medrhos paused. "Indeed, we may well never see spaghetti the same way again, if ever, but there's only one way to find out; only one way to try and save our own necks and hers."

For a moment, none of them offered a comment.

"Well," Marc said at length. "It's every captain's judgment to make for themselves." He pressed the switch on the general intercom. "If anyone on this ship would rather not take the leap and would prefer to take your chances with the Mercenaries, Pell will organize shuttle departures."

The other captains followed his lead. It was soon discovered that the balance of the mere possibility of spaghettification and whatever came after, was considered relatively equal to the dangers of the Hawk. Even for those who would have chosen it, they quickly realized there was a far greater chance of being stranded in a time rift without a hospitable place to colonize; not to mention, no way of even calling home, should the mother ships not return. It was all or nothing now.

The *Harbinger* took the lead and was soon swallowed by the gaping maw. The *Lumenara* followed, flanked by the *Galateia* and the *Delta*, surrounded by the metallic sea that was the fleet. They were engulfed in a roaring silence that seemed to seep through minute cracks between the hull plating. It was followed by a rattling that increased with twice the fury of the vortex. Marc's eyes went to the walls of the ship, expecting them to buckle inwards as the ships were drawn in a slow spiral. The creaks and groans of metal against dark energy were enough to deafen everyone.

Gravity was all at once uprooted and slammed down on its head, spinning as all the instruments' readings were inverted. The power flickered and went out, plunging them all in darkness. Aiyra, no longer quite sure where she was on the bridge after being tipped off the sofa, called out for Konstan and her father. They reached for her and, finding her in the dark, lifted her back into her seat despite what gravity had to say about it.

Everyone went still, and even the prayers ceased for a moment as the noise died down. The *Lumenara* was no longer spiraling. A dim blue glow hesitated to fill the room as the emergency lights rose to the occasion. They threw a watery light over the tense faces there.

Aiyra, still clasping Konstan's hand, felt him spasm. She turned to him in concern and saw his other hand go to his heart. A grimace etched itself into his features.

"Konstan? Are you hurting?"

He sucked in his breath, bent nearly double. "I feel – pressure," he said, faintly. "Do you feel it too?"

"I-" Aiyra found herself pressing a hand to her own heart as a void seemed to grow inside her chest, shoving at her ribcage and leading all her bones to ache. Her heart struggled to beat against the pressure and her head began to spin. "I feel it." She tightened her hold on his hand as everyone wondered if it were the end, and the end of hope.

"Konstan – there is something, in case we do not make it-" she paused to listen to the noise. Something shook the ship and made it scream like a panther. She lost her train of thought.

"Is – is it stretching us?" Aiyra wanted to know, yet wasn't sure whether she really did.

"Aiyra baby, give me your hand." Her father reached back and took her other hand reassuringly. "This black hole should have destroyed us by now, if it were normal. . . maybe, if we could get the ship's life support and pressurization stabilized, it would help, but the emergency power doesn't seem to be doing the job."

Aiyra said nothing. She understood what her father was thinking and closed her eyes. If only the implant would come in handy again – just once more – she could feel the accustomed aggravation shooting through her nerves. The implant was so close to breaking her, but just once, if only she could – she tried to ignore the migrating migraine and the cold fire flooding her veins as she fought to make the connection.

Both men felt her hands grow cold in theirs, but it was only a moment later that a low hum in the midst of the eerie silence announced the repressurization and the return of life support. The hint of stretching pains eased. Aiyra drew a crackling breath, slumping against Konstan's shoulder.

"I – tried – the other ships," she whispered. "Too many – I do not know."

Marc dropped everything and faced her in trepidation at the weakness of her voice. That she had tried for far more than the *Lumenara*, all at once, was unthinkable – what had it cost?

The lights flashed on and the engines whirred to life, interrupting his fears as Briggs gave a shout. Marc exhaled shakily and glanced out the viewports, realizing with a start that he was seeing infinitesimal points of light ahead. The mouth of the hole! And the *Harbinger* was gliding safely through it.

"Nine-hundred *c*, Ensign! Get us out of here!"

Topping complied with alacrity.

Radio contact was established with the other ships as soon as power returned, and it was ascertained that everyone was in decent condition. It would be another twenty minutes of waiting until the last ship exited the gate.

"Konstan? Are you alright?"

Konstan glanced down at the girl in confusion. She was still pale and struggling to straighten from his shoulder.

"You're asking me that when you just damaged yourself for us?" He shook his head. "I'll be alright, my heart just needs to size down again."

He pulled her back onto his shoulder as Marc swiveled his seat around. The captain laid his hand on the right side of Aiyra's face as though he could heal the pain.

"Are you alright, sweetie?" He searched her eyes, afraid he'd find an answer there that she would not voice.

Aiyra gave a weary nod against Konstan's shoulder. "I will be alright-" A smile alighted on her lips. She slipped her hand more securely into Konstan's. "-Like I always have to be."

"If we have the chance, then we'll fix this for you as soon as may be," her father said quietly. "I fear that either way, you don't have much left to suffer." He turned away again as the last of the ships exited the maw.

"Ok, Marauder, your call," he said briefly. The animosity between them had faded but remained somewhat difficult to bypass.

Konstan looked to Aiyra again and whispered, "Weren't you trying to tell me something?"

Aiyra's eyes lowered and she wouldn't meet his gaze. "Nothing."

"Hm, just when it was getting interesting," the boy sighed, and rested his chin on her hair.

"We've scanned the system," Medrhos' voice came at last, seeming as though he were still exiting a dizzy spell. "There's only one planet deemed directly anywhere from here; and that's directly – down."

The *Harbinger* nosedived and for a moment everyone forgot they were in space, craning their necks to see whether she were in danger.

"Is that down?" Aiyra questioned.

"Or up?" Konstan finished.

"Could be right or left," Vidara surmised.

Marc only shook his head and asked Topping to make the plunge a trifle less destructively. The change of course was made and a dusty red orb settled into view. It was unmarred by clouds or even a drop of ocean.

"Do you know this place?" Marc's eyes studied the planet, praying and aching to know whether Samantha was there; did her heart still beat?

"If you think I've made a habit of assimilating with spaghetti and diving headfirst into Hell's Gate, hardly," Medrhos drawled. "But do I know *of* it, yes. A place once thought only to exist in legend; one without a name, which ironically gave it one: Dyhsx‾z. What I know of it, I'd rather not say; only that it's one of the triune birthplaces of my people, and where we first received the crystals. It's . . . Rätha's homeworld."

Konstan, head on hand, looked at the planet and muttered, "Amazing" as though hardly disturbed at this point. Either that, or the devil having a physical home other than a body was terribly hard for him to imagine.

Medrhos had the scanners going as they made the initial approach. It soon became evident that Dyhsx‾z was tidally locked to a nearby dwarf star.

"All in favor of death by immediate frying, take the bright side – all in favor of instant relation to a glacier, you can brave the dark side," Medrhos announced. "There's only one place we can go and that's a twenty mile strip between the zones. Ember squadron, enter at mach omega-7 and give a full scan of the belt."

The squadron was away, scarcely visible as it ran the barriers of time. They returned a quarter of an hour later, reporting an anomalous reading over the central-south quadrant on the far side. Instruments had responded in a fashion not unlike within the Gate.

"Dark energy, surely," Medrhos said to himself, unconsciously digging his nails into the console before him. The scratch marks never did come out.

The planet was hellishly quiet and the sky all too red as they made their way around it. It was agreed that Medrhos' vast armada should remain in orbit, accompanied by the *Galateia* and *Lumenara*. Three of Medrhos' lighter CX-3 class warships, plus the *Icebreaker* and the *Torment,* Cajetan's lead ship, would join the *Harbinger* on the surface.

Marc closed his eyes for a moment of procrastination, just for a few seconds. He unbuckled himself and arose, nodding at Konstan. The boy had already read his mind. So had Aiyra.

Part of her felt so inadvertently betrayed that she didn't want to look at them. Marc crouched and kissed his daughter's fingers. They were still frigid. He tried to say something reassuring but nothing came.

"You cannot promise me anything," Aiyra reminded him again, still looking away.

Marc glanced down at her hands, pressing them gently and running his thumb over Talitha's bracelet. "And I know I can ask nothing of you."

Aiyra finally met his gaze.

"At least – try – to save her from dying like A'ma," she whispered. "I love you, A'da."

She pulled her hands away to let him go. Marc's kiss and pounding heartbeat were the only reply he could make.

Konstan, too, had nothing he could say, and stood staring out the veiwport in a vain attempt not to count the passing seconds. He felt Aiyra's fingertips brush the ring still bound on his left hand. His eyes met hers with a poignant clarity unlike all the promises they couldn't make, and all the words left unsaid. He stooped and laid his head alongside hers for just a breath. He stepped to follow Marc out.

"Konstan!" Aiyra caught his hand and he looked back. "I was going to tell you that I love you." She almost bit her lip but gazed at him steadily as she said it.

The old glow jumped into Konstan's eyes. He smiled, but said only, "My little girl," and didn't need to say any more. There was no more time.

Once again, Marc and Konstan joined the Marauder aboard his ship, and the vessel winged her way into the dusty atmosphere. They left Aiyra standing on the bridge, clasping her arms and staring into the shadows of the dark side of Dyhsxˉz.

XVII

Revenant

The *Harbinger* broke through the dust storm she had created and settled cautiously on the sandstone plains. Crawling vines straggled here and there, blackened by the ultraviolet rays streaming through the fragile atmosphere.

Medrhos kicked a chargrilled mushroom out of his way as he stepped from the ramp. There had been no signs of man-made structures anywhere, only a massive plateau guarded by seven soaring mountains. Scans had picked up a subterranean network cutting through it. That was all the information they could gain from the otherwise befuddled instruments. That much info was itself an anomaly that heightened everyone's suspicions.

"Sire?" One of Medrhos' aides poked his head through the doorway as Marc, Konstan, and the guards filed down the ramp. "The handmaids are asking to accompany you for the Queen's sake."

Medrhos' dark eyes looked at him a moment, expression hidden by the masked cloak pulled over his mouth and nose to filter the dusty air.

"No. Lock them in the Queen's cabin if you have to. I don't want them to get hurt. Varclav!"

The ensign appeared.

"Be ready to take off at the slightest sign of anything, understand? Be prepared to swoop in if I signal, whether for pick-up or for battle."

Varclav saluted and vanished to set the remaining men at their posts. As they were joined by groups from the other five ships, Medrhos swung around and surveyed the landscape before him.

They had landed south of the plateau, drawn there by an odd formation, or rather, deformation. The rock had been gouged away as though massive claws had sunk into the earth and torn its way backwards into the cliff. Drawn, right back into a collapsed protrusion of stone, that still stood in eerie resemblance to half of a laughing skull. What had been the left jaw had been shattered, blocking an entrance to the cave system.

Medrhos strode across the gap, finding the dust so deep that in some pockets he sank up to his ankles. Marc glanced over into one of the dual ravines and saw that its depths were littered with bits of quartz and iridium.

They halted at the mound of rubble. The narrow gap that remained wouldn't allow any of them through.

"Can you do something?" It was Cobalt who asked. It seemed his opinion of Medrhos' usefulness was improving.

"That would be beautiful, using Rätha's power in his land," Medrhos muttered. "How well do you think that's going to work?"

He grasped the nearest block of rubble and together, they heaved it aside. With the others' help, the opening was soon widened. If the hollow eyesocket winked above them, they didn't notice as they filed through.

The heavy odor of molten minerals and charred fungi lingered on the damp air. Marc switched on his flashlight and beamed it around on the walls. The corridor was narrow and the walls oozed a substance that smelled of rancid meat. More than one man slipped and had to modify the grip of their tactical boots.

The cave continued to snake its way through the plateau, slanting downwards, the stone worn smoother than a meteor's path across the starry sky. No further grip adjustments could be made. Medrhos lost his footing and soon chains of the hundred-and-forty were sliding uncontrollably down the chute.

It split, sending men off in seven directions through streams of rushing water. Stone, stone, and more stone whizzed by, suddenly broken by a phosphorescent glow, and then they were falling down, down, and landed with a thud and a splash.

Marc, dizzy, had the presence of mind to throw himself away from the landing zone as the men behind him were subjected to their own share of drenching and bruises.

Groans and splashes echoed through the warmly lit cavern. They had landed in a shallow lagoon that sent steam rolling up to the roof some three hundred feet above.

Medrhos shoved himself upright, dripping and aching all over.

"This is most definitely not the welcome I was expecting," he sighed. He felt the shifting, weighted substance that was enveloping his hands beneath the water, and brought up a fistful.

Gelatinous, berry-sized crystals glowed an electric shade of mint in his hand. They were half-formed and unripe like a green apple, but no less deadly. Medrhos flung them away in disgust.

"I have a bad feeling about this." Konstan had noticed it too, and stood up, shaking the water from his hair. He whipped around, searching the rock formation with his eyes for the nearest exit. "The quicker we move, the less danger we're in of not finding her before it's over for all of us," he said sharply.

"I agree with you, for once." Medrhos pulled himself to his feet.

Marc picked himself up likewise, rubbing his neck, now jammed out of position. "That's twice today, if we're counting, and I hope it's not the last time."

He waved the men towards the exit Konstan had found. It branched out repeatedly, until they were all forced to halt once more.

"Split up, seven by seven. If she's in here, or there's a sign to her, we'll find her. But mark!" Medrhos warned. "Mark every turn you take, because if anyone gets lost, I can't promise the same for them."

The men wandered the sprawling maze. In the distance one could hear the echoing footfalls of the other groups, and their voices as they called to one another. The air shivered with heat. Wavering steam hung over everything, and hot springs littered the ground, bubbling like a kettle left on for too long.

The farther they pressed, the hotter it became, and charcoal ruins of lava hid the ground from sight. The thick mist was crawling and curling, gushing aside as the men stepped through it, so reflective anyone would have sworn they saw moving figures within.

Konstan jumped and listened, body tense as a man's shouts echoed their way to his ears. It was one of the Kedrian men; he was too distant to make out much, but he did catch something about orange juice. Nose wrinkled in confusion, he popped into the adjoining cavern.

A Marauder soldier was using all his strength to prevent the young Kedrian from precipitating himself into the gelatinous pool before his feet. The Marauder caught Konstan's eye.

"Overheated and delusional, thinks it's a pond of orange juice for-Rätha-knows-why," he said in exasperation.

Konstan frowned. "Cedros! Let him take you out. That refreshing 'orange juice' will scald you alive."

Meanwhile, Marc was having as little luck as anyone else. There were no signs of life anywhere, beyond the occasional cave crawler, and nothing human, even a scratch in the walls like the ones they were using to map their way back among the twists and turns.

He found his mind, beneath its unending calculations and worries, comparing the caves to the pictures he had seen of the Crucifixion mount. Was it more than a coincidence that the cave mouth, too, was a skull? Or did Rätha wish for a thousand lesser crucifixions, to wash the stone with blood that would aid no one if they failed?

Medrhos wasn't far away, occasionally striking the walls in vain for hidden passages. The narrow run of rock he followed circled a pool, and on the other side was Cajetan. The prince had similarly been studying the crevasses in the walls. His dark eyes met the King's. Without a word, nor taking his gaze from the Marauder, he skirted the pool and vanished into the next cavern.

Medrhos muttered to himself, a faint vision of Cajetan's sister flitting before his eyes. He rounded the stalagmite on his left and ran into Marc. The sudden urge to slap the captain took Medrhos over. Marc gave him a look as the Marauder pitched forward and seized him by the collar.

"You!" he snarled, giving Marc a shake. "You found her and you're hiding her from me! Where is she?!"

"Oh please, if I'd found her, don't you think I'd look happier than I do?" Marc asked in disgust. "I'd tell you to cool your jets, but this steam isn't helping, is it."

Medrhos struck him, hard, across the face, half-confused as to why he did it and wondering why he was only superficially angry. Marc caught his breath as his jaw blistered and jerked his knee upwards, kicking Medrhos back with such force that the King stumbled into the pool. The boiling liquid splashed up to his calves, his boots just barely saving his skin.

Medrhos' eyes dropped to his gloved hands and he realized he was sweating. He peeled the gloves off and traced the curling steam up to the ceiling, where the condensation pearled into stalactites.

"It's the crystals in the water," he said slowly. "The steam is building them into every inch of rock." He looked back at Marc. "We need to get out of here, quickly."

"You don't say," Marc drawled, rubbing his jaw. He gave Medrhos his hand and helped him out of the sauna.

Something shook the earth and Medrhos swayed on his feet. He froze.

"Did you feel that?"

"Hardly couldn't have," Marc replied.

Medrhos seized his arm, staring down the corridor.

"Samantha!" His yell bounced back to their ears. "No, why'd she run?!"

Cajetan's low voice interrupted Marc's vain attempt to find his girl through the mist. "You do realize, I hope, that you're the tenth person who's seen her in the past five minutes, covering an area of three miles."

Medrhos glanced at him in despair as the wildness faded from his eyes.

"It must have been the steam," he said reluctantly. "But still! I can't take the risk that it *might* be her! She could be seeing things."

Marc followed him down the passageway at a run, praying that the maze would give the missing maiden up.

~~~

It was, in fact, Samantha, and she had been seeing things. What she had seen was far from relieving. It was a mystery to her why Aniceda had dropped her down a pit into this place to begin with. She had expected much worse. Not that this was a vacation by any stretch of the imagination, she thought, as she crouched on a rise behind a boulder and watched for her pursuers.

With no way of escaping the territory, she had been dodging Aniceda and a couple of creeps for several hours now, or so she thought. She was never more than a few seconds ahead, and her nerves were stretched to capacity by the constant edge and the heat. Worse, she had been experiencing the constant threat of heatstroke, and how she hadn't collapsed was in itself a mystery. She ducked behind the boulder as her pursuers ran past her hiding place.

With the coast clear, it was back to the endless game of cat and mouse. She had wondered whether anyone could possibly rescue her from this Godforsaken place. Aniceda had not said one way or the other, but she had made it very clear just how far away the nearest souls were.

Fear was an emotion which Samantha had never felt with such strength before. Even her heart, once racing from the chase, seemed to be shivering now, and she couldn't stop calculating whether running was worth it at this point.

But then, Medrhos and Marc were not the kind to let even a fire-breathing dragon, or whatever Rätha proved to be, stand in their way. Marc's love and Medrhos' unorthodox approach might come through for her again, she hoped. She had to try and hold out.

In the very least, she needed to gain the time to make her best act of contrition, should she be about to face the scythe. But did Rätha have the power to kill? was a question she kept turning over in her mind. Even if he didn't, Aniceda did, being human.

Samantha came to a fork in the cave and debated the path to take. She was almost certain she had been down the lefthand path some seventy-five turns ago, so she chose the right. The engineer halted abruptly. Something had caught her eye as being out of place as she passed.

Two steps backwards placed the wall with its freshly crumbling carvings before her. Samantha's eyes widened and as her fingers reached upwards to feel the engraving, the memory of another cavern wall, gray with time, flashed before her eyes. On it was the ghost of the same markings.

Samantha's fingers pressed desperately into the Cultic numbers, the directional, and there, the crescent moon! The braided moon that only Almedrans carved, placed like a delicate afterthought, the symbol that only one Marauder would use. Her cry cut the cavern walls.

"Medrhoooos!"

~~~

The two men had split up when the left side of the fork had led into a chain of magma pits and hot lakes. It was then that Marc came face to face with one of Aniceda's pets. The reptilian humanoid froze for just a heartbeat, silhouetted against the cavern wall, and ran.

"No you don't!" Marc muttered, drawing his blaster. He chased it down, cornering it in one of the lava pits.

The air was so unstable that Marc could scarcely see a few feet ahead of him, and a slow stream of viscous lava flowed through the columns, leaving stepping stones precariously placed in its midst. There was nowhere for the creature to go but the doorway behind Marc.

With a growling hiss it rushed him before he could fire a shot, colliding with him when he didn't move aside. Marc caught at the creature as they both pitched backwards, falling flat at the magma's edge.

Marc pinned it down. "Where is she?" he growled. "Where did Aniceda take her? If you know and can speak, answer me!" He shoved the creature's shoulders deeper into the sand as it hissed wordlessly in his face.

"Samantha!" Medrhos' cry rang through the room as his momentum sent the steam rolling back. He stared. "Hesslin!" he fairly screamed. "That's *Samantha*! Let go of her!"

"What on earth! This is *not* Samantha!" Marc growled.

"What the – Hesslin, you're seeing things!" Medrhos said furiously.

Marc grit his teeth, no longer certain. It was Konstan's timely arrival that proved Medrhos right.

"Sahma!" he shouted, and ran down to the bank, pulling Marc away and scooping Samantha up from the sand.

Apparently the creature recognized him, unlike Medrhos and Marc, and curled its head against his shoulder, hissing softly.

"Samantha, it's alright, it's Marc, and here is Medrhos, too," Konstan said softly. "This crystal steam has been messing with all of us today."

Marc took a step back, searching the reptilian face as Konstan lifted the creature to its feet.

"Samantha?" the captain asked slowly. "If it's you, I can't see or hear you."

"She can't see or hear you either." Medrhos restlessly clenched his hands.

"Give her a kiss," was Konstan's recommendation.

Marc scowled. "Seriously?"

"Trust me!" Konstan called over his shoulder, disappearing into the steam. "It's the second-best spell-breaker, you know."

Marc found himself shaking his head and Medrhos was glaring at him.

"Well, do something, will you please?"

Marc leaned forward and kissed the creature's brow. Then he heard Samantha's voice coming from its lips as she spoke his name hesitantly.

"Samantha?" Marc touched the face in front of him and the mirage faded, leaving Samantha's despairing eyes looking into his. "Samantha!"

He flung his arms around her and kissed her hair, much to Medrhos' annoyance.

"I – I thought you were one of Aniceda's monsters," Samantha whispered. "Is it really you?"

"Yes," Marc whispered, his fingers brushing her scar. His heart ached for the desperation in her eyes. "Yes, my darling! I promised I would always come for you!"

Medrhos glowered, arms folded as he watched the reunion. "Yes, it's the both of you, and will you *both* please remember that we should be leaving?"

"He's right." Marc set Samantha on her feet. Medrhos quickly stole her back as Konstan poked his head into the cave.

"Gather the men together. I found the exit."

Collectively, it took an hour for them to gather the wandering hundred-and-forty. While they waited, Medrhos unslung a small pouch from beneath his cloak and handed it to Samantha.

"I thought you might need it."

The girl reached inside and drew out the coil of silk from the Almedran grotto. A smile tugged on one corner of her lips as she twined the silken strands.

She looked up as she said, "It's your sixth sense again, Rhos."

One question remained on her mind, that of Aniceda's whereabouts and her strange silence. It was the silent receding of an ocean bay before a hurricane. Medrhos seemed to share her thoughts, dropping one hand on her shoulder.

Samantha flinched as something cold, then all at once warm, spread through her skin. She stared down at herself as the tattered ivory linen melded into sapphire blue and alabaster. Medrhos jerked his hand away, eyes widening at the fear of what might have gone into it.

"I'm sorry," he said sharply. "I wasn't trying to do that." He looked at his hand, still gloveless. "I was just thinking... how you're probably wishing you were wearing something more suitable."

"Well, I can't say you're wrong." The riding skirt and blouse were definitely an improvement in mobility.

"I don't think I've ever told you that you look good in blue," Medrhos said, glancing away as the last company marched in. "Consider yourself told."

"Mm, well, I might have been thinking about Marc's eyes," Samantha murmured. "Thank you."

Medrhos snorted. "Why am I not surprised?"

"Everyone here?" Konstan called, and took a head check. "Alright then, follow me!"

He led them up a steep passageway that stretched upwards, straighter and slicker than a pin. As Konstan himself admitted, something about it still felt too easy.

Sighting true daylight at last outweighed their misgivings and they broke out into the sunlight, and comparatively cool air, with an outburst of relief.

They found themselves upon the flattop of the plateau, its guardian mountains ringing it in all their gloomy glory like a throneback.

Medrhos and Marc were holding Samantha's arms, for both had learned what happened if they let go of her for more than two seconds. The girl's eyes darted to the mountains on either side and felt that familiar frightened chill numbing her brain as the carvings on the wall once again flashed before her eyes. She seized Medrhos' arm.

"Rhos – this is Mal-lon!" He felt her forehead and she pushed his hand away. "You don't understand! *This is Mal-lon*! The carvings you made in the cave are the ancient ones I found in Mal-lon! Just look around you! Erosion will wear away *five* of these seven mountains."

Medrhos cautiously measured his surroundings and the color drained from his face.

"What have we done?"

And then his eyes fell to the central mountain's base, where a colossal iron door was set in the stone, rusted and draped in sooty moss. And before it on a rise stood a figure wrapped in sable.

Aniceda's eyebrows arched. "Welcome. . . to your trap."

A clicking, as of setting guns, came from behind. Medrhos closed his eyes and didn't need to turn his head to see the *Callista*, her sibling ships, and a wall of Cults and mercenaries.

"Do me a favor, and don't shoot me in the back, Flotjvik."

"Raa, that would be terribly disappointing for more than one of us, wouldn't it, fyrc?"

"It's been a beautiful little game, Ancilla. . . I wasn't meant to give you the time you need to die," Aniceda admitted, her voice carrying clearly on the noiseless wind. "But it gives me the pleasure of watching you dive into despair."

"We're hardly surprised by your trap," Samantha sighed, audibly bored as she gripped Marc and Medrhos' hands. From the corner of her eye she glimpsed Medrhos' fingers inching towards his blaster, ready to fire the signal shot for the *Harbinger* if the chance came. "I'm sure we're not the only ones who'd like to go home, so can we skip to the end please?"

"Why do I feel like we'll regret that," Konstan murmured.

"It was unavoidable to begin with," Marc said softly, slipping his hand around the wrist on which Samantha still wore her bracelet.

Aniceda smiled.

"I'm glad you asked!"

She raised her hand to the *Callista*.

The sound of her war drums rolled across the flat and crashed against the great doorway. Samantha's eyes locked on it, not daring to look away. Medrhos tensed and Marc stiffened as Konstan moved to block Samantha.

A sound began to grow from the rock, like the reversal of an echo. Something was coming.

Iron creaked and bent against its foundations. Something was trying to get out.

The metal splintered and slammed upwards, expelling a cloud of blackened maroon and midnight smoke. Something larger than life and limb bent through the gap.

The head raised and eyes of hellfire gleamed scarlet.

The shadow of Rätha had fallen.

XVIII

Armageddon

It wasn't the kind of fear one speaks of. It was the kind that allows you to do nothing but resign yourself to whatever is coming, because there is no way of running. All hope of a life without nightmares, should they even live to sleep one more night, was gone. Except, possibly, for Konstan. He had very little personal knowledge of nightmares.

The soldiers clustered closer together, unwillingly but unable to help themselves. Rätha's shadow fell over them and darkened the whole of the plateau as his torso emerged from the confines of the earth. His lower limbs remained out of sight, though one guessed it might have been some useless extremity for land, perhaps a serpentine tail too dead to do much good. He was not something that should ever be described, no image that should ever been seen.

He was a gargantuan creature of myth that had lain in death before its possession. Mottled, dead flesh was riddled by veins of crimson. Hollow eyes of flame and darksmoke looked at them from a skull split between that of an ancient titan, face slashed upwards and elongated by a dragonian touch, and teeth for which fangs hardly managed as a noun.

But the left side of its body was hung together by metal plating, colossal mechanisms just barely visible between the joints, and the formed skull was that of Samantha's nightmares. And in the center

of the monster's chest was the power source, a triple heart of crystal: a heart which was the living source of the crystals of death.

Amid the gushing smoke the behemoth stooped and one massive hand cupped softly around Aniceda like a shelter. She smiled, without looking into that face, a face which was to Medrhos' battle mask what that mask had been in comparison to Orion's. The voice Samantha had come to know too well rolled through the still air.

"There now, Aniceda. . . they won't be giving you any more trouble. You did your best to spare them and I'm pleased. Now, it's my turn."

Aniceda closed her eyes and rested her cheek on the tip of the claw that touched her gently. Being Rätha's princess had its perks.

Then the monster turned his head and withdrew his hand. His eyes seemed to spark when they fell on his Emperor.

"Ah, my son," he purred, as softly as a behemoth could.

Medrhos moved around Konstan and approached. It was some ninety yards to where Rätha awaited him.

Samantha instinctively clutched the medal that Aniceda had not dared to touch.

"Have you come to apologize for the frustration you've given my princess by not accepting our offer, and for the ruin that you've caused my plans? I'd like to restore you as my true emperor. . . make you. . ." the eyes glowed and he seemed to draw a breath in a gutteral hiss. "-*Better*, than you ever were."

The face hovered low to the ground, too large to ever be eye to eye with anyone. The silence began to stretch as Medrhos' eyes settled on the skull's bared fangs.

Another Face hovered before him, one as unlike to this as the sea was to the desert. The pleading, staring, binding depth of love and no reproach seemed to scorch the deadly visage in front of him, that spoke of a proposed love in the middle of a visible cacophony of hate and darkness.

There was the face that had bound his people in murder, that which had bled Samantha and tortured the breath from her lungs, while soft brown eyes of another Being seemed to carry them through. Medrhos' hand was curling at his side.

Without any detectable warning, his fist crashed into Rätha's unbearable grin and the leviathan swung back with a scream. Two fangs shattered into Rätha's mouth and Medrhos went leaping backwards.

The claws swung down and struck into the earth with the sound of crumbling rock, narrowly missing Medrhos. But the creature didn't say a word. The smoke thickened.

Aniceda raised her head and her arms. The silence was worse than the pronunciation of the verdict would have been. Rätha knew it. The quiet stretched.

Konstan clapped his hands together. "So, let's wrap this up so we can go home, shall we?" He looked at Rätha with the faintest glimmer of contempt and said, "We deal with you every day you know, and we do pretty decently against you, I think. We'll do pretty decently against you again. Come on fellows!" he called. "For anyone who's wanted to punch the devil in the face the way Medrhos just did, I dare say this is the best chance we'll get in the next thousand years."

For just a moment, the wall of fear broke and a shimmer of a laugh echoed through the men. Even Samantha smiled, and for an instant the problem seemed as small as the only half-conscious temptation. But then it loomed as large as the struggle to erase even the smallest, nagging thought that wouldn't lose itself in hell.

Then the wall of soldiers behind them opened fire.

Medrhos shoved Samantha to the ground, whipping out his blaster and firing a xanthic flare into the air. If the ships didn't reach them with their firepower in the next sixty seconds, they'd be worse off than toast in a malfunctioning microwave.

"Exactly how are we planning on doing this?" Cobalt demanded.

"Kill the body and scare him back to hell where he belongs," Cajetan responded. His hand was on his blade.

"You're forgetting we're completely surrounded by sorcerers and pirates!" Cobalt growled.

Firebolts and curses came raining down, forcing the Marauders to deploy the shields generated by their armor. Even the Realtra had access to such shields from their many raids. The shoulder plating of Konstan and Cajetan's armor slid upwards, forming helmets struck with channels of electric aqua and amber plasma. Medrhos generated his own suit of armor, but this time it did not bear a helmet.

Samantha was the only one left vulnerable and Aniceda was taking amusement in targeting her. Marc ripped off one of his shield-forming gauntlets and slapped it on Samantha's wrist to provide some protection as he, Medrhos, and Konstan strove to deflect the blows that came her way. She felt useless until she thought of the medal around her neck. She seized it and jerked on Konstan's sleeve.

"I'm – an explosion, look out!" he yelled. Samantha was deeply confused until he tackled her to the ground as a grenade ripped up the rock. "As I was saying, I'm kind of busy, what?" he asked, dragging her to her feet.

"Maybe if we can get my medal to him it will drive him away, or at least do damage!"

"It's worth a shot!"

Marc looked over and snatched the medal from her hand, snapping the cord around his own neck at the same time, the cross swinging free. He strung them together and passed them back to the girl.

Another explosion just feet away sent men flying, but it was only the attackers who found themselves airborne. The *Harbinger* swooped low, followed by her companion ships, and they were soon taking on the mounted snipers and the mercenary fleet. The ground forces were still outnumbered and Rätha was only playing games. If only his power was broken! Would any of the mercenaries turn?

The *Callista* managed to unleash a spiked train of magnetized weights that spun outwards, locking end to end like a dog chasing its tail. It spun through the fray to deadly effect. Everyone who had time fell flat, saved by the mere sixteen inches of hover room. Medrhos' grapple locked on the train's side and its force jerked him high into the air as it spun overhead, landing him squarely astride it.

One of the men had deposited Samantha in the cradle of the nearest rock formation. She held both her silks and the strung cross and medal in her hand.

"Medrhos, can you get me closer?" she called, as he tried to influence the train's path of destruction. "We need to do what we do best!"

Medrhos was busy keeping his balance on the circling train. "I don't know what your idea of my best is! What do you and I do best?!"

"Sparring!"

"Precisely! I catch your drift-"

Medrhos held out his hands as Samantha hurled herself from the peak – he caught her and threw her. A thread of shimmering silk flew from her hand and caught on the mountainside. Wind whistling in her ears, she landed precariously perpendicular to the ground and hung there comfortably.

She was higher than Rätha's head now. She could swing, make her target with the chain, and parachute to a safe distance on the opposite end of the plateau. Silent prayer to the angels was the only breather she could take. Whether any good would be done by the presence of the metal sacramentals in her hand was a question she kept trying not to ask. Whether any good could be done at all in this fight, was another one.

Despite the cold knot in her stomach, she released her hold on the mountain and arched out over the melee below. Rätha turned and greeted her with one monstrous hand that came rushing up to meet her. She lost her hold on the silks and the medal slipped from her grip. A moment later the yellowed claws closed around her in a prison of dead flesh.

Or, at least, that's what would have happened if Medrhos had not ordered the *Harbinger* to magnetize her underside and collide fields with the train, sending it rocketing into Rätha's hand.

Samantha twisted the path of her fall and plunged straight downwards. There was a flash of rose and then she appeared in Marc's arms out of nowhere, startling them both. He was forced to drop her immediately as Serengoch came out of the crowd.

Hand to hand combat commenced while the men boxed the weaponless Samantha in. But when she saw them being overwhelmed, she took her silk and in half a minute had lassoed three offenders together, granting them an accumulated headache. That was something, anyway.

The battle was an opportunity the Hawk had been desiring for years. To him, he only saw the chance to test Medrhos' skill with a blade and see whether the Emperor was worthy of being the Empire's warrior in comparison to himself. As it turned out, they were far too evenly matched to get much of anywhere, to the frustration of each party.

Flashes of multicolored light were bursting off shields as stormwalls were spontaneously formed in an attempt to corral the rebellion; traps were being sprung around their feet, and a few unlucky men found themselves suspended upside-down while the blood rushed to their heads, until their comrades managed to pull them down to earth again.

Samantha was busy deflecting Aniceda's gleeful enchantments off her wrist-shield. They were getting nowhere, and the fleet had made no signs of rescue. A brief thought that something might have happened, that something had happened to Aiyra, flickered in her mind and she pushed it away.

"We need to get it closer!" she shouted to Marc. He whipped around and kicked Serengoch in the ribs, sending him flying into the nearest cluster of mercenaries and gaining a breather.

"Throw it to me!"

She tossed it and he caught it in his outstretched hand.

"Cajetan, incoming!" he called, as Cajetan dispatched a mercenary and likewise gained an opening.

The battlefield became a game board as the chain was juggled from hand to hand, inching closer to the edge of the melee, where hopefully someone had a slingshot blaster that would fire it nicely.

But Rätha seemed to know that it was time for him to add to the sport. He bent and exhaled a violent breath. It was not dragonfire but a familiar swirl of azure and cherry-pink, the eddies of which burst into vortexes at will. Those sucked inside found themselves hurtling groundwards anywhere from Timbuktu, wherever that was, to the creation of Andromeda, to the destruction of Almedra, to the dreadful battle of Maltara.

A frustrated Medrhos found his hands busy between the duel and repeatedly reopening the vortex to bring everyone back onto the battlefield. Konstan was busy fighting off the mercenaries' massive battle wolves, one arm already torn to shreds by their fangs. The weight of two wolves at once was enough to shatter even Marauder shields. The same were circling Marc as he fought Serengoch's seven blades, and the dogs dove in to nip at his legs at every opening. Cajetan and Samantha were similarly getting nowhere. Everywhere one looked, they were failing fast.

Cobalt glanced up as he blocked a blow from a mercenary electroblade. "About time!" he yelled, and everyone, even the antagonists, gave pause to see what he was shouting about.

The seven hundred ships of Medrhos' battle fleet broke through the whirling clouds the Cult had created. Two Malevolent-Z7's were shielding the *Lumenara* at the head and above them loomed the *Galateia*. Even Rätha seemed surprised. More so were those onboard.

As the sunstrikers and Z-17s peeled off to take on the tidal wave of mercenary bulldogs, Aiyra's hands came down on the console before her as her breath shivered in her lungs. No one needed a definition of what Rätha was, least of all her.

Vague, vague memories of a priestess came back as from a million miles away in another life, and fire echoed through her skull. Her vision faded statically as her temples throbbed. Yet her face did not betray her dawning realizations as she noted Rätha's composition. She laid her hand on the com.

"*Lumenara* to *Galateia*. Open fire on Rätha."

XIX

Cataclysm

An explosion of light flooded the air and three spiraling beams of white energy converged, striking the first chamber of Rätha's heart. The monster gave a violent shudder, then a laugh of pain.

"Do you think a little energy will end me? Aniceda!" He twisted a little but was unable to break free, and the fleet's ships had shields that protected them from unwanted time changes. The wall of his ships was being dismantled and Medrhos and Marc alone had dispatched far too many men. He grit his teeth.

"Bring me. . . a young son of the Cult. We need more power to deal the pain they deserve!"

Aniceda reached down from her perch and plucked a mercenary teen from the wall that protected her. The boy stared at her.

"Will he do, love?" the woman asked.

". . . Ahh, nicely," Rätha murmured, bringing his face down to scrutinize the youth, who had barely reached the age of fifteen. "Bring him to the stone and I will make him mine."

Aniceda put her hands on the boy's shoulders, seeing the fear in his eyes. "Don't be afraid," she crooned. "He won't hurt you. We only need your help. Your part in this fight is coming, as you've longed." She began to guide him over the rocks.

"Aniceda!" a voice bellowed. She swung around to find that Flotjvik had abandoned his duel and leapt through the wall. His eyes blazed and his blade was still ignited. *"That's my son!"*

Aniceda's expression remained cold. "What part of you. . . thinks that I don't know that?"

The Hawk's face tightened. "Curse you, princess! What part of you thinks I won't rebel if you do this?! My son is mine to -"

"He's also mine!" Aniceda was furious now. "You've kept him from me long enough, Hawk."

Rätha's hot breath almost scorched the pirate's face as the monster stooped to speak. "Young Erol. . . may well win the war and make you proud."

Flotjvik flung down his sabre. "Confound it all! I don't want a war hero, I want him to have his mother! I don't like you anymore than they do out there!" He jerked his hand towards the battlefield. "But I don't mind working for you - *if you leave my son out of it!* He's not even of age!" He glared at Aniceda, who was still gripping Erol's arm.

"Erol deserves the choice," she snapped, and pulled the boy closer to Rätha and away from his father. But Rätha wasn't bent on giving anyone a choice, least of all a boy who couldn't possibly choose his own way, or so he said to himself.

One hand came down, blocking Flotjvik out. Rätha was still being burned by the purgation beam and Aniceda could see the crystals of the first chamber beginning to blacken and crack.

"Bring him here," came the hiss, and the priestess, without feeling herself move, found that she was forcing Erol to kneel on the great obsidian stone. His eyes, so like hers, were wide and he wasn't sure what would happen if he protested.

"Mother-"

But Aniceda didn't seem to see him, standing with eyes fastened on the beating heart of Rätha. A pulsing light began to shift its colors, falling on the boy who flinched.

"Aniceda!" Flotjvik yelled from the other side of Rätha's barricade. He had had enough. "*Aniceda, wake up!*"

Something in his voice jerked a nerve and her eyes went down to Erol, who would soon be too far gone.

"Rätha!" Her own frightened voice startled her. "That's my son! Please, take someone else!"

The skull's mouth twisted upwards ever so slightly as he echoed her own words. "What part of you. . . thinks that I don't know that?"

Aniceda raised her eyes as though he had dumped the entirety of the chilled Tal-Estilla upon her.

Erol blinked as he landed hard beyond Rätha's reach. His mother had done the only thing she could to save him. She had become Rätha's victim.

The leviathan didn't have enough time to stop once he realized it was his bride who was taking the pain of transfer and conformity. In the end, it didn't matter because the heart he bore was of rock and metal, pulsating only with its end goal.

Flotjvik took one look at the spectre that was taking shape and moaned aloud. It was little better than it would have been, and now Rätha's shadow had unleashed power and a passion to end Samantha, Marc, and the rebellion that loomed larger with the mercenaries willing to despise the radical side of their hate.

In one breath, Aniceda had scythed a path through the men and come face to face with Samantha. But one face was a mask, worse than Medrhos', as a scepter flamed in her hand. Fire streamed from it and spilled around the shield as Samantha blocked, scorching her arm and drawing a cry that interrupted Marc and Medrhos' battle with Serengoch.

"Samantha, catch!" Medrhos hurled a fallen blade her way but it was frozen in a wall of ice before it reached her.

Thorns bloomed and straggled, larger than a man's arm, jabbing fighters and forcing them out of the ring. The spectre casually rained fiery coals down on the Realtra with special attention for the ringleaders, who could already scarcely manage their now malfunctioning shields amidst adversaries' blows.

Most of the mercenaries may have turned, but with the Cult's power, Rätha had summoned creatures of stone and bones to pick up where his army had left off. Destroying rock was a more daunting task for a decent portion of the men, and the tide was turning back again.

Aiyra stopped there on the heights, silhouetted by the sun and the shadows of the battle cruisers above her as she took in the bloodshed. The wind whipped her hair. Everything was wrong, all wrong, always wrong! There was only one way to make it right. Her stomach turned.

Samantha was faring no better than her companions. Aniceda's blows were digging the ground up from beneath her feet, threatening to plunge her back into the caverns below.

Thinking quickly, the maiden vaulted over the forming hole as Aniceda ducked. As Samantha came down, she caught the mask's diadem and jerked it with her, bringing the beaded strands around Aniceda's throat and forcing her to fall backwards with her. It was

Samantha's intention to grab the scepter as it fell from Aniceda's hand, but it didn't happen.

Energy bound it to the spectre like glue, and as they struggled in a tangled heap, Aniceda wrested one arm free and pointed it at the fleet.

"*Voyanya!*" she yelled.

The shadow that fell now was not Rätha's.

With the silence of a dreadful realization, the lights on every last non-Cultic ship went out. The *Galateia's* beams flickered, sputtered, and vanished.

Rätha roared in triumph, despite the heart chamber that shattered.

The ships' noses tipped down.

"Look out!" more than one man screamed. The thorn wall was abruptly incinerated, an arm came around Samantha's waist, and she was dragged, but nowhere on the plateau was safe. It was a mass graveyard, ready to happen in fifteen seconds.

The falling ships forced the air down in a rushing wind that tore many off their feet as the sun blacked out.

Hardly had a final collective breath been taken before everyone ducked, as the snowlight ray blazed out above them and slammed into the turf, scorching it white as the cannons of the fleet crashed volleys into the cliffside, sending rubble raining down on Rätha's head. The shadows jerked back with a rumble of engine-fire as quickly as they had fallen.

Samantha looked up from under Konstan's good arm. She shook her hair out of her eyes to free her vision.

"Aiyra?"

Her gasp drew Konstan's eyes back from his grimace of pain. The maid still stood on the rise, the wind whipping her hair, twisting her skirt about her, her eyes unseeing. Every fiber of her being was straining to do more than what she had nearly failed to do within the maw.

An angel's hand might have hurled those ships aloft, pitching their noses skyward, might have lent its heart and power to the girl, to do what her mind and body could not withstand.

Sweat was pearling on Aiyra's face despite the chill of the wind. Every heartbeat seemed a gong that threatened to break the link, so she tried not to breathe, but if she didn't it would break anyway.

And yet, she needed to stretch it further because the Cult's cursed rays were still focused on the rebellion. Her face tremored as she tried to open a channel to the Cult's ships, reaching out for anything that would turn off or redirect those guns.

Something clicked.

"What the – they're firing on their own creatures?" Cobalt cried in disbelief.

Rätha screamed at Aniceda in frustration as the rock-beings he had brought forth were burst by blows of dark energy.

"How long can she keep this up?" Konstan breathed.

Samantha had no answer. She no longer knew what Aiyra's state of health was. She scrambled to her feet, pulling Konstan upright. Rätha didn't seem to have any further tricks up his sleeve. If they could keep Aniceda, Serept and the rest of the Cult busy long enough for the *Galateia* to finish her task, everything might end well. *If* Aiyra could last.

Rätha's laugh was heard for the third time. It rolled over the battlefield with the cannons that continued to blast away.

"How did I know. . . that you would spring her on me, Hesslin?"

Marc froze and his eyes found his daughter, still statuesque as she struggled to keep the ships aloft.

"Your only fault," the titan snarled with sudden contempt, "is that you love too much." His smile twisted as the battle slowed to a halt. Everyone seemed intent on hearing just what the monster meant to say.

"Had you never crossed me, had you never intercepted the destruction of the *one* world which love chose to birth in, your daughter would never have suffered, your wife would still live – yes, your people died. . . because of *you*. And your little one I took to destroy you, my bride was to raise her against you to take back what was mine, but the girl took after you too much." He spat the words.

"Now, feel the pain she went through because of you! In every most deadly place I put her, willing to break her! And now. . . understand why I let her go."

Marc's eyes widened in fear as the flame leapt up in Rätha's eyes and all was still, deadly still, as Aiyra's concentration shattered with a scream and the ships went black, shuddering with the deadly intent to fall if the final thread were cut.

Aiyra tried so hard to keep from breaking as the agonizing energy burned through her. Only Samantha, in her torture in Tapinak-Raebzalom, knew what the girl was feeling. The weight of a thousand ships creaked and strained and her nerves felt like a net with every last thread splintering as the weight of a titan fell down upon it, with fire and hate and memory and pain – all the pain she had forgotten, all the horror she had known: her mother's death, every moment of her torment flashed through her mind in blinding frequency, filling a glass ready to break. It reached the top, and overflowed, and suddenly it shattered.

Aiyra's body snapped double. The ships plunged groundwards. As they did, she straightened slowly, taut like a zitar string, but tears were streaming down her face. The guns that had been trained on death itself now turned upon her people. Every last shield burst.

Even at that distance, Aiyra's frightened eyes caught Konstan's as his helmet retracted.

"Aiyra, break it!" he pleaded. In his horror his own pain was forgotten. They should have saved her before they had entered the void.

"Marc, go!" Samantha tore her silk strands in two and flung one coil to him. Marc was galvanized into action, sprinting through the mass of men to reach his daughter's side, Serengoch forgotten. He had only thirty seconds.

Serept, however, had no intention of allowing Orion to interfere. A bolt of lightning struck the ground beneath his feat and froze around him in an electrified cage.

"No, Aiyra!" he cried desperately. "Aiyra! Don't let him hurt you!" The fear he hadn't known since the burning of Cytha ripped through his veins. His eyes blurred with hot tears. He couldn't lose her, not like this.

"God, save her! I can't!" he whispered. He was failing, again, and again, even though he had done nothing wrong! It couldn't end this way, not for Aiyra – he raised his eyes as a faint wail reached down from the rise.

"A'da. . . help me!" She had crumpled to her knees, yet she must have been fighting still or she never could have cried out that way. Thankfully Serengoch didn't have a silencing spell.

"Aiyra!" He pressed as close to the cage as he dared, praying for something, anything, any words that could break the killing force that was upon her. "*God loves you! God loves you!*" In the end, it was all that could be said.

Aiyra's torn breathing suddenly staggered. The dark images began to flicker. The Face she had always wanted to see. . . for just a moment, a breath of wind blew through the pain.

"Let go, Aiyra, let go!"

And she stopped fighting, sank into the pain and the sigh of the breeze.

"Aiyra – Aiyra – Aiyra. . . Aiyra!" Her father's voice echoed in her mind, melding with Samantha's and Konstan's; and then the sweet lilt of her mother's voice seemed to come back to her, layered with a voice she had never heard but longed to know.

"Aiyra. . . Aiyra!"

There it was, the Face she had been struggling to see all along! Her eyes snapped open and her hand upwards.

And then, inexplicably, a bolt of something that wasn't dark energy, came from the crowd and struck the fleet, flooding outwards, as though a Marauder king had suddenly been broken as she. Between them the ghastly mist that had clung to the blackened ships peeled back.

The lights came on and the pilots jerked the craft upwards, missing the plateau by the mere width of the *Icebreaker*. A loud hum announced the return of the shields, and a shatter, the second chamber of Rätha's heart.

Aiyra raised her head and was not surprised to find that the titan was glaring directly at her as the smoke thickened around him.

So comes your end, destroyer. You're the last failure I'll ever make!

Aiyra only lowered her gaze to the last remaining crystal chamber. The *Galateia* alone could not destroy it, even as she refocused her rays. Every enchantment had been laid upon this one, rather than spreading them thin over the three. To destroy it as the others was virtually impossible.

She raised her eyes to the left of Rätha's skull, unaware that Medrhos had yanked Marc out of the cage as the battle resumed, nor that Rätha had called upon Aniceda to destroy her once-would-have-been child.

Aniceda was of no use. In the despair of escaping the plateau at the ships' plunge, Flotjvik and Erol had managed to corner the spectre and maim the mask on her face. It had broken her own curse, whereupon they had held her tight and would not let her go, lest Rätha try to reclaim her.

All Aiyra knew was the end reason for all her suffering. No, it was not Rätha's doing. But it was Rätha who had written his own downfall, thrice. Somehow she got to her feet and slid down the slope. This time there was no coming back.

The fighting parted in a wave of confusion at something in the girl's face as she moved steadily forward, stopping unscathed just out of Rätha's reach.

"Aiyra!" Marc saw her, and having passed Serengoch off to Medrhos, ran to her and seized her shoulders. He peered into those iridescent eyes, which now glowed blue like his with the gas still curling over the field, reading the ruin done to her that she seemed unconscious of.

"It is the only way, A'da," she said. She hesitated. "Will you protect me?"

Marc felt his throat tighten. He didn't need to ask what she meant to do. "Yes, baby. I will always protect you, if I may!"

Deep down, he knew he could raise no protest at her role. No one had the time left to risk. Ships were coming down in balls of flame and too many men had fallen to curses and blades. Marc took up his place at her side to fend off any blow that threatened his child. Aiyra turned away. And then she began.

It took Rätha a moment to feel the sudden shivers running through the wiring. He reared back, the *Galateia's* rays remaining locked on his heart.

"You dare-?!"

I dare. There was almost a smile on Aiyra's lips.

The ground shook as the monster began to pull himself free from the cavern. His left eye was sputtering in its argyle flames as though the mechanism spawning them was threatening to burst.

Medrhos came out of the crowd. The power Samantha had convinced him to find had destroyed Serengoch at last, sending him down into the lava caverns where he belonged.

Medrhos' eyes caught Aiyra's. He seemed to understand the thought in them. Of the same mind, he raised his left hand towards the titan that was breaking free. No jewels glowed this time as he unleashed the power which he had bent on the fleet, concentrating all his mind and energy on the terra side of the undead.

The latter screamed again, wordlessly, as his flesh began to burn away, as though some white-hot acid were drowning him. The crystal chambers were flashing violent streaks of vermilion and azure and jade over the landscape, pulse creeping higher and higher. His neck jerked forward as he broke every last strand of power he had put out into the battleground and threw it into Aiyra and Medrhos.

The King's limbs seemed to freeze solid amid the screaming in his head. It was all he could do to dimly remain on his feet, concentrating, trying with all his might to destroy the thing that had crushed his people with all its weight.

Aiyra's mind was breaking again, and the color was being sucked from her skin with every pulse of the crystals. Her vision was closing in on Rätha's face as he pulled his way out of the mountain, rising to his full height. She could hear him screaming darkness in her ears. Every nerve in her body felt as though it was being ripped from her skin.

She was only truly conscious of one thing. Those five faces that had been hurt by him; those five faces, and the anger she felt welling up at the sight of his, and the love that couldn't, *wouldn't*, let her loved ones be hurt again. She pressed her eyelids shut against the threatening shadows, memorizing every line of those faces.

Rätha's claws were coming down, reaching for earth and survival by digging them up with it. Marc saw it coming.

"Don't touch my daughter!" he snarled, and snatching Samantha's silks, caught up a failed grenade and whipped it around, around, until he released it – it flew and collided with the hand as it came down to kill them. The collision ended with an explosion.

"Get it in, now!" Konstan was yelling. "Go, go, go!" He pitched the medal back to Samantha, who ducked as a shot went over her head, and the silk was back in her hands to do as Marc had done, for he was occupied by a trio of fallen mercenaries. They were backing him farther and farther away from Aiyra.

"Go back whence you came!" Samantha cried, and the cross and medal made their mark, falling into the dying flames of one eyesocket.

At the same instant, Medrhos' power and Aiyra's hacking came to a head. Men went running as a typhoon of sparks shattered skywards as though it were the ejection of a supernova. The great metal jaw unhinged and snapped downwards as gases came pouring from its mechanical veins. His body wracked and shivered.

Air and matter came rushing out of it, hissing like a burst pipe, but ten-thousand fold. No one wanted to watch as the dead limbs suddenly decomposed before them like ash on a burning wind. The casing of the heart broke and the *Galateia's* beam struck the final nest of absinthe crystals at full force.

Every sound on the plateau was silenced. A vacuum swirled everything into itself. Everything was spinning, earth, sky, mountains, the ships and the sun overhead.

A mounting roar came rumbling upwards. A wave of refracted light burst across the plateau, striking every eye blind. The sounds ground the war to a halt. There was a terrifying cracking that threatened to join deafness to the predicament.

Cult and mercenary alike realized, split seconds before the wave hit them, that Rätha had been banished. As the men were engulfed, any crystals or effects thereof were erased. Most stood stupefied, as well as blinded, weapons and curses forgotten. Some drowned in anger. These last were not seen again.

Marc raised his weary head, shaking it to clear his vision. The color was fading back in a swarm of spots. All around he was beginning to make out the destruction of death.

Marauders, mercenaries, Realtra, Vestar, Cult and wolves alike lay scattered. Some lay in the peace of a death well-paid, despite never having the chance to know the Man they'd meet. Others were to be pitied for the freedom they had not yet been granted.

Only God knows, he thought, and then his exhausted mind remembered Samantha, Konstan, Aiyra –

He stumbled to his feet, swaying as the wolf wound on his left leg growled at him physically. His vision faded in and out again. His jaw, too, was aching sharply. He was pretty sure Serengoch had fractured it.

Many were finding their own wounds as they picked themselves up from the ruins of war. The rumbling was fainter now.

"Aiyra, Samantha! Konstan!" He felt his way around the boulders strewn across the plateau.

"Marc?" Samantha came running, stumbling once or twice over debris.

Marc swept her up in relief. He had lost track of her after Rätha's attack on Aiyra. He pressed his face against Samantha's tangled hair. She was safe, with only a badly burned forearm and bruised ribs, courtesy of Aniceda. She wasn't with Talitha, not yet.

"I haven't heard Aiyra or Konstan," Marc said tersely, setting Samantha back on her feet. That was when they noticed.

The cacophony they had heard had been caused by the rock collapsing beneath the tyrant's remains, crumbling away right up to the war zone, forming a shifting lake of red gases, the excrement of the broken crystals. Medrhos and Aiyra lay crumpled at its edge. Before anyone had a chance to move, the earth had crumbled away beneath them.

"AIYRA!"

Marc lunged for her. The distance was too great. The pit had swallowed both man and maiden with scarcely a sound. The couple froze.

"Oh Father, no, please no," Marc whispered, shutting his eyes as he envisioned Aiyra lying somewhere below among the scattered bones. She hadn't fallen on the rise, that prayer had been answered; she'd be with Talitha, he was only her guardian, but still – he was feeling the silk still wrapped around his hand, and Samantha had been thinking of hers, too. But Marc's hand fell limp at his side, realizing as his heart seemed to be cut in twain, that it was no use.

Konstan was standing at the pit edge, staring down into its depths. He, too, had seen it happen and his face was drawn. The fall, however long it proved to be, and the crystal gas were a deadly combination. No one could get down there. Almost no one.

Something broke inside of him. His helmet clasped itself around his face as he stepped back. One, two, three running steps and he had plunged into the mist.

"Konstan, no!" Samantha shrieked, tearing away from Marc. Aiyra, Medrhos, now Konstan - how could she be losing all three of them?

Marc jerked her back as the black figure vanished.

"Don't, Konstan is the only one I know who is immune to the crystals," he breathed shakily, pressing her head anxiously to his heart. Neither of them took their eyes away from where their hearts had fallen.

It was an eternity of ever-ticking yet never passing seconds as the couple stood there, waiting. Waiting for the worst with hopes that didn't dare be put into words. Not anymore.

All around them the dead were being taken aboard the ships which had now landed. A fifth of those who had fought for Rätha now slept and a third had vanished without a trace. The remaining twenty-three thousand returned to their cruisers, nursing injuries and blanking on how much of their lives they had lost. Ten thousand Marauders had fallen, trying to save their people and their queen. Nearly half of the Realtra and Vestar force had also paid their last debts.

Aniceda sat with Flotjvik and their son, her priestess garb in tatters, the diadem and pendant burnt away, as was much of her former personality.

Marc and Samantha's nerves were being stretched too far. It had been too long since their loved ones had disappeared in the mist.

A sound came from the pit. A little more earth crumbled away and a hand came over the edge, grasping for a hold. Medrhos drew himself to his feet, cloak gone, face worn, nursing a headache. The blood rushed to Samantha's head and finally broke the shock she had been stuck in.

"Rhos!" she gasped, and would have thrown herself into his arms, had he not stooped and hauled upward the silk ladder he had created.

Konstan appeared, helmet retracted. There was a limp body in his arms. Tears streaked his face; tears for the girl whose love had caused the implant to explode.

XX

Aftershock

Instrumental lights faded in and out in rainbow shades. They seemed as tired as the *Lumenara* and those on board her. The ICU was dark, save for those lights. It was as if no one wanted to use their eyes, not to see the aftermath that lay before them, anyway. It was the state in which one has panicked so long and so deeply that it ceases to exist, and is replaced by a deep, dull, aching waiting.

Victory was not something in anyone's minds. Too many lay silent in a temporary state of burial in the crypt, for it to be comprehended that the shadow had been withdrawn, the slave empire left behind, and the state of galaxy-wide fear put at rest.

Samantha and Marc stood with their backs to the wall, unconscious of their bodies' needs to rest, leaving their injuries to the side for the many who were worse wounded. Since fewer Vestar members had been in the fight and thus, fewer wounded, the *Lumenara* had taken some of the Realtra on board to care for them in her larger medical facilities.

Marc was unaware, too, that his arm was wrapped around Samantha, pressing her closer every few moments with each nervous wave. She was safe, after so long – he could feel her painful thoughts that it was her fault – he couldn't let her feel that way, the way he had for all those years.

He was aware of the dull aching of his heart, which beat only unwillingly. He must have strained it in the fight. Or it was carrying too much weight again.

Everything seemed muffled now. Behind them, through the winding infirmary corridors, they could hear the faint sounds of traffic moving to and fro as the *Lumenara* left Dyhsx⁻z behind. No one in the room was saying anything. Even the illuminated clock on the wall made no sound.

Ahead of them, Marc and Samantha could make out Konstan, dimly silhouetted against the lights. He was leaning on the counter of one of the sinks, his left arm plunged into a bath of ice water, per Elise's orders to numb the pain while he waited. The light carbon plating of Konstan's armor, movable at will due to the nanobots in their construction, had clamped over the limb, exerting enough pressure to keep it together for now. The bleeding had eventually been forced to a halt.

Medrhos stood there too, wrapped in the shadows. He would have been on his own vessel, checking up on his own men; but when Konstan had placed that limp figure in Marc's arms, the father had pressed his head to her and found a heart scarcely beating. The right side of her skull had been shattered outwards and her brown tresses were wet with blood.

Samantha had raised her eyes with trembling lips. "You healed me in Arce'Atelane," she had whispered. "Please, Rhos, do something!"

His eyes had stayed on her for a moment, then on Aiyra. The thought that in the end, he had brought her to that, brought all of them to that, brought thousands to that-

"I can promise you nothing," Medrhos had said darkly, looking back at them. "I've never done more than that which I did for you."

Samantha had bit her lip, on the verge of tears, eyes still pleading.

Then Marc had stepped forward, staring at Medrhos, and done something he thought he'd never do. He had laid Aiyra in Medrhos' arms.

"Please. . . you're the only one who can. Try to save my daughter!"

The Marauder had been taken aback. His jaw had tightened and he had borne the girl up into the *Lumenara*, ordering the fleet back to Mal-lon.

The Maw had vanished, as had the time rift in which the Cult had lived, lives frozen. There had been no need to open a vortex to Mal-lon. The fields of Borania had probably been destroyed, too. It remained to be seen what effect it would have on getting everyone home. For now, silence remained settled as a blanket.

The green glow of the scanners flickered and Elise finally turned on the lights. She straightened and slid the scanner ring back from Aiyra and off to the side. The doctor peeled off her gloves and washed her hands in the opposite sink before she said anything.

At last she turned around and leaned back against the counter.

"There is extensive damage to the frontal and temporal lobes, as well as to the greater part of her nervous system."

She picked up a remote and everyone's eyes went to the screen on the wall. Images of the scan appeared.

"As you can see," Elise continued quietly, "the explosion, however small, sent shrapnel throughout the right side of her head, bursting a portion of the skull and virtually erasing much of the brain tissue in this area."

The doctor faced them.

"You must realize," she said soberly, "that even if there's a chance. . . these portions of the brain are responsible for everything that makes Aiyra herself. Personality, social skills, arts and music, movement, speech, hearing. . . and memory." She let that sink in. "Even if the tissue could be restored, you won't know her, nor her, you." She took a deep breath.

"Unless your friend here really does have a capacity for over-and-above miracles. If we're going to have any chance at all, we need to remove the remains of that implant, and quickly." She called in two nurses to help her.

"Konstan witnessed the implant's installation." It was the first time Marc had spoken since handing Aiyra to Medrhos.

"It wasn't in shards then," Konstan muttered, pulling his arm out of the ice bath. "And the nerves it was attached to weren't half-destroyed." He rubbed his arm, sufficiently frozen. "But. . . they used nanobots to finish the assembly on the inside."

"Nanobots," Elise muttered, and went to the chest in which they were organized by injection size and programming. She pulled out a case. "Empira, Dido, put Aiyra in the stasis chamber. We need time. Samantha, Konstan – if you're up to it, I need you to rewrite the code on these. I don't have any for dismantling shrapnel."

Konstan took the box without a word about his arm. A hand fell on his shoulder as he went to take the seat at the nearest computer.

"That arm is of little use to her, isn't it."

Konstan reached up and forced the plating back from his arm, revealing the flesh, torn from shoulder to wrist with flashes of bone beneath, mangled with the tattered leather of his suit. Samantha made a sound but Marc put her into one of the seats, squeezing her shoulders.

Medrhos examined the lacerations for a moment. If he tried, it would either make or break the hope they had that he could bring Aiyra back. He laid his hand on the limb, ignoring the blood.

Samantha waited, holding her breath while she attempted to focus on the coding in front of her. Aiyra had been removed from the room. Elise was busy preparing the surgical computer for repairing Aiyra's skull, should the injection work. Then a gloved hand covered Samantha's.

She looked up from the screen into Konstan's eyes. He pressed her fingers, and her gaze traveled down his arm. The cloth had been repaired and lay dry against his skin. Samantha glanced up at Medrhos, who was nodding methodically at the relief in her face.

Yes, he would try.

Between the two engineers, it didn't take long to reprogram the nanobots. Aiyra was removed from stasis, replaced on life support, and the bots were injected into the rupture. Elise monitored the progress on the live scan.

"It's working," she murmured. The debris was being shredded into molecules of iron, which was left in the bloodstream due to the level of blood loss. That which couldn't be converted was siphoned out by a filter inserted at the neck.

Eventually it was done, and the surgical computer set to repairing the bone, filling the empty space with titanium plating. Elise glanced at the monitors.

"She's getting weaker," she said tersely. "Captain, you said something about a quicker repair for nerve damage. Get on that." She looked at Medrhos. "Unless you can take care of *everything*."

"We're too close to Mal-lon for me to begin now," he said quietly. "It would be better not to be interrupted by arriving. We'll get her to Almedran-town. It's quieter than in the city."

Marc spoke to Tryphena, who had been listening over his watch, waiting for the verdict on her niece. The *Galateia's* infirmary didn't have any brethil on hand.

"It's still growing on the cliffs of Maedra," Konstan offered. "Aiyra and I saw it when we climbed to the ruins."

Medrhos snapped on his own watch. "Coran. Try sending a man to Maedra, please. Brethil is growing on the cliffs."

Scarcely two minutes later a vortex opened in the wall, proving that it was still functioning, and one of his aides, Bran, exited, a knapsack slung over one shoulder.

"Sorry for being off by two minutes. The governor's son was trying to kill me. It seems he heard we have the Queen," he said dryly. He handed the bag to Marc.

Tryphena spoke again. "Marc, she should be moved to the *Galateia*. We can keep her stable until we reach Mal-lon."

Medrhos recalculated the vortex and the *Galateia's* open, spa-like infirmary appeared on the other side. With everyone's help, Aiyra was carefully shifted across the gap. Tryphena took the herbs and began to crush some of them with jojoba oil, honey, and frankincense to make a lotion. Since the girl was unable to ingest it the way Talitha had made it, her skin would have to do the work. The lotion was applied to Aiyra's face and limbs.

The remaining herbs were crushed and scattered into one of the shallow thermal pools. Aiyra was laid in the water, submerged save for her head, supported by a cushioned ledge. Here her temperature and heart rate would be monitored by the water itself. She would remain stable until they reached Mal-lon in the next two hours. Beyond that, there were no further promises which could be made.

There was nothing Marc or Samantha could do except pray as they were treated for their own injuries. Konstan knelt at the pool and remained there, Aiyra's hand clasped in his as he made sure she breathed.

"Please come back to me, my Aurora!" he whispered, pressing his lips to her fingertips. "I'm only a slave without you. . . my midnight sun, please take my night away!"

~~~

It was early morning when the ships made landfall, and Mal-lon was a welcome sight. It had been twenty-four hours since anyone had slept. The Marauder fleet returned to the city, but the *Harbinger*, *Lumenara*, *Delta*, and the Realtra split off.

The fields were wide in Almedran country, whitened by the winter season as the group landed near the mountains of Elduor. The forest draping the slopes was home to the healing houses of Almedra.

Snow fell noiselessly outside, dusting the tree branches as with sugar while Aiyra was taken inside. A spacious flat was given for her, so wide and open with the view of the snow-powdered courtyard that the child seemed even more fragile.

Medrhos went in and took up a seat at her bedside. Aiyra's breathing was scarcely even shallow by this time. Her heart was still winding down.

The King looked into her sleeping face and thought of many things. Mostly he thought of the man whose heart was breaking twice, and how his own was as well. Medrhos didn't stir from that seat. The snow was building up; the sun was rolling down.

The trio, joined by Tryphena, waited just inside the doorway in the foyer, until Marc's wound cramped. They forced themselves to take a walk along the raised pathways and balconies of the complex. Marc would go down and plunge his knee into the snow until it numbed enough to bear a few more hours of waiting. The pattern repeated, with an otherwise ignorance of their own needs, until Samantha nearly collapsed in front of them.

Elise appeared to threaten the men with a sleeping drug if they didn't care for themselves. Coran came with the handmaids in tow and removed Samantha to a chamber of her own.

Tryphena returned to the *Galateia* for the night, summoned to aid some of her ailing patients. Konstan stretched out on a window-seat through the archway to Aiyra's room. The captain's restless mind was soon forced to sleep by his weary heart, leaving the sun to set in icy watercolors across the snowscape.

Sunrise found a warmer day, and the thin sheets of ice were already melting, revealing winter blooms in shades of cranberry, grape, gold and ivory. Rosy snapdragons entwined with the mauve of heather under the evergreens, bejeweled by the scattered richness of violets and irises. Jasmine climbed the walls, perfuming the crystal-crisp winter air while snowdrops bobbed below, with the bells of lily-of-the-valley. The appearance of holly and Christmas roses normally would have reminded those present of the upcoming Earth calendar date.

It was the mid-month of Elur-thel in Mal-lon, the rough equivalent of December. Blossoms, berries, and silk garlands were strung throughout the halls and beeswax candles of fuschia, grape and cream burned in every latticed window. Scents of herbs, fruits and spices lingered from the dried, decorative ropes over every doorway. Almedran airspace, normally peaceful, was crisscrossed by vessels of all sizes. The roads, too, were bustling in the distance.

Some of it was due to the Empire's plan of reparation, outlined by Medrhos to Coran, which was well underway. The records of every slave in the Empire were being organized and the slaves themselves gathered. They would be returned to their respective times and homes as soon as possible.

The Realtra were free to return to their kingdoms; Cajetan departed to ensure that his people were doing well as their relationship with the Empire was altered. Konstan, too, would have to leave. Eventually.

Meanwhile, someone, probably Pell, had thought to put a call through to Admiral Flynn, to inform him of what was taking place. The Marauders had adjusted the frequency of the *Lumenara's* signal to make sure Vestar actually received the message in due time.

The Mercenaries and the Cult were floundering to find anything of their lives that could be salvaged. The mercenaries had trailed along in the return from battle, perhaps out of a nagging sense of guilt and duty. They had been unofficially readmitted to the Empire, so that was of some help.

According to rumor, Flotjvik had convinced a now-gentled, dismayed Aniceda to clear her confusion by officially marrying him, for Erol's sake. They had a little girl, too, whom Aniceda had kept in the relatively safe confines of the Cult nursery. Now that the Cultic city was effectively out of commission, they would all have to find new homes.

But for now, there was only the man and the girl in the quiet room. Medrhos had not slept, nor ever risen from his seat. The hours continued to tick by with no change. Marc had remained, and soon Konstan awakened. By now, they were only waiting for Medrhos to inform them that it was time to say goodbye.

Samantha and Tryphena returned and the vigil continued.

Samantha sat on the floor at Marc's feet, leaning her head on his knee. Her body was struggling to heal from the torture she had undergone. Her mind and emotions seemed damaged. Sleep was riddled with nightmares, and consciousness with flashbacks, racing heartbeats, and wild anxieties she had never known.

Every sound made her jump, and Marc would lay his hand on her hair to make her feel safe again. Gelert had been brought in to comfort her and he kept his head in her lap, letting her stroke his ears unfeelingly. If they lost Aiyra. . . she doubted anything could ever heal her again.

Both Tryphena and Konstan remained in prayer and the day crept on.

Night was falling once more. Marc had sent Samantha to bed, but this time she, too, found a windowseat. Konstan had been directed outside. The youth was still getting cramps as well, and had hardly risen from his knees that day. Tryphena stood at the window, wrapped in silence.

Medrhos had finally slumped over in sleep. He wasn't sure if it was a sound, or the warmth against his palm that awakened him. The courtyard clock hadn't yet chimed eight bells, he was sure of that. He raised his head, wondering if he could stay awake to continue what he ought to have been doing.

There was the rasping of a chair being pushed back. Marc raised his head at the sound. The new glow of a pillar candle was warming the room beyond.

Medrhos' dark figure came wearily to the carved pine archway and leaned upon it, eyes glimmering in the vague lighting. He spoke not a word as both Marc and Tryphena arose and brushed past him.

Thought was something almost alien in Marc's mind after these many hours. The prayer of a broken heartbeat had become his closest friend. Blue eyes roved unseeingly through the shadows dancing on the walls. One hand touched the light switch, flicking it only slightly. The lamps on the walls brightened just enough to steady the shivering. Marc's gaze turned, no longer able to hesitate, to his daughter.

Aiyra lay still, hair draped over the cushions and a silken coverlet drawn up to her heart. Marc knelt at the bedside and laid his lips on Aiyra's cheek. Her skin was oddly warm to his touch. He drew back. Yes, there was color in her face. Her breathing – he watched, and it seemed no longer shallow.

"Aiyra?" He whispered, and found he was looking into her eyes. He raised himself and sat on the edge of the bed. His heart was suddenly pounding heavier than it had before. "Aiyra, sweetie, do you know me?"

The girl gazed up at him and then sat up, studying the room with the air of a tired kitten. She turned her head towards him with a smile.

"You are my A'da," she said sweetly, wrapping her arms around his neck. She dropped a kiss on his bruised jaw. "Poor A'da, you look so tired."

Her eyes fell on her aunt. It took her a few moments. The struggle of memory was evident in her eyes as she looked from one to the other.

"Aiyra," Tryphena murmured, and laid her hand on the girl's forehead. Aiyra smiled at this and finally recognized her with a kiss. She cocked her head at her father.

"Where are Konstan and Sahma?" She laughed at the way his eyes lit up, as if she knew what he had been fearing.

"I just sent them to bed," he answered, trying to keep his voice level as he cuddled her. Just how much of her had been restored? This was higher than any of his hopes yet. "No one has been getting enough sleep, worrying about you."

"Just my luck!" Aiyra shook her hair over her shoulders. "The moment I wake up, everyone is going to sleep. Well, I guess I must sing lullabies to you all."

A door had banged as she was speaking. Konstan stood in the entryway, eyes wide as he took in the scene. Aiyra smiled at him over her father's shoulder.

"You, go lay down over there, right now," she said, pointing to a couch across the room. He opened his mouth to protest and she repeated, "*Right* now." The mischievous sparkle in her eye seemed so foreign to her as she added, "You too, A'da!"

Konstan began laughing uncontrollably.

"Medrhos, what have you done to my daughter?" Marc cried, cracking up with the mere giddiness of welcome relief.

"Don't blame me!" Medrhos protested, reappearing behind Konstan.

Aiyra stopped and slipped out of bed despite Marc's anxiety. She crossed the chilled floor to the Marauder, and looked at him for only a moment before putting her arms around his waist. Medrhos' dark head bent over hers to hide the tears that came unbidden.

"Aiyra?" Samantha's voice broke the moment. She came forward hesitantly, certain that she was dreaming and that it would soon tumble into a nightmare.

Aiyra instantly abandoned the King, pressing herself into the engineer's arms and her head into Samantha's shoulder.

"Sahma. . . please never get taken again."

Samantha took the girl's face in her hands and kissed her forehead. "And don't you go and get another implant!" she whispered, and held her close.

A grin tugged on Aiyra's lips, hidden against the engineer's shoulder.

"I was not. . . *plant*ing on it."

Konstan, waiting impatiently for his turn, broke down again hopelessly until Aiyra was finally wrapped safely in her Daystar's arms.

XXI

Unchained

Another day was taken in rest. Marc was finally able to check up on his people, Vestar and Realtra alike. Aiyra refused to let him go without her. After such a scare, he'd have it no other way. Konstan was forced to take a day to see his kingdom, and managed to pass the crown to the nobleman who had taken care of things in his absence.

Samantha continued to waver between trauma and thoughts of the home and the family she no longer needed to protect from herself. She remembered the way the lights were hung across the open villa, like dew-dripped webs; the scent of rosemary, citrus and pine, and the flowers scattering the floor for the Christ-Child's first tread.

Medrhos was in constant motion. His past left him, seemingly, with no time to rest. Former slaves were being returned home, freed from every planet in his rule and his sphere beyond; conquered worlds were being offered freedom, and those who chose it given stabilized transitions; and a great deal of purgation was made.

The crystal caverns had thankfully been incinerated at the breakage. The Marauder, who no longer was, wondered if Mal-lon should be abandoned. Surely between its roots and the trauma they all felt upon seeing the city, there was enough cause. Konstan wisely said no, that it should be reclaimed and given a future better than its past.

Speaking of the youth, he had finally received the answer to a long-pondered mystery.

"One thing still puzzles me," he had mused aloud as they all sat in the garden sunshine for a few borrowed moments. "How my death was reversed in the attack on the *Lumenara*. But I may never know; I guess I'll take it for a miracle."

"You could call it that," Medrhos' voice rose from behind, as he inspected a vine of jasmine that was late in blooming. Konstan turned.

"You had something to do with it?"

Medrhos snorted. "You could say that. One of those random vortexes dropped me straight into one of the Starkindler's. I had told those Mercenary dogs not to shoot to kill anyway. Do they listen to half the things I say? Apparently not."

He dropped the vine and circled around to Aiyra, laying his hand on her forehead, for she felt dizzy at times. Konstan's eyes followed, smiling.

"Thank you. For her sake especially."

Medrhos didn't answer, but he didn't argue, either.

Things were being patched up with Vestar, too, as much as might be. There wasn't much trust yet, but Maltara's hero establishing a friendship with the Emperor did wonders.

One pillar hadn't cracked yet, one which troubled Samantha and left Marc silent when he was with her. Many times the engineer had moved to answer that long-ago question of Esta and Sacra. She didn't need to ask now who held her heart; but to the Marauder people, she was still married. More than that, she had become one of them and promised to make them her people. She might not be married, but she was as good as engaged.

~~~

The group soon moved into the city, for Medrhos had much to do and wanted to keep an eye on Aiyra. She was doing well, but it remained to be seen just what her condition was.

"The city needs to see its Queen," Medrhos said, coming to Samantha on the second day. "I need to speak with them of these things that have happened. You will accompany me?"

Samantha's heart sank a little but she went. Medrhos took her out into the courtyard overlooking the city, the same spot where she had been presented as his bride. The city had already turned out to hear what their Emperor had to say. He switched on the microphone before him.

"We all know of the changes that have occurred for our lives and those of our descendants," Medrhos began. His voice carried out over the streets below. "I know that this is a difficult and confusing time for all of us. Many pieces of our lives have been removed, and left with nothing to replace them. I ask your forgiveness for placing you in this state, but in the end I believe it will be better than it began. I'm doing my best to make the transition easier, and will continue to do so, as far as I am able." He took a deep breath.

"There are few things which we can hold onto now, I know this. I regret that I have to ask you to accept one last change." Medrhos paused. "I confess," he said slowly, "that the Queen you had awaited for so long was taken as unwillingly from her life as the slaves we've been sending home. I took her from her own people, yes, because I loved her and because I needed her. Yet I loved her enough... to ruin my own wedding. I meant to protect her from our enemies until she was ready. . . but I failed. She is not truly my wife. I know how much you need her, how much you love her. . . but I ask that with me, you be willing to let her go, for the role she has played in freeing us from Rätha's shadow."

The crowd gave no answer for a moment, while Medrhos waited painfully. Then there was a soft ripple of an answer, and Medrhos faced Samantha.

"Samantha Mariel Anselle, I release you from every promise you have made to me."

With a curious expression, he pulled off his winter gloves, cupping his hand over her scarred brow. A soft warmth blew away the morning chill from her skin. There was the sensation of something being drawn out from her and Medrhos removed his hand, nodding slightly as the long-scarred skin healed over without a trace of the sign which had marked her life. He read the mixture of joy and bewilderment in the woman's eyes.

"I release you from *everything*," he repeated. "Except, you will remain as a Queen to us, as has been the tradition of our people. But I return you to your own. Samantha, forgive me! For all the things I have been to you."

A smile was his answer. "Many things you have been to me, Rhos, and one of them you shall always be: my brother." She gave him a kiss and then the King took her shoulders and pivoted her to face Marc.

Konstan and Aiyra were bouncing unreservedly behind one of the columns. Some things never changed, even with princedom and implants.

"Take care of her." Medrhos spoke in a low voice. He placed Samantha in Marc's arms.

The captain met his eyes.

"I will."

~~~

As everything was being cleared up and the Vestar ships readied for the return home, Medrhos continued to heal his empire as best he could, leaving his friends to rest and recuperate as much as possible.

Estill had been tagging along with Medrhos everywhere, getting somewhat adorably underfoot until at last he was forced to stop her. He crouched and took her hands.

"I need to get you set to go home, Estill. We'll bring up your file next."

She frowned and shook her head, hugging the stuffed animal he had given her.

"I can't go home."

"Why not?"

"'Cause I don't have any. My parents gone, my grandparents gone, my aunts and uncles gone, my cousins gone-" she ticked them off on her fingers.

"What do you mean, gone?" Medrhos was thinking they, too, were probably somewhere in the systems. A reunion could quickly be arranged, in that event.

"All dead," Estill said. "A big bad virus came and killed everybody." She hugged her animal tighter and wouldn't meet his gaze. "You. . . be my daddy now?"

"What – but don't you want to go with your Uncle Orion, then?"

"No!" Estill insisted fiercely. "*You* adopted me! Want to stay." She was almost in tears.

Medrhos was at his wits' end, he could hardly be fit to play father to her, not now – but he was left with no choice.

"Then stay," he said softly, and drew the child into his arms.

~~~

Samantha and Marc stood on the terrace, watching the wind ripple the snow in the gardens below.

Another blessing had come that day in the form of the return of Aiyra's family, the Citharas. Her grandparents, King Mered and Queen Edyin, Princess Tirzah, and Prince Hezron had all been found safe, along with most of Aiyra's cousins. Some, including Prince Kenan, had been lost to accidents or natural death. Those who had survived, as well as all the other Cythians found in the system, would be returned on the *Galateia*.

News of Talitha's death had come hard to them, but at the same time all had believed the rest of the family to have perished.

"If not for Talitha," Samantha mulled, as she absentmindedly measured her hand against Marc's, "Aiyra would have fallen to the Cult. . . and I shudder to think where we'd all be."

"Yes," Marc murmured, eyes following the flight of a distant falcon. "She played her part and helped us to play ours." He rested his chin on her hair thoughtfully. "I can have no regrets now that I understand why it was written thus. And now that God keeps her safe, I just have to worry about you and Aiyra," he teased.

She laughed and then they fell into thought once more, taking in the peace of nature, which they hadn't been able to enjoy in many months. They didn't have much more time to spend in Mal-lon; those of the *Lumenara* and *Delta* were expected at Vestar headquarters on Zorrastra the following day to make the full report.

Everyone would be leaving; everyone except Ransomme, who had chosen to remain and administer to the city's needs. The handmaids insisted on coming along, for soon enough, they would be divided by the timeline and twelve systems.

At any rate, when they reached headquarters, it would be Christmas.

"I wish I could be home for Christmas," Samantha said wistfully as she leaned on Marc's arm. "They've waited too long for me."

Marc squeezed her hand.

"I'll get you home soon." An idea was forming in his mind, and shortly thereafter he and Medrhos vanished for several hours. Coran and Pell were left to organize the departure.

The *Harbinger* would be accompanying the *Galateia*, *Lumenara* and *Delta*, as well as a cruiser carrying captives from that particular system. Two overnight stops would be made: one to pick up those *Lumenara* crewmembers dropped off on the Earth's moon, and one to retrieve the bodies aboard the *Remnant*, including Jack Hesslin's. These would be taken for proper burial on Zorrastra.

When Marc and Medrhos reappeared that evening, they only said that they'd been working on some final preparations. Konstan seemed to know what that meant, but he wasn't telling.

A few minutes' time found their nighttime course set through a magenta haze. Aiyra was happy to retire to her room and snuggle with Sage and Pyrrho.

Samantha had been gifted Lyona, who had previously been Berron's wife's cat. The warm bundle of fur curled in a knot at her side, some comfort in the midst of the flickering nightmares she'd endure for a while yet.

Silmä, too, would remain hers, but the *Lumenara* was not adjusted for carrying free-roaming tigers, and so the creature remained on the *Harbinger*, along with Gelert, for now.

It was good to hear the hum of the *Lumenara's* engines; good to see Aiyra breathe and laugh, free and happy and safe, free from the personality training of the implant. Much of the Aiyra they knew remained, sweet and fragile, but playful. She knew her own mind, knew what she had been through, and was stronger for it, someone who could shelter others in pain. The girl had some issues with memory and vocabulary, but she was quickly relearning it with her father's constant support.

Yes, Samantha thought, it was good, good to have Marc here once more and to have his arms around her more often than not; to hear his strong voice when her mind was threatened with the memory of torture on her skin. It was good to be able to be free from fear, free to go home – home!

She fell asleep thinking these things, thinking of the One Who held her and made all these things good. For that night her nightmares were lost in the soft glow of time.

XXII

Starlight

Morning came – it would have been sunrise for those on board, but Zorrastra had already broken its fast and Vestar was well busied. The atmosphere of the planet still colored the sky with sunrise tints, reflected in the placid ponds and lakes dotting the emerald hills.

De'ngelos, the city of Andromedan Vestar Control, marked the landscape with its gleaming terraces of steel and glass towers. The city edges were melted into towns and suburbs, ringed by swathes of farmland. The three vessels were welcomed in the spaceport north of the boundary.

Scarcely had anyone disembarked when Marc, Berron, Medrhos and Coran were whisked off to Vestar Control, just on the far edge of the port. The others were left on their own with the handmaids and Estill in tow.

Exploring the spaceport seemed a wise idea until they, too, were whisked off to accommodations in the nearest luxury hotel. Aiyra had never seen one before, so the surroundings provided plenty of interest while awaiting the men. They wandered the lobbies, admiring the decadent upholstery, numerous fountains, and starstrung ceilings.

Holiday décor was everywhere, even in the streets below. There was the usual greenery, lights and ribbons, candies and Santa figurines, even a reindeer or two, and child-made snowmen in the park below.

Aiyra had about as much experience as Medrhos when it came to the keeping of Christmas. Her eyes were wide and she ran to look at everything, touching the branches of the little trees everywhere, the sparkling snowflake garlands, and then there were the plates of spiced breads and cookies for guests.

Estill, meanwhile, was half out of her mind with glee and kept shouting, "Christmas, Christmas, CHRISTMAS!"

If it weren't for the handmaids and the Citharas, Samantha and Konstan might have had their hands full. The King and Queen, and Adora and Konstan gently taught Aiyra about everything she saw, and took in her delight with great pleasure. Samantha and the other handmaids, however, were all over the place trying to disentangle Estill from the various lights, curtains, and pearl vines she got caught up in.

They rounded a corner and were confronted by the grandest of all sights yet. A live evergreen soared to the ceiling, twinkling with many colored lights and the sparkling of baubles, icicles, and bows. A skirt of poinsettia velvet was swathed about its trunk, a blanket on which rested a nearly lifelike scene of Love's Nativity.

"Well, that's a rare sight these days," Konstan remarked.

"But – there is no Baby," Aiyra said anxiously, upon further inspection.

"Mm, He'll be there tomorrow night," Adora promised. "He comes at midnight every year."

"Go, I'll take your picture," Samantha told them cheerfully, and shooed them off to pose with the figures. The handmaids declined at first but were eventually convinced.

Samantha stepped back to fit the tree into the frame of her new phone's camera. Marc had given her one, now that she had no reason to worry about keeping her relationships.

A group had come behind her and seemed equally surprised at the scene. Estill was staring up at the golden star sparkling overhead.

"Estill!" Samantha laughed. "Could you look at the camera please?" She barely snapped the photo in time.

"Daddy!" Estill cried, and scrambled impatiently over Konstan, who was kneeling near the shepherd. The child's foot caught on the tree skirt and pulled it out from under Aiyra, dumping her into Dyra. The second picture showed everyone in mid-fall with Estill only a blur as she ran to Medrhos.

Samantha was debilitated by laughter until someone's arms laced around her waist. She glanced up, thinking it was Marc. She froze so sharply she choked on her own heartbeat. It was her mother.

"Amara?"

"My sweet girl, we're here now," Lyr Lynne Anselle whispered, and Dün Andolin, Samantha's father, wrapped his arms around them both.

"You don't need to run away from us anymore, little Sahma."

"Daro!"

Marc and Medrhos fist-bumped each other as Samantha hid her face in her father's shoulder and cried. A hand wove itself playfully into her hair and she glanced around, blinking, lashes drenched.

"Seraph!"

A smile dawned across her brother' face. "Didn't think I'd forget you, I hope, little Moonstone."

"No, I knew you wouldn't, Wings," came the teary answer.

The infant on Seraph's arm leaned in and obediently gave Samantha a kiss.

"Vora?" Samantha asked helplessly, not sure who to look at or what to say as the child was bundled into her arms. "You were only a baby when I saw you last. Look at you, such a big girl now!"

She was trying in vain to end the tears that had finally been released, but maybe she had bottled them up for too long, and it felt so good! Her family didn't tell her not to cry; they felt the same way.

"I'm sorry – for everything and for hurting you for so long. I couldn't – I didn't know what would happen," Samantha whispered.

Seraph's wife, Erana, slipped in to give her sister a kiss.

"Everything's alright now, dear. . . we understand and it's over now."

"But how – you couldn't possibly have happened to all be here," Samantha pointed out, drying her cheeks.

"Certainly was no coincidence," Dün Andolin smiled, smoothing his daughter's now dampened hair. He nodded towards the two men who were feigning innocence amongst Aiyra's unending holiday inquiries and Estill's fascination with a rocking baby reindeer.

"They explained everything, briefly, and your old friend was able to send us here in just an hour," Lyr Anselle said. She smiled into Samantha's finally dry eyes. "We wouldn't have missed seeing you for Christmas for *anything* and all the holidays on Danya."

Samantha smiled, and then she knew she needed to thank the men.

"Hey-" she appeared between them and pulled them back under a branch of mistletoe discreetly suspended from the ceiling. She dropped a kiss on each man's cheek. "Thank you." And then she pushed them in opposite directions, laughing.

"Daddy, Daddy!" Estill started tugging on Medrhos' coat. "Did you get me lots of presents?"

"Did I – I don't want to think of how ridiculously many I got you," he replied, feigning a headache, but it was obvious he was enjoying himself.

"Yayyy! Daddy, when we go home, can we get a tree like that?"

"Uhhh. . . Coran? Do we even have Christmas trees on Mal-lon?"

"Uhhh. . . I don't know, do they come with lights and things on them? I'm sure we have something we could make work."

"You could always get one from somewhere that does," Estill suggested hopefully.

"Interplanetary Christmas trees? That's one way to boost the economy," Medrhos said in amusement. "You're turning out to be a real little princess. And to think, you used to be so quiet."

The child hugged his right knee and tilted her head back to look up at him. "That's 'cause I was all alone, but now I have you." Her eyes saddened. "Would you like me to still be quiet?"

Medrhos pried her from his knee only to scoop her up. "Quiet is the last thing I want you to be," he grinned, and Estill started laughing again.

"Samantha?"

The girl turned at the sound of Marc's voice. Beside him stood a woman, tall and shapely like a willow, her blond hair swept up to crown her regal head. Her eyes were the deepest blue, identical to Marc's.

"This is my mother."

Samantha and Zendira measured each other with a smile and then Zendira raised her white hands and gracefully drew Samantha closer.

"I thank you, for bringing him home once more and making him happy again," she murmured. Her eyes turned to Marc with almost a laugh, but her hand went out to Aiyra who had seen her and stood, waiting uncertainly.

"And my little Granda! It's been too long since I held you in my arms."

Aiyra bolted, on fire for the fact that at last, she had a fuller family again, and someone of her father's.

Once the reunions were somewhat completed, leaving everyone just a little bit hyper, Estill managed to turn the talk back to presents.

"Oh no!" Samantha gasped, and she, Konstan, and Aiyra voiced the same thought about needing to find presents of their own. "And I don't even have my card, thanks to *someone*," she groaned.

"Oops, my fault," Medrhos grinned.

"Relax, sisia, the Vestar bank is right behind the hotel so we can get you a new one. And we'll get to hunting for presents right away," Konstan consoled her. "We have most of the day anyway."

"Good luck avoiding the paparazzi," Marc chuckled, slipping his arms around Samantha from behind. "I'm surprised you haven't been mobbed yet. The three of us, and Berron too, had some narrow escapes. I think they're gathered outside the hotel doors, but Vestar is keeping them out. Have you been up to the rooms yet?"

"No, we ended up wandering around down here," Aiyra confessed, finally leaving her grandmother's arms and hijacking her father's embrace. He laughed.

"Well, that can wait for a little, I suppose. Why don't we give the hounds outside time to disperse and get something to celebrate?"

Everyone was in favor of this motion, but when a trip to one of the hotel's cafes and bakery resulted in frothy mugs of hot chocolate and an array of holiday pastries, Medrhos was dismayed. Estill kept trying to convince him to drink the chocolate and finally, laughing, Samantha pushed a slice of yule log towards him, decorated with marshmallow mushrooms and red tapioca pearls for holly.

"Come on, Rhos, eat something, please," she entreated him.

"No, no, no, no!" Medrhos pushed it back. "I don't want to remember the *last* time you gave me sugar."

"Hey, you're the one who ate the ice cream, and the chocolate milk wasn't my doing."

"Maybe so, but you *were* the one who shoved strawberry shortcake in my mouth."

Samantha dissolved into a fit of giggles as Estill demanded to hear an account of the incident. Eventually the King was somewhat convinced that sugar was not, in fact, poison, and was able to eat the cake.

Sitting next to her parents, Samantha noticed their eyes often fell on Marc, and his gaze would turn to her. Zendira smiled at her from across the stable while stroking Aiyra's curls.

A pang of anxiety stabbed Samantha for just a moment as she inspected a piece of snowbell candy. She had yet to speak to her family about Marc, but she wasn't sure how much he had told them.

Surely, after all he had done, it would be alright – and Zendira seemed happy.

Then it was time to settle in their suites, have their things brought from the ships, obtain a new credit card for Samantha, and then, at last, slip out into the chill for Christmas shopping.

Bells chimed merrily on every corner, and faint familiar songs spilled from garlanded storefronts. Passerby called cheerily to one another, and even the inconvenienced seemed not to mind.

Why was Christmas the one time when everyone seemed to be friends, with few differences in religion and government considered enough to bar the way? Even the secular here felt warmly enough to tip their hats to any creche they should happen upon.

A song playing in the square theorized that the world fell in love at Christmastime; one wished it were always the holidays, for the universe was wrapped in peace, joy and unity like a bow. It was the one time of year when the world became a fantasy, hung with lights, flowers, ribbons and greenery, and pretty clothing worn, by many, for just that one month of the calendar.

Caring and giving and loving and laughing were the pastimes everyone adored in these days, and even the most mundane everyday tasks sparkled with the beauty of life.

The group realized they were standing still and collecting snow on their shoulders.

"It seems we are safe," Tryphena said cheerfully. "Now, how to obtain presents for everyone without anyone knowing?"

"How to obtain presents, period, might be a better question," Medrhos said under his breath.

"I doubt you can find anything we haven't already bought," Marc coughed.

Samantha arched her eyebrows at the pair. "What did you do, spend a million dollars?"

"We respectfully choose not to answer," Coran and the Anselles chorused, proving themselves to be accomplices.

Eventually it began working out, with much splitting up and resplitting and regathering. Zendira and Marc were well acquainted with the city and its stores, and knew of gems which much of the public was unaware of. They made visits to a dozen stores plus the mall, which Aiyra and Estill found fascinating.

That is, until they were hunted down by the paparazzi. Someone had snapped a picture of the group and posted it on SpaceVibe and Starchat, quite inconsiderately.

At this point, the handmaids, the Citharas, and Konstan had disappeared to find something, leaving the flash mob to descend on the winter wonderland courtyard where the girls were playing. The adults were enjoying spiced coffees when they heard the onset of the mob.

"Yikes, hide!" Samantha yelped, and they all dove behind the nearest snowy evergreen. Aiyra, Vora, and Estill were already hiding in a brightly painted sleigh.

"You know they already spotted us," Seraph said, as they ducked in vain through the branches.

"Not to mention, they saw us hide back here," his father added.

"Aaand there's no place to go," Marc commented, knocking on the wall behind them.

Medrhos only pulled out his blaster and aimed it over his shoulder. "Not anymore!"

"Girls, come!" Erana called, and they all jumped into the vortex.

Medrhos herded them down a brief corridor and they hopped out into the middle of what appeared to be an antique store.

"Where are we?" Aiyra inquired, instantly drawn to a wooden stand covered in gloriously vintage books. One had a soft lilac cover, with a double rainbow arching over irises, and seemed softly romantic. The paper cover was fading in an attractive way and she picked it up.

"A store your father and I visited earlier," Medrhos answered airily. "Close to the hotel, and now our friends the paparazzi are successfully shouting questions at a tree."

"I daresay the shop owner is a little disconcerted at our sudden appearance," Samantha said wryly, investigating an array of pretty hats and headwear.

Medrhos scoffed. "Please give me credit, my dear – he's extremely disconcerted. I'll buy something again to make him feel better."

"Medrhos, you bought half the store this morning," Marc reminded him.

"Well, I didn't buy this hat," Medrhos said, plucking several white swanfeather picture hats from the rack and spinning them to Marc. "Here, suits your sisters. "

Samantha was contemplating a number in ivory with rose and raspberry accents – he took this, too. He spied Vora tugging on a long beaded necklace.

"And that, I guess."

Aiyra was hugging the book she had found. She gently touched his sleeve.

"May I please have this, Uncle Rhos?"

His eyes softened. "You can have whatever you want, Princess."

Samantha was clinging to Marc's arm in a rush of happiness. Seeing her favorite people get along with each other as well as she did was more than she had long hoped for.

With the final purchases made, including something sparkly for Estill because it was impossible for Medrhos to leave her out, they returned to the hotel. They were soon joined by Konstan and the others. The remainder of the day was spent wondering who had the wrapping paper, the scissors, and the tape at any given moment.

~~~

Midnight crept closer, with Samantha and her companions grateful not to have needed an interview with Flynn. Their captains had taken care of everything, including video footage from the ships' cameras, to lift the burden of further explanation from their companions' shoulders.

A knock on the door stirred Samantha from where she sat quietly with her family, Lyona curled in her lap and Gelert lounging on the floor. Silmä wasn't present, as the hotel staff had justly been a trifle concerned about the presence of even the most docile tiger.

Samantha had finally been able to tell her parents everything, filling in what Marc and Medrhos had sketched, and told them of her love. They had taken it with no displeasure.

She glanced up at the time. The church Zendira attended halfway across the city was offering the ancient midnight Mass. It was nearly ten; soon they'd be readying to depart.

Marc was at the door, dressed to go out. His father's medallion hung around his neck. He smiled at her.

"Could you get your wrap, dear? I want to take you somewhere."

Samantha nodded and ducked into her room for the ivory caped coat. Soon she was buckled snugly in Marc's sedan. She had forgotten that this had been homebase for him; where he came for conferences and assignments every six months, and where his mother lived. She wondered, briefly, if this would be homebase for her, too.

Marc slid behind the wheel and pulled the car out of the lot. He flicked on the radio. Carols played quietly as they drove through the chilly streets.

"There's a place I've been wanting to show you," Marc confided, as they left the city. "It's not a far drive, so we'll be back in time for you to dress for Mass."

Samantha didn't answer, snuggling her arms deeper into the fur blanket he had tucked around her. The countryside passed by in shades of periwinkle and purple under the budding moon. Cityglow was fading, leaving the stars to come out in thick clusters, like berries crystallized on a wandering vine. The land curved away as the road spiraled and turned up a hill behind De'ngelos. Marc parked at its crest and got out, opening Samantha's door and aiding her to free herself from the blankets.

"Just behind these trees," he whispered, and they ducked through the draping branches of willow and jasmine.

A grotto fell away before them, arched on the hillside. In the rock was nestled an ancient representation of Lourdes on Earth, so seldom visited that luminescent pearluna blossoms ran free through the icicles, draping the trees and traipsing in halos around the Blessed Mother's image. A spring bubbled quietly in the snow, shimmering with the blue haze. Bernadette seemed serene despite the ivy that adorned her dress.

The valley was falling deep before them, the lakes painted silver with golden constellations marked there, and the city lights glowed warmly like a castle that was safe and familiar.

"Few come here, save Mother and I," Marc murmured, his voice barely separating from the hushed blowing of the breeze. It rang iced leaves against each other, like fairy chimes. "I came always when I needed to be alone. . . when no other place offered solace."

He was listening to the dancing of the night, the orchestration of the water and the ice.

"And I wanted to show you. . . ." He nudged her head back, tilting it up towards the sky.

A familiar star was set in the velvet backdrop, and beside it, almost upon it, a point of golden-rose. Esta and Sacra were together just as on Mal-lon, even across a thousand years. Samantha could see her breath hanging in the air, like the answer that seemed to hang in her heart, paused in the fear of being the first to speak. But Marc didn't seem to notice.

"They're so close," he said, almost to himself. "I could reach out and touch them. . . ."

He raised his hand and the sky-diamonds vanished from Samantha's view, and then his hand came down, drawing her eyes with it. Marc uncurled his gloved fingers and there, shining in his palm, were twin stars, bound on a band of rose-gold.

Then he was kneeling in the snow at her feet, eyes glowing at the look on her face as he told her again that nothing in the world, nor any words on his tongue, could bear testament to his love, except his heart's beat. But his heart was everything.

Samantha's lips didn't know whether to laugh with joy, as her eyes wondered whether to cry, so there was a little bit of both as she sank down on his knee and said yes. Marc might have cried too, as he put the ring on her finger. He cuddled her for a minute, as they tried to quiet their racing hearts and plan at least a little for the sake of the questions soon to be asked.

After everything he and Medrhos had told Samantha's parents, Marc said, the couple had not had anything to say save to tell him, smilingly, that Samantha's ring size was a seven. Both had expected that they'd formally court, but it seemed no one wanted to waste any more of Samantha's heart and time when she was free and knew what she wanted, and needed.

"At least six months, I think," Samantha said, when she was finally capable of speaking coherently. "Time enough for preparing the celebration, my trousseau, and my dresses, and it fulfills the requirements on Danya, were we to wed there. But -" She hesitated.

Marc kissed her ringed finger.

"Don't worry about a home," he murmured. "I'm leaving Zorrastra because I'm never taking you away from your family again. I'll build a home for you on Danya where you can be happy, and

Aiyra will have a family. Mother has agreed to come too, and then that will only leave visiting the Citharas on Alnilam."

Samantha leaned her head on his and sighed, watching the diamonds sparkle in the moonlight. It seemed so surreal, as did the passing time.

"Let's plan tomorrow then, when daylight clears our minds, for I'm too happy to know much of anything right now."

"Mm, I second that motion," Marc replied, and gathering her up, carried her back to the car. He nestled her warm and safe in the blankets once more, and they returned to the hotel with just time left to change.

Aiyra was almost late, for the moment her eyes caught on the diamonds, she was indisposed to do anything but cling to Samantha as she cried for the joy that was her father's, and hers, and her future mother's.

 Bundled in warm wraps and handmade holiday dresses they had found while shopping, the girls were escorted into the complimentary limousines at quarter past eleven. Those four families attending Midnight Mass together seemed like a welcome dream, and they were happy to spend the ride with one another.

Medrhos brought Coran along, and the rest of the brethren and handmaidens would follow. It was to be only the second Mass Medrhos and his men had known, and the first which they'd begin to understand.

Snowflakes had begun to fall, turning to crystal in the Christmaslight and icing the cathedral stairs and guardian statues as they pulled up. The echoing interior of the church was lit only by the golden glow of a thousand candles, with the light flickering on the trees guarding the tabernacle, and the star that hovered above the Nativity.

"On the darkest midnight in December. . ." a lone voice rose in song, followed by others and the hymn of a harp like the piping of the stars which turned high above the cathedral spire.

There were men and women of every age and race, who sat there in silence, enraptured by that Face – the One that's never seen yet forever lingers before the eyes.

Thoughts of love and freedom, and cold Christmas nights where the only warmth was in the Mother's arms; the only earth-sound the lowing of gentle stable-kind; and the only song the lullaby, and the knowing that all was well, truly well, at last.

The Child Ever-Holy had ransomed them that night, giving up all of heaven to set things aright. Joseph kept Him safe and sound; the shepherds and the angels watched with bated breath; and the Blessed Virgin Mary had given Him His rest, in a night that felt such peace as had never yet been blessed.

A peace which came back, like a living memory, as a galaxy healed its wounds and took its first free breaths. Beneath the warm blanket of candleglow and the fading carols, Aiyra's head sank onto her father's shoulder as she took the gift to heart, and slept.

Epilogue

Six months later, Samantha was contemplating the lake from her balconnaded windows. She let the cool spring air caress her carefully coiffed hair as she leaned out to take in the perfume of the morning. The sun had only just begun to send a few tentative sparkles across the water. Birds were sleepily serenading the lilac-shaded city. All was well on her wedding day.

Medrhos' empire had trained itself to replace slavery with honest, well-paid work, and the economy was better off than before. Vestar had turned to lighter things for the keeping of the peace.

Marc had all but retired, save for occasionally aiding with classes of cadets, and served now as a city counselor in Couerdoré, where he had built a home. It stood up on the rise, away from the town, warm and gentle in its embrace of Cytha and Almedra, where the pain of the past was only a strengthening memory.

The *Lumenara's* helm had been passed to Pell, who had married Elise a few months prior, a relationship having been started while Aiyra was in charge. Whether it was a coincidence, no one would say.

Truitt had remained happily aboard his pride and joy.

Konstan had stayed on Danya, keeping the promise he had made to Aiyra. He had been welcomed into the Anselles' home at Samantha's behest, and readily adopted them all as his family, not to their displeasure. His days were spent working in the research center of the city, or willingly running tech calls. When he wasn't working or with the family, he was up at the home, helping Marc to prepare it for Samantha, and confirming his heart's feelings towards Aiyra after fourteen years of painful wondering.

Aiyra herself was having the time of her life decorating her new, true home and settling the gardens with Zendira and Erana. Her recovery was almost full, except for occasional nerve pains and headaches that would make her feel as though she were asleep and dreaming all that she did. Uncle Medrhos was never more than five minutes away at these times, and under his hand the pain would cease.

Everyone had enjoyed seeing just how Aiyra would turn out to be, now that nothing was controlling her; each day was a new chapter of finding out how her heart and mind thought. She didn't seem to notice, as she cheerfully volunteered to aid Samantha with wedding preparations.

Samantha, for her part, had her hands full while her heart sang. Flowers, gowns, bridal showers and receptions were hers to plan, with Marc's help. Her entire family, too, were enjoying the busyness as much as she.

Yes, all was well in her world! she thought, as she scooped up Lyona and cuddled her. The cat had come up to visit her on the balustrade, and purred as her mistress scratched her ears.

Medrhos and his brethren had chosen baptism, and Samantha smiled as she remembered how he had acquired his new name, for he was no longer Medrhos – though many continued to call him by that name out of habit.

"What, I have to change my name?" the King had exclaimed upon hearing the revelation. "I've had it for nearly three decades at this point!"

Samantha nodded, trying not to laugh. "It's to demonstrate your newness in Christ," she reminded him.

Medrhos sighed. "Ugh, fine, what's a good name then?"

"Mm, I think Michael might suit you, what's that in Mândrauer?"

Medrhos frowned, for it was a good question. "Uhh, computer, translate Michael."

"Mikrhos," came the automated reply.

"What it said."

"Yayy, I can still call you Rhos!" Samantha said in relief.

Medrhos chuckled. "Yayyy, me."

Aiyra, who had been at Medrhos' arm listening, had promptly translated his name again into Cythian. "Uncle Rhosiel!"

"Oh no, not roses!"

"Yayyyy!" Samantha had laughed, and they had smothered him with a hug.

All the slaves had successfully been returned home, too. Or rather, all but one.

Her mind went back now, to the galaxy-wide celebration that had followed that Christmas day. The Mândrauers had mingled freely with Vestar, amidst music, dance, and festivities. Another Marauder ship had come in that morning to join the celebration.

Medrhos had wandered to the terrace and looked down upon the cheerful city below, but his thoughts seemed lost in the chalice of wine in his hand. Samantha had followed him, leaving Marc with Aiyra.

"What is it, Rhos?"

He had turned his head at the touch of her hand.

"I'm just thinking. . . don't think, little Rose, that I regret it, but there is a pain lower than my relief. Some king I am," he sighed, gazing out over the towers draped in crystal ice. "I said I'd be a Marauder like no king before me. All I've brought to my people is confusion and change. . . and there's all those whom I've killed and enslaved. My heart wonders what the worth of my change is, even to try and remain for them. . . I looked at God's Face in the manger last night, and wondered how I could have done those things in His sight, and how I could look at Him now."

Yet Samantha's hand felt comfortingly safe on his shoulder as she straightened his collar.

"Yes, you were right, Medrhos," she said softly. "There has never been such a Marauder King as you: you freed your people, defeating the monster that made you do all those things, and you abolished slavery-" She was smiling now. "You can always look into the Face of that Child without fear. He'll never chase you away, and will only look at you with love as you change for His sake."

Medrhos looked up. "Guess you're right," he murmured, with just the ghost of that old arrogant smile, that faded into one of tenderness as he looked into his glass and saw again in his heart the Face, and the eyes that spoke of love.

Karthos had appeared behind the pair, also bearing wine glass in hand as he perched on the wall beside them. He had come on the ship that morning.

"I correct myself, that *that's* the truest thing you've said, my almost-granddaughter."

Medrhos scowled, out of habit – the pair had been relearning a better relationship, but it was coming harder at times than Medrhos' friendship with Marc.

"I'm sorry but I still can't stop thinking about it," he muttered.

"Look on the bright side," Samantha reminded them, draping her arms over their shoulders. "If your grandfather hadn't been that way, we wouldn't be here. At least now you two don't have to spend your time seeing which one of you can throw the other into the nearest incinerator fastest."

Her eyes were twinkling and Medrhos and Karthos were forced to smile.

"That's true," Medrhos admitted. "You're so good for me, Samantha, good for my people, good for the slaves, good for everything except marrying me," he said wryly.

"Aw, you'll find someone someday who's better for you at that," Samantha consoled him. "Besides, you'll always be my brother!" She playfully punched him in the arm.

"Not that I'll be that for long," Medrhos replied gravely, and instantly regretted it.

"What do you mean?" The smile faded from the girl's lips.

Medrhos' eyes turned away from her again across the landscape, as though he were seeing all of time, and would rather face it than her.

"As the slaves from each period are returned, that piece of the timeline is shut to us. Once the last from your time has been returned, Samantha, the timeline will be closed." His eyes roved.

"Technically I'm dead to you," he laughed a little. "I will be seeing you sooner than you think! But for now, Adora is from this time, and so has agreed to be the last to be officially returned, and will only visit home for now; that will allow us to be present at your wedding." He met her gaze once more.

"And then, little Ancilla-" He stopped, for the woman was on the verge of tears. She had expected that this would happen, but when it had not happened at Rätha's fall, she had begun to hope.

"Don't cry, be happy with the time we are meant to have left," he said kindly. "And promise me," he added sternly, "that you won't go and look up Mal-lon's present situation so you can immediately visit my tomb. I don't want you to spend your honeymoon there, nor to spend it weeping. Promise me!" He touched her cheek. "It will be alright, Samantha, everything will work out the way the stars were meant to dance."

It was the only shadow to darken the day, Samantha thought, returning to the present with a wince. He would be there for a while anyway, maybe a week or two. So, she could put off her sorrow until after the happiest day of her life.

She moved nervously through her room, knowing she should be replacing her silk nightrobe with the wedding garments laid out on the bed. The sun was now tinting the skyline across the lake; the wedding was in golden hour and there was not much time.

Despite the knowledge that she'd soon be saying goodbye, Samantha's heart rose again, with some trembling as her eyes fell upon the layers of smooth silks and chiffon, the crystals, pearls and the trailing veil finer than the daintiest web.

She began to prepare for the wedding, donning the gracefully draped waterfall gown, the jewelry, and the veil. Her father had made her every adornment, from the necklace, to the jewels in her hair, to the crown of flowers woven with pearls and gems.

As for the bridal party, Estill had volunteered to play flower girl, decked out as a full-fledged Mândrauer princess, post-purgation style. Her bridesmaids were Silvestra, Adora, Erana, and Aiyra, who remained at Samantha's side. Each maiden wore a diaphanous dress of pastel hue – all was airy and light, like wind and water.

Samantha had chosen a less formal setting. She felt that they had all been through so much, yet had not had much time to rest due to the work of those six months. Softness and an emphasis on what was taking place were her priorities. Restrictive garments, as well as guests who weren't close to the parties and their families, would have been distracting. Thus, the attendees would be few.

As the sky was being painted, the bridal party set out, walking a winding path through the cobbled streets, strewn with flower petals. Seraph and Dün Andolin had evidently risen even earlier than the women.

The city was only slowly waking, and the walk was a peaceful one, not made a spectacle. Those who happened to be awake, however, naturally admired the dresses from their windows or the nearest cafe. The women murmured the Aves and Glorias of the rosary at every turn to keep Samantha's mind off the restless butterflies in her stomach.

Seraph and Dün Andolin were awaiting them on the steps winging the church. Samantha's brother handed her the bouquet of lilacs, peonies, forget-me-nots, moon roses, ferns and ivy, sprinkled with pearl dust and wrapped with a silken ribbon the color of Marc's eyes, with a dainty raindrop charm tied on. It was Aiyra's signature shade of rose, and the maid smiled when she saw it.

Samantha's father took the bride's arm and the glass doors swung open before them. The nave stretched away, the ceiling rapidly vanishing upwards with latticed columns like blossoming trees. Stained glass windows illuminated the church, turning it into a bejeweled tapestry.

The airy webbing of Almedra was in its influence; all was light upon the ivory stone, the barely blue paint and the hint of gilded décor, and the mirage-like paintings on the walls. Behind the altar rose an image of the new Eden in pastel tones, with the Queen and her Child there, surrounded by God's creation.

The church itself blended into that painting, with wisteria, mountain laurel, cherry and apple blossom branches arranged all around, strung with teardrop beads like rain. Ferns and snapdragons were lushly scattered, so that the place felt like an embracing, enchanted forest.

The extended Anselle family was there, and some close friends; the Citharas were present, as were Pell, Elise, Vidara, Truitt, Briggs and Topping (who, of course, had baked a magnificent cake for the occasion).

Medrhos turned and smiled at the bride. The former Marauder wore his princely garb, but had begun to trade his favored black and red for variations of red and blue, or orange and brown. All his brethren were there, similarly attired and smiling as their former and forever Queen halted.

Marc was standing at the sanctuary gate, Vestar uniform discarded in favor of a Cythian tunic of ocean-sky and silver. Konstan, Cajetan, and Pell were his only companions.

Samantha felt rooted to the carpet lining the aisle. She turned helplessly to her father, finding his hand and slipping hers into it.

"Don't be afraid, little Sahma," he whispered tenderly. "I'll always be here for you to lean on, as much as you need. Both of your Kings will take care of you."

Aiyra hugged Samantha then, bringing a smile back to the bride's face.

"Come down the aisle beside me," Samantha whispered. "This is just as much a new union for you as for your father and I."

She drew Aiyra along, finally lifting her gaze shyly to meet Marc's. He was smiling at what she had done and no one objected when Aiyra was ushered up to the sanctuary and another chair was brought for her.

Marc extended his hand to Samantha; but he would not take it until she offered it, waiting patiently as the bride drew a questioning breath. A glance at the tabernacle and she was at peace. She lifted her hand with a smile and placed it in his.

This time, the vows were full and true. Samantha felt no need to hesitate with her promise. Marc slipped the ring he had made onto her finger; the moonstone shone, embraced by tiny amethysts and diamonds, and the band was a twist of polished willow and rose-gold.

It seemed only a few minutes before they were being pelted with rose petals and glitter as they ran down the outside steps, even though they were only going as far as the church gardens and grottos, and the lakeside for photos.

The reception was held at the Anselles' villa, with the music of harps and lyres, dancing, and much time spent sitting, talking and laughing. Samantha sat without speaking, listening to the others and trying to realize that she was Marc's, and Aiyra was hers. Marc's arm was around his wife, and he wouldn't leave her side. Aiyra hesitated, not knowing whether they would rather be alone, but Samantha caught her daughter's arm as she began to leave, and drew her back into her arms.

"What should I call you?" Aiyra inquired, tilting her head.

The bride looked down at her and smoothed the girl's forehead. She wasn't about to request being called mother, or A'ma; the fact that Aiyra had chosen her to be loved by was gift enough.

"You may call me whatever you wish, dear."

A smile spread over Aiyra's lips. "I love you, Amara."

It was the name which Samantha hadn't dared hope she'd hear given to her, ever since that long-ago day on Almedra.

"I love you too. . . my daughter!"

Gifts were brought forth; the trio laughed when Medrhos presented them with not one, but four baby Almedran spiders. They would be released into a controlled habitat in the mountains, with the city's approval. One day, the Almedran gift of spider-silk would return.

The king had brought gowns and pretty things for Aiyra too, and some of Samantha's possessions from Mal-lon, those which did not bring bad memories with them. He laughingly produced Orion's cracked battle helmet for Marc, previously lost on the battlefield, supplemented by the finest Marauder wines.

There were other gifts from the guests, some practical, others not. For his part, Topping proudly unveiled the wedding cake, breathtaking in its white loveliness. It was time for the bride to serve it to her guests along with tea and fruit for a suitable breakfast.

The wedding feast was held at noon, an array of fresh spring foods, warm and sweet. There was lavender lemonade to accompany citrus and strawberries, salads of blossoms, fruits and greens; chickpeas and mushrooms in a rich alfredo cream; and chilled chicken salad served over warm pasta.

Rustic homemade bread was spread with fresh yellow butter from the Anselles' own cows, and there were treats of mini tartlets, candied flowers, chocolate-dipped berries and chips, and clover and lingonberry muffins drizzled with honey. The Mândrauer men were happy to find that there were heavy meat and potato tarts too, to fall back on if they had too much sugar.

Silmä and Gelert were prowling the party, turning their pleading eyes on anyone who might let a scrap fall. Vora and Estill quickly won the rank of most generous, innocently willing to let entire helpings of any dish fall to the floor. Samantha watched as Estill stroked the supposedly starving hound's ears. The bride called Medrhos over.

"Rhos, when you leave, it is my wish that you take Gelert with you." She stopped him as he moved to protest. "He's been with you longer than he's been with me," she said gently. "I wish you to have something of mine to remember me by, and Estill loves him so. Please, say you'll take him."

The King looked down at her gravely. Taking both her hands in his, he kissed them.

"As you wish, my Rose."

He departed to inform Estill of her latest gift, upon which she shrieked with happiness and Gelert, regardless of whether he actually understood, was only too happy to follow the child onto the dance floor to spin in circles.

Samantha swallowed hard to clear the choking sob from her throat. She would keep the promise she had made, and there was time enough to spend with Medrhos and the child before it was time for goodbye. Silmä yawned and laid down at her mistress' feet as though she sensed the barely suppressed tears. Samantha reached down to stroke the cat's head.

"Good kitty!"

Marc leaned over with a knowing glance and his hand enveloped Samantha's. The bride was content to let him whisper sweet nothings in her ear for the remainder of the reception.

Medrhos returned some time later, after the first dances had been had, bearing with him another gift. It was the blaster which Samantha had worn for the invasion, but left unused.

"I thought this might be of use. It may not bridge times, but in occasions of need it will allow you to travel swiftly. I'm not sure how long it will last; I've brought extra parts as the technology doesn't exist in your time. Should you run out, being the engineer that you are, I'm sure you could come up with something. I hope it will help protect you and Aiyra, should either of you be endangered again."

He was watching Aiyra as he spoke. The girl had been dancing in and out of the crowd with Konstan in tow. Now a group dance was beginning as Aiyra's cousins joined in a circle and began to teach the pair.

"I wish I could continue to be here to finish her healing," he sighed. "But I've had something prepared which may be of help. It's been taken up to the house, and you'll find instructions with it."

Samantha thanked him with as much gravity as he had thanked her for Gelert. Evening was coming on now, and after a lighter meal, this time prepared by the Citharas in fine Cythian style, the final event of the reception was set.

It was a wedding game, one which Marc had played with Talitha so many years before. In the vibrant, shadowing hazes of evening, luminescent luna moths were released into the courtyard gardens, and the newlyweds needed to try and catch three of the silent, swiftly fluttering creatures. It took thirty minutes to hunt them down, and innumerable times of Marc freeing a laughing Samantha when her silks or beads caught on grasping branches and statuary.

Once they had succeeded, the couple vanished inside, leaving the guests to try their luck with the remaining moths. Konstan and Aiyra came running up to the newlyweds after a time, displaying their half dozen captures, including the Queen moth, the trickiest of them all.

As the last band of violet and turquoise faded from the sky, the crew of the *Lumenara* and Samantha's friends began to leave, giving a last hand with the clean-up. When they had gone, Marc wrapped a shawl around his daughter's shoulders and they, too, departed to prepare the homecoming ceremony for the bride. Konstan was quick to follow, the ever-helpful guardian.

Samantha was left to exchange her wedding gown for a flowing dress of lace, silk and velvet, and lingered with her family, bridesmaids, and the Mândrauer men. Coran came forward with Silvestra, asking for the bride's blessing on the new promise of their own future union. Silvestra was of Coran's time, so there was no loss of family for her in remaining in Mal-lon.

Samantha laid a hand on each and kissed them, saying, "I pray you will have peace and joy in whatever God brings to you. I know you will be as happy as I," she added fondly, and the couple smiled at each other.

One by one, each of Medrhos' brethren, including the captain from her escapade, came forward to kiss their Queen goodnight and to wish her well. Each struggled to force a smile as he did so. The captain hugged her, but didn't say a word, and she thought she saw tears in his eyes. When Medrhos' turn came, his arms lingered around her as he studied her face.

"Be happy, little Samantha," he said finally. "I have no sorrow in giving you to Marc. May he give you more than I ever could, and may your love heal you of all sorrow, and all the trauma you've been through. I love you, my sister, and may God bless you abundantly for what you've done for me, for my people, and for the world. Goodnight, my Samantha, my Ancilla, my Queen, my Angel-Rose!"

Leaning forward, he kissed the place where the scar had once been.

"Then please don't be sad, my brother." Samantha put her hands on his heart, where the tiger pendant had once hung. It had been replaced by a medal of the Veil he had come to love. "I pray you'll have the life now that you always were meant to have, and lost. I know you'll find another heart for yours, one that will help you to take care of your people, and help you to come even closer to Him, more than I could. So please don't be scared, I'll always love you!"

She leaned her head on him and thought she felt him crying, but when she looked up she couldn't see any tears. Maybe he would be happier tomorrow, she hoped. The pain in his eyes was hurting her even though he was doing his best to hide it. She would have enough time, though, to say all the things she needed and wanted to say. She wisely changed the subject.

"You'll. . . come to the redo of the well-wishing ceremony, won't you?" she asked, certain the memory would bring a smile into his eyes. "I think it will be on Tuesday."

"Mm." His face creased with a little smile. "I trust you'll do it properly this time?"

Samantha laughed, and so did he. He lifted Estill to give her once-mother a goodnight kiss. The bride cuddled her for a moment, wondering whether she'd ever have a little girl like Estill, a sister for Aiyra at last. Visions of losing Estill to time flitted though her mind and she blinked them away before the tears could come, tightening her hold on the girl. Then it was time for the men to go.

About an hour later, when the sky was of midnight color and the stars were at play, the bridal party set out for the last time, with Seraph and Dün Andolin following behind, symbolically bearing the last of Samantha's possessions.

Each woman held a candle, and as they walked they sang the final song of the bride, of hope and webs of stardust and dreams. Well-wishers showered them with confetti and roses from the windows as they passed through the town, then through the countryside and up the rise.

Marc awaited them at the gate. He lifted Samantha and bore her into the home. Aiyra, Zendira, Konstan, and the Citharas were there, as Marc set Samantha on her feet in the welcoming glow of a plethora of candles.

A table was draped in golden lace and strewn with flowers. On it were pitchers of rose eggnog, for the royalty she had become; passionflower tea for love; dark chocolate for the bitter sweetness of life; whole grain loaves for the home that was now hers to tend; and a bowl of holy water to sprinkle the home with, for the souls which were now hers to nurture more than ever.

When the last toast was made and the last chant of blessing sung, the Anselles kissed Samantha and took their leave. Adora and Silvestra bade the bride a tender goodnight, the Citharas gave the last welcoming embrace, and they were gone. Konstan lingered to keep Aiyra company as Marc and Samantha wandered the gardens.

In the distance they could hear the rolling of the lake. A single nightingale was singing from the branch of a sycamore, and the crickets began to softly synchronize with the sparkling stars and the bubbling of the fountains. The moon slipped from behind a curtain of clouds, lining the leaves with silver and rippling tantalizingly near in the waters.

Marc glanced down at his bride as the bloom of white grew and glowed on her skin. Samantha gasped very softly, raising her hands and letting the wide sleeves of her gown fall back to frame the vines and star-like flowers there.

"Your scars – they've changed," Marc breathed wonderingly. His fingers traced the blossom that had appeared on her forehead.

"I haven't seen them since the night you first showed me Esta," Samantha murmured. "He's happy, Marc."

"Mm. . ." Marc smiled down at her. "So am I! . . . They've changed from your suffering, then?"

Samantha lifted her face to him with a smile.

"And my love."

Marc offered her a kiss as the moon watched over them.

The bridegroom turned his head and listened to the orchestration of the evening as many thoughts ran and flowered in his mind. He was glad that Samantha and Aiyra had been saved, glad that Talitha was safe and home, glad that his family was his to care for and keep for some time yet. How long didn't matter so much as how well.

"I hope I can guard you -" Marc paused, as though searching the night sky for the words. "It sounds wrong to say as well as I guarded Talitha. But that's what it was. . . everything I did was to guard the path God had placed before her, and it was done and she was safe. I pray that I may guard your path as well."

He looked down into her eyes, dark in the night but trembling with the reflection of stars like tears that fell in the rain.

"Whatever happens in the future, never be afraid, my love!" he whispered. "For we have seen all fear, and we know it now. It cannot touch us again to the depths it once held."

"No," Samantha whispered, laying her head on his breast. "No, I never need to be afraid again."

~~~

Far away, in the meadows across the lake, the great black ship sat silent in the night, save for the aura of purple at her thrusters. A figure stood at the foot of the hatch's ramp, wrapped in a velvet mantle, eyes watching the glimmering lights of the distant home on the rise. Medrhos, too, listened to the sounds of the night.

The waves lapped and faded in and out, as steadily as a heartbeat. The moon seemed to sympathize as she rested on the tops of the newly green-sprung trees on the opposite shore. He listened, and thought he could hear the bride's joy in the singing of the night birds, and tears that would come, in the whispering of the wind.

It was time to let her go. She was safe, and always would be, now that she had Marc's heart to guard her. He lifted his eyes to the dark sky.

Yes, it was time. Time for his time to be a thing of the past. Time for him to be in a place where he could do them all more good than now. Time, as far as they knew, to see the Face he had begun to dream of. Time to finish whatever was asked. . . time to be here again in the blink of an eye to watch over them all, to repay them for what he had done, and be what he should always have been. . . who he was made to be.

He dropped his hand on Estill's curls as she stood quietly beside him, her hand buried in Gelert's ruff.

"Come, my precious daughter. It's time to go home."

The hatch raised with a gentle hiss and the engines purred, lifting the once-*Harbinger*, now the *Ancilla*, into the darkened sky.

A familiar streak of rose was all that was seen from the home. It was a battle not to cry. But it was the one day on which he knew she'd be able to keep her promise, as goodbyes fell silently into the void.

High above, the stars laughed as though to say that they'd all spoken too soon.

Appendix

For more information on the devotion to the Holy Face, promises, and prayers given by Our Lord, please visit: holyfacedevotion.com

To join the Archconfraternity of the Holy Face, a form may be filled out here:
https://hisholyface.com/archconfraternity-of-the-holy-face-of-jesus

For information on the Holy Face Medal and its graces, please see:
holyface.org.uk

www.ingramcontent.com/pod-product-compliance
Lightning Source LLC
Chambersburg PA
CBHW010805250626
47156CB00010B/2999